Praise for *Tell Us*

"The result is a slow-burn psych[...] well-developed characters that [...] unsettling, conclusion. Sterling is a writer to watch."

—*Publishers Weekly*

"Set in 1970 at a girls' boarding school in Lenox, Massachusetts, Sterling's novel is both a gripping psychological thriller and a not-so-nostalgic look back at a time of massive social upheaval . . . Both evocative and provocative, Sterling's blend of thriller and coming-of-age tale is deeply affecting and full of unexpected twists."

—*Booklist* (starred review)

"*Tell Us No Secrets*, the debut novel by American journalist Siena Sterling, has all the ingredients for a slow-simmering stew of teenage angst that will leave readers relieved that they are no longer in high school."

—Crime Fiction Lover

The Game She Plays

ALSO BY SIENA STERLING

Tell Us No Secrets

The
Game
She
Plays

A NOVEL

SIENA STERLING

wm

WILLIAM MORROW

An Imprint of HarperCollinsPublishers

HarperCollins books may be purchased for educational, business, or sales promotional use. For information, please email the Special Markets Department at SPsales@harpercollins.com.

FIRST EDITION

Designed by Diahann Sturge

Photography throughout © Rory Bowcott / Shutterstock

Library of Congress Cataloging-in-Publication Data has been applied for.

ISBN 978-0-06-316184-9

22 23 24 25 26 LBC 5 4 3 2 1

For Violet, Aya, Arturo, and Santiago.
Present and future stars of the galaxy.

PART ONE

It fell from the sky in a straight line, hurtling to the ground like a skydiver without a chute. Was there that moment midflight when it felt the bullet hit, a consciousness of doom as its wings stopped flapping?

It would land in a heap without splattering: a limp body that would then find itself in the careful jaws of a dog. Later it would be plucked, every feather torn off it until it was bald, ready to be shoved into an oven and roasted.

Then eaten. By people drinking wine and talking and laughing and very occasionally finding their teeth crunching down on the remnant of a lead bullet hidden in the flesh. A little reminder of death.

They should be reminded of death.

Because accidents can happen on a shooting weekend.

And accidents can be arranged.

Chapter One

October 1980

NICOLA

W hen I meet Hugo and Trez, am I supposed to curt-sey?"

"No." James laughed. "You bow and curtsey only to royalty—like the Queen or Prince Philip and their children. Hugo and Trez are going to be an earl and a countess, but they're not royal. They're just normal people who will have a title someday. Hugo's a good bloke. He can be a little gruff sometimes, but that's just his way. And you'll love Trez. Like I said on the plane, she's the salt of the earth."

"I don't know any normal people who are going to have a title."

"Well, you'll meet Nigel and Badger too. They'll never

have titles, so they qualify as normal. And Nigel has a new girlfriend, apparently. Her name is Bella." James took one hand off the steering wheel and put it on her knee. "I know it's a lot, meeting my friends all together like this, but I can't keep you to myself forever."

I wish you could. Our relationship has gone so quickly in such a short time I feel winded. One day I meet you when I'm sitting beside you on a plane to Paris, eight hours later I'm traveling with you to your parents' house in the South of France, a week later I'm living with you in London, and two weeks after that here I am in your car on the way to an earl-to-be's house for a shooting weekend in the English countryside. This is nuts. Completely crazy. Until I met you on the plane, I didn't even know people shot pheasants.

And I had no idea I could fall in love so fast and so hard.

"You're not nervous about the weekend, are you?"

"A little."

"Don't be. Really. I promise. This is going to be fun. There'll only be the seven of us—you and me, Hugo and Trez, Nigel and Bella, and Badger. You'll get to know everyone quickly. It will be a blast. And I promise we won't spend all the time telling stories about our Cambridge days."

Cambridge—the Harvard or Yale of England. James and his friends had all been there together, sharing their college days. How could they not reminisce? She'd sit and listen and try to laugh with them, but she'd have no idea of what they were talking about.

Oh, let me tell you about the time my best friend Sue and I went to this amazing party in our Elmira college days. You've never heard of Elmira? I can't believe it! That would be a great way to fit in.

Calm down, Nic. Relax.

I'm trying, Daniel.

Try harder.

They were speeding along in James's dark green Jaguar. She thought of her old gray Toyota back in Buffalo, a heap of a car. Once she'd let it get so dirty with leftover snow slush, someone had written PLEASE CLEAN ME on the filthy windscreen.

The Toyota would still be sitting on the street outside her apartment, the apartment she'd shared with her boyfriend Greg until he'd ditched her for another woman, an older divorcée, and walked out. The apartment where she'd get ready every morning for work until she ended up punching Tony Kellow, her sleazy boss, after yet another one of his endless sexual innuendoes, thereby losing her job.

The day after she'd thrown that punch, she'd called TWA and made a reservation on a plane to Paris, desperate to escape from the wreck of her life and lose herself for a few weeks in a foreign country. Instead, she'd lost herself in the kind of love she'd never imagined possible, the terrifying kind of love where her whole life felt at stake.

Of course she was nervous about the weekend. His friends would be sizing her up. An American woman.

An American woman who knew nothing about shooting, nothing about weekend parties in the country, next to
nothing about England.

She'd never been to a dinner party before, much less a
weekend at a "country house." Yes, friends had come over
for lunch or dinner when she was living with Greg. But
they'd order some pizza and sit and eat slices out of the box
and drink beer. This was a whole different ball game, with
a man who was going to have a title someday and his wife
who would have one too and Nigel plus his girlfriend and
a man who sounded like he belonged in *The Wind in the
Willows*—Badger.

"I'm sure the weekend will be great. But why do you
have to kill the birds?" They had come to a sudden halt in
standstill traffic on the highway. A part of her hoped they
would stay so stuck they wouldn't be able to get there, that
they'd have to turn and go back to London, and she could
have some more time before she faced all these new people.

"A little hard to eat them if they're not dead." He laughed
again. "We eat the pheasants we shoot. It's like fishing, really. Come on. You're not a vegetarian. I've seen you tuck-
ing into a big steak. The cow dies, you know. Someone
kills that cow."

"But not me personally. I don't witness it."

"Exactly. You're removed from it, so you don't have to
think about it. Think about this, though. The cow doesn't
have a chance. A pheasant does. Not every pheasant dies
in a shoot, you know. A lot of them fly away to live peace-

ful, happy pheasant lives. Maybe they have pheasant tea parties."

That made her laugh. And he was right: she was a meat eater, so she couldn't complain about any animal being killed for food. But she still wasn't sure she wanted to watch birds being slaughtered.

"It's beautiful countryside, lots of fresh air, delicious dinners. A good lunch too during the shoot. Honestly— you'll love it. Plus, you'll get to tell your American friends how eccentric and mad the English are."

"That's true."

I'll get to tell them. When? When I go back? Is that a hint? A clue telling me I'll be going back—soon? That this relationship is a fling for you, not one that has any chance of lasting?

"Listen—you can stay in the house while we go out if you want to. Coming with me on the shoot isn't manda- tory. But I'd like you to be with me." He turned his eyes to her, then back to the road.

"I'll come with you. It will be exciting. In a ghoulish way."

"Don't say that to Hugo. He takes his shooting very seri- ously. He runs the shoot, in fact. It's a business for him."

"People pay to go?"

"Absolutely. Hugo said there is a German man coming tomorrow morning. He's more or less testing it out, to see if he wants to hire it for his own shooting party. It's not cheap, I can tell you. And your compatriots like it too—

more and more Americans are paying a lot of money to come on a shoot."

Not any Americans she'd ever met. But then she'd never met anyone who was going to inherit a title, or anyone who owned a huge house in the country. This was a whole different world, and she was entirely on his turf. Calls to the United States were expensive. She would have liked to call Sue, but she'd have to have a long conversation to explain what had happened, which would cost a bomb. Besides, what could Sue say to help her feel less foreign?

James was funny. James was smart. James was sexy. James was generous. James was kind. James was attractive.

Yeah, right, Nic. AND he has an English accent. What the hell do you want? Have you called to hear how jealous I am? To gloat?

Why don't you tell me about going to an earl's house? How tough that's going to be? Or are you upset because Prince Charles might not be there?

It would be hard to explain that she wasn't looking for sympathy. More like she needed to touch base with her life back home to make sure it still existed, that there were people who cared about her, that she'd have something to go back to if all this collapsed.

And, okay, maybe some sympathy.

I have no idea how long this is going to last. He hasn't told me he loves me yet.

Wow, Nic, that's horrible. It's been what? Three whole weeks? Christ, he should have proposed by now. You should be out buying a wedding dress.

The traffic began to move again. She saw what had held them up: it wasn't a normal jam; there had been a crash on the other side of the highway. She could see a motorcycle on its side, an ambulance, two police cars.

"Rubberneckers," James stated. "I'm afraid we'll be late for dinner because of them."

"I've always wondered how it's possible *not* to rubberneck when you see something like that. Are you supposed to drive on as if nothing has happened? I don't think it's ghoulish. I think it's a normal human instinct."

"Ah, we're back to 'ghoulish,' are we? I think it's ghoulish, frankly. Our first disagreement." He put his hand on her thigh and squeezed it.

She'd never seen him in a bad mood. He could be quiet; there were times when she sensed he wanted to be left alone, but he hadn't even come close to losing his temper.

It was hard to imagine having a real argument with him, ever. Would he shout, go red in the face? Greg hadn't shouted; he'd used the patronizing tone of voice of a teacher with a recalcitrant child whenever they fought. Which was guaranteed to drive her even crazier.

"What would make you really angry?"

"I don't know. Maybe if someone hurt someone I care about."

"That's fair." She nodded.

"I might also be a little bit angry if we're late for dinner, but that's only because I'm a punctuality freak. You should know that about me. I can't stand being late for anything."

"I'm the same."

"Then again, I might be enraged if I thought I had a free seat beside me on the plane and some random Englishman came late and took it."

"Justifiably enraged."

"Absolutely."

They were past the accident. He stepped on the gas, sped down the highway.

Off the highway, they drove down smaller roads, then even smaller, narrower ones, with hedges hemming them in on either side.

Obviously, he'd done this trip many times before, because he was still speeding along, negotiating the twists and turns with ease.

Then they made a sharp right-hand turn through big gates and were on a driveway, heading toward what looked in the dark like the looming hulk of a monstrous ship. As they approached it and she could make out just how massive it was, she could tell that in the daylight it would be even more frightening in its majesty.

James's house in London was a small mews house in South Kensington with a tiny kitchen and two bedrooms. He'd explained that mews houses were where the stables used to be; then, when cars took over from horses, they'd been converted into houses. The area was lovely, especially the cobbled street of the mews, and nothing about it made her nervous. Not like this frighteningly huge house. She'd wished before that the traffic jam would have made them turn back, and now, when they pulled up and came to a stop, she wished she could stay in the car.

God, Daniel, I'm out of my depth. Help.

Calm down, Nic. They're people. Just people. Incredibly rich people, granted. But still . . . you can always do that old trick of picturing them naked.

"Hi, hi, hello!" A tiny woman with short dark hair that framed a round, friendly, bespectacled face was at the door, her arms outstretched. "James! Just in time!"

"There was an accident on the M3. A lot of rubberneckers, who are either normal people or ghoulish people, depending on your point of view. That's a long way of saying we got stuck in traffic." He gave the woman a brief hug, kissed her on both cheeks. "Trez—this is Nicola Harris. Nicola, this is Trez Langley."

"Nicola, what a pleasure." The woman then stepped forward, kissed her on both cheeks. She was wearing a black wool maxi skirt that flared out and was embroidered with white buttons in the shape of a poodle, topped by a blue mohair sweater that could have been a thrift-shop reject.

"James, grab her suitcase like a good boy. Now come in. I'll show you to your room; you can get your bags settled and come down to dinner. Everyone's here except Badger."

"Badger's always late."

"That's because Badger has no sense of time. You know that. Come on in."

When they went through the door into a large hall, what

first struck her was how dark it was inside despite lights
being on. The walls were all paneled in dark wood, and
there were oil paintings with dark backgrounds, and dark
red velvet tapestries.

As Trez led the way up a wide flight of stairs, they passed
what looked like deer heads with pointy antlers and beady
eyes. Nicola felt glowered at, as if the walls and gloomy
paintings and the dead deer were angry with this intrusion.
When they reached the first landing, they turned right.
They must have passed three bedrooms on each side of the
hallway before Trez turned into one on the left.

"Here you are. I hope you like it."

"It's beautiful."

The room could have fit three double beds. It had a sink,
two big armchairs, and a dainty dressing table with little
glass bottles, a brush, a comb, and a mirror on top. Heavy
pale blue velvet curtains covered the windows at the back.

Each bedside table had a lamp and a small jug of water
with a glass beside it on a tray. And there were two hot
water bottles lying side by side on top of the bed.

"Get yourselves settled and then come down. Maybe
Badger will have arrived by then."

"I bet you he won't."

"I'm not about to take that bet, James," Trez smiled. "It
really is nice to meet you, Nicola."

"You too."

"Oh, damn. I forgot. James, can you move your car
around to the front of the garage, please?"

"Your wish is my command." He saluted her and left the room.

Nicola stood with Trez, not sure what to say.

"Do you—?" she started, but Trez was already talking.

"I'm so happy James has finally found someone. He deserves to be happy, and I'm sure you'll make him very happy."

"I hope so." The way Trez had said it made Nicola ask: "Was he unhappy before?"

"He had his heart broken a little. A long time ago."

"Oh."

What did that mean? His heart was broken a little? Trez was clearly being protective. She must have been around when whoever it was had broken his heart. A little. A long time ago.

"Anyway." She clapped her hands. "Our friend Nigel has a new girlfriend too—her name is Bella. It's a pretty name—so is 'Nicola.' I was unfortunate enough to be christened Jane. Not so pretty. Oh God, enough about names. Sometimes I do bang on. What I'm trying to say is that you won't be the only one who hasn't met anyone here. Bella's in the same boat. I should go down now. Hugo is probably banging on about shooting and boring Bella rigid. See you in a few minutes."

Her big black poodle skirt swished and off she went. James had said she was the salt of the earth, and she did seem straightforward and friendly, but also a bizarre combination of very much younger than she was and very much older. She could have been fifteen or fifty. Nicola knew she'd have to get used to the way people spoke and the words they used. She'd never heard the phrase "bang on" or anyone boring anyone else "rigid."

"She's really nice," she said when James came back.

"I told you. Hugo can be a little bullish sometimes, but he's nice too. Deep down. You'll like my friends, Nic."

"I know I will."

But will they like me?

Chapter Two

The living room was enormous. Nicola's entire apartment in Buffalo could have fit in it with room to spare. There were three large couches, two armchairs, a grand piano, a bookcase that stretched all the way across one wall, a glass table, and three standing lamps, all sitting on what was clearly a Persian rug of immense proportions. Paintings of hunting scenes were on the non-bookcase walls, and there was a massive stone fireplace, with logs blazing. The room, despite being so big, was warm.

The fact that there was dog hair all over one of the couches made her feel a little less anxious, but still—the house had looked like a ship in the dark, and now it felt as if she were actually on that ship and it was an ocean liner. Definitely not someone's house.

Trez approached them, guided them to where two men and a woman were standing on the left of the fire.

"Nicola, this is my husband, Hugo." She reached out, put her hand on his arm. He was tall, but slightly stooped, and he was wearing pink trousers and a bright blue shirt.

In the car she'd imagined Trez wearing a ball gown and tiara, Hugo a tuxedo.

"Pleased to meet you." He put out his hand. "You're from the United States of America, I gather."

"Yes, I'm from Maine, but I live in New York."

"New York. Great city, I've been told." He shook her hand with a seriously firm grip.

"I don't live in Manhattan, I live in Buffalo, which is Upstate New York."

"Buffalo. Lots of Red Indians there?"

Red Indians? Who is this man?

"You met James on a plane, I gather. You've landed on your feet, haven't you?"

She was too stunned to reply.

"Hugo . . ." Trez turned to her. "I'm sorry, Nicola. My husband does not have a way with words. To put it mildly. He thinks anyone who doesn't live here in England is disadvantaged, so what he meant was that anyone who is here now is fortunate."

Really? Is that what he meant? He obviously thinks I'm some scheming gold digger. Is that what they all think?

"Hugo, for Christ's sake, you can be such a prat sometimes." James shook his head. "You should apologize to Nic."

"I'm fine, honestly. No apology necessary."

Picture him naked, Nic.

Do I have to?

"And this is Nigel and Bella." Trez was introducing her to the two others. "Bella, you haven't met James either."

They all shook hands. Bella was thin, with long blonde hair and a very pretty, petite face. She was wearing a see-through blouse, black trousers, and stiletto heels. Nigel was almost as thin and good-looking as she was; his hair was albino blond, so blond it made Bella look like a brunette.

An older man appeared, carrying a silver tray with glasses of champagne on it. At the same time, a black Labrador ran into the room, straight up to Hugo, who reached down, patted its head, then pointed to the door, saying, "Leave, Buster. Now."

No one introduced the older man to anyone else. He passed around the tray and left the room.

A *waiter*, she couldn't help but think, though she realized he was a servant. They were in their early thirties, and they had waiters.

Hugo and Trez were both one-offs, people she'd expect to see in an old Sherlock Holmes movie, but they seemed entirely comfortable in this wealth-laden setting. They'd obviously grown up in this world; they'd probably never had to worry about money or anything mundane. She couldn't imagine either of them ever going to a shrink or having neuroses.

Go for a walk with the dog, she could imagine them saying to themselves if they ever felt depressed. That's the answer. Probably to everything.

After a few seconds, the men gravitated to one another on the other side of the fireplace and started talking about some soccer match while she and Trez and Bella stood in their own little group.

"Badger's always late," Trez said once again. "It would be annoying if it weren't so predictable."

Nicola could see Bella crossing her arms, trying to hide her clearly visible white lacy bra.

"How did Badger get his nickname?" she asked.

"No clue." Trez shrugged. "He looks more like a mole than a badger, but one of our group of friends in Cambridge already had the mole nickname."

"Badger was at Cambridge too?" Bella asked.

"Yes. In a manner of speaking. He spent most of his time drinking and the rest of his time reading, but never the books he was supposed to be reading."

"Well, I understand not doing what you're supposed to do at school." Bella smiled. "Anyway, I'm a pavement person. The countryside gives me the creeps. Moles, badgers, rats. They're so ugly. And bats. You know I heard about a woman and this bat flew into her hair and got stuck. It nested there and laid little bat eggs."

"Wait a minute!" Trez exclaimed. "Wouldn't you know a bat was in your hair? Wouldn't you get rid of it? And bats don't lay eggs."

"How much hair would you have to have to make a bat nest? It's hard to picture," Nicola added.

"Yeah, I guess that might not be a true story." Bella

laughed. Trez laughed with her, and Nicola thought: *This might turn out to be a fun night. Bella seems unpretentious and friendly, Trez is making an effort with us both. I can start to relax.*

"There's another story I heard, it's even more disgusting, it's about—"

Bella was interrupted by the arrival of a man in the room. He had reddish hair and a face that did indeed resemble a mole's.

"Badger. About bloody time. We're all starving," Hugo said, striding toward him.

"I barged in without knocking, sorry. Because I've brought an extra guest as a surprise. I hope you don't mind."

"Another supposed extra man?" Trez asked him, then turned back to Nicola and Bella. "The last time Badger came, he said he'd brought an extra man with him, and he *had* brought a male, but it was a male puppy."

"No, this time it's an extra woman." Looking behind him, he said: "Come in. Surprise, everyone! She's back!"

A woman walked into the room. She had long, thick black hair; she was wearing a simple black dress, black stockings, and ballet shoes.

God, she's stunning. Who is she?

"Jules! Oh my God. It's you. I don't believe it!" Hugo walked up to her, enveloped her in a bear hug.

"Easy, Huge." She stepped back out of his embrace. "Christ, you've put on weight." She poked him in the stomach, then surveyed the room.

"Trez, what have you been feeding him? And how can you not have aged one bit in seven years?"

Trez ran to her, hugged her so tightly and for so long Nicola began to think she'd never let go. When she finally did, she had tears on her face.

"And wait a second . . ." The woman surveyed the room, her eyes traveling from Nigel to James, then to Bella and herself. "Two other gorgeous women. I thought this was a dinner party. Have I walked into a photo shoot? Hello, Nigel. And Jimmy." She walked over to James, kissed him on both cheeks. "Long time, no see. I hope you don't mind me showing up like this."

"Jimmy"? She calls him Jimmy?

Nicola stood staring at James's face. This wasn't the woman who had broken his heart a little. This had to be the woman who'd taken a sledgehammer to it.

Chapter Three

A gong sounded. Everyone started to move out of the room. That must be how they knew it was time for dinner. They had someone ring a gong.

Nicola's brain was on fire.

Had she avoided talking about exes with James on purpose? Knowing there would be some amazing Englishwoman in the background? A woman who understood his world, had no problem with waiters and gongs.

A woman who called him "Jimmy."

Had *he* avoided the topic because it was still so painful for him?

Trez and Hugo clearly adored her.

How long had they been together? How had it ended?

How was she supposed to get through this dinner when she was freaking out?

If he had to have an ex-girlfriend show up, why did it have to be such a stunning one? Except Juliet's looks were, like Trez's, a seeming contradiction. If she were being critical, she'd say that Juliet's nose was a little too pointy and her eyes were too close together and she had these big bushy black eyebrows, all features that should have disqualified her from being stunning. Yet they worked together in an unfathomable way, making any critique just plain wrong.

She was standing there in her perfect black dress, looking chic and striking and getting away with ballet slippers. Not just getting away with them but making them look like what any woman with any taste would wear.

Why did it have to be this woman? And why now?

All eight of them filed like little soldiers into the dining room, which was yet another enormous room with a table that could have seated twenty people, all laid out with china plates and silver cutlery. The table was made of some expensive wood, and it gleamed. Some poor person had probably spent hours polishing it.

How many people did Hugo and Trez employ? How had Hugo's family made their money in the first place? She'd like to know, but knew the question would be frowned upon. People like this didn't like to talk about money, they liked to spend it.

Trez had found another waiter, a young man, to bring an extra set of plates now that there were eight of them instead of seven. They would be sitting in the middle of the table, four facing four.

"You're here, Bella," Trez said, pointing at a chair. "And James, you sit beside Bella. Then I'll be beside James, and Nicola can be on his other side. Hugo, you sit opposite

Bella; Juliet, you can have the pleasure of sitting beside Hugo and Nigel, and then me, and then Badger. That works, doesn't it?"

Sitting down, Nicola looked at all the cutlery in front of her—two knives, two forks, two spoons. Yet more evidence of what a foreign world this was. But then James put his hand on her knee and squeezed it. His face was back to normal.

It's James. Remember how incredible the time you've spent together has been. This is only a weekend. You can get through it.

The young waiter was pouring wine into their glasses. Maybe the man serving the champagne in the living room was his father. They looked similar, but she couldn't be sure.

Both men were so silent and deft at their jobs, serving and disappearing, serving and disappearing.

No one was speaking. Trez kept looking at Juliet, shaking her head in evident joy and bewilderment.

"Right, well, I'll jump in and ask the only question worth asking." Juliet pushed her thick black hair back, leaned forward. "How did you two meet—Nigel—and it's Bella, isn't it? What's the story?"

"He picked me up in Boots. I work behind the counter there. The Boots on Piccadilly."

"No shit." Juliet laughed. "Nice one, Nigel. And you two? Jimmy and Nicola?"

"We met on a plane," James said. "From New York to

Paris. Nic thought she was going to get a free seat beside her, but then I came in late and took it. So she was stuck with me for seven hours."

"You were late? Not like you, Jimmy."

"I sat beside an MI5 agent on a plane once."

"Badger, I doubt he or she was an MI5 agent if he or she told you that." James laughed.

"Speaking of counterfeits, do you remember how you pretended to be with the mayor of Cambridge when we first met, Jules?" Hugo asked. "You dragged some poor man in off the street."

"The 'poor man' got a free drink. No, wait, he got *two* free drinks." Juliet laughed. "Don't forget that part."

"No one's going to forget that night. It was the first night James met . . ." Trez stopped.

"Me, Trez was going to say, Nicola." Juliet was looking straight at her. Her stare was disarmingly friendly. "The first night Jimmy and I met. But that's hardly like meeting on a transatlantic trip. Now, that sounds truly romantic. Not like some grotty Cambridge pub. I suppose I shouldn't ask if you two joined the Mile High Club."

Nicola could feel herself blushing.

"Did you know that 'Lawrence Sperry, born in 1892, invented the autopilot? He was a pilot and took advantage of his invention to become a Mile High Club member himself. Poor bloke died when he was only thirty-one."

"Badger. What a relief. Nothing's changed. You're still coming out with these ridiculous facts."

"Hardly ridiculous, Jules," Badger protested. "Knowledge is knowledge. I, for one, would never have guessed the Mile High Club existed before World War One if I hadn't stumbled across that fact."

Badger's red hair stood up on his head like a sort of comb, like a rooster's comb. His face was freckled, and his shirt was too large for him, and he constantly fidgeted—moving his fork around, turning his wineglass in a circle, snapping the elastic band on his wrist. He looked as if he wanted to get out and go roaming. But to where?

Did he actually have a job? James had told her that Badger "didn't do much of anything," so he must be rich enough to be happily unemployed.

Had Juliet broken his heart as well as everyone else's? What happened when you went to a university like Cambridge? Did you end up lusting after heartbreaking women for the rest of your life?

"I always said you'd come back from Hong Kong, Jules. Everyone comes back home eventually. Or if they don't, they regret it. We should toast to your homecoming."

"No, Huge, let's toast to the Special Relationship instead." Juliet lifted her glass and so did everyone else. "Hang on. Before we drink, do they call it the Special Relationship in the States?"

She looked directly at Nicola again.

"I'm sorry, I don't know what you're talking about." Her blush was now, she could feel, raging.

"The relationship between Britain and the US. We call it

the Special Relationship here. So you've answered my question, Nic. If you've never heard that expression, I guess we don't rate so much across the pond."

"Let's drink to it anyway," Badger put in.

Nic. Juliet had said it so naturally. She couldn't object without sounding petulant.

"To the Special Relationship." Hugo stood up. "Cheers." He took a sip of wine. They all did. "And you can't stop me making a toast to you, Jules. God, it's good to have you back. A toast to Juliet."

"Hear, hear. Here's to Jules. A jolly good fellow," Badger said. Everyone drank. Nicola wished she could go upstairs and get in bed, pull the covers up, and cry.

Clearly, Juliet had been with them all in Cambridge, then gone to Hong Kong. And now she was back.

What does she want?

To get together again with James? Jimmy?

If that were the case, though, it didn't make sense that everything Juliet had said to her, aside from the Mile High joke, had been nice. She'd been the reverse of bitchy, complimenting her and drawing her in with those eyes when she talked to her.

Jesus, Daniel, what do I do now?

Get ahold of yourself. She's an ex-girlfriend. You have an ex-boyfriend. James has nothing to fear from Greg; why should it be different with Juliet?

She's here with Badger. Maybe she's in love with him?

I doubt that.

"Nicola?" She turned to the voice, and saw Badger look-ing at her, seemingly baffled. "Sorry, but did you hear me? I asked you whether it's true, whether Americans have no sense of irony?"

"Is that what people think?" was all she could manage to respond.

The whole table was staring at her. She hadn't known about the "Special Relationship," and now she was sup-posed to prove that Americans could be ironic. How was she supposed to do that? By saying something ironic, obvi-ously. But what?

"Oh, Christ, Badge. Don't be so stupid. I met plenty of Americans in Hong Kong, and they were funny as hell. They were ironic as hell too. Think of the stereotype Eng-lishman we all know. The Hooray Henry. Believe me, the Hooray Henrys don't have much of an appetite for irony."

She came to my rescue. Another act of kindness. But couldn't it have been someone else? Couldn't James have rescued me?

She was sitting at a ridiculously large dining table in an absurdly huge house with someone who asked about Red Indians in Buffalo, a red-haired man who knew random facts and thought all Americans had no sense of irony, and a woman who literally shed tears of joy when she saw James's ex had walked into the room. It didn't get any worse. Except it did.

Now that young waiter in a white shirt and black suit is serving smoked salmon.

All these knives and forks. Which fucking one do I use to eat it?

Chapter Four

Nicola didn't understand. After they'd finished dinner, all the women had gone back into the living room, but all the men had stayed at the dinner table.

"Aren't the men coming with us?" she asked Bella, who was by her side as they walked out.

"Doesn't look that way. Looks like the blokes want to talk about bloke stuff while we sit and knit."

"But that's so—"

"It's English, Nic. Can I call you 'Nic'?"

"Yes, of course."

Bella could. Juliet couldn't. But Juliet already had. It wasn't as if she could stop her now.

"Englishmen aren't that keen on talking to women, you know. It's as if we spoil their fun."

"Really?"

"Really. Here, come sit down beside me." Bella went to one of the large sofas, sat down, patted the cushion beside her. "Must be a little tricky having the ex show up like this."

"I heard that." Juliet and Trez were walking into the room together, arm in arm. "Nic, it's not tricky for you, is it? I mean, I wanted to surprise my old friends, and Badger didn't tell me Jimmy had a new girlfriend. I didn't plan this, you know."

"Yes. I mean, yes, I know. Of course you didn't plan it. And it's all fine, really. Nothing is tricky. It's fine. Really."

Why does every word that comes out of my mouth sound stupid? Because they're all lies?

"We're going to be great friends. There's no law against that, is there? I don't understand why women can't get along just because they've slept with the same man."

"Jules." Trez laughed. "You're incorrigible."

"I'm honest. Seriously, I think men want us woman to be rivals." She unhooked her arm from Trez's, came and sat on the other side of Nicola, leaned across her a little, and addressed Bella. "What do you think, Bell? The men are sitting there smoking cigars and talking about stupid shit. We should talk about interesting things. Like jealousy. It's a terrible emotion, isn't it?"

"It's shitty, I give you that. But everyone feels jealous at some point. You can't help it."

"Really, Bell? I've never felt jealous. I don't mean to sound smug, but if someone likes someone more than they like me, well, that's the way it is. Good luck to them." Juliet shrugged.

Is that the way I should have reacted to Greg and his

divorcée? Good luck to them? *Should I be sitting here now thinking,* Hey, if James prefers Juliet, wants her back again, no sweat?

"Women always blame other women for stealing their man. And that works out well for men, doesn't it? Pit the women against one another. So much for female solidarity."

"I'd blame Hugo if he cheated, Jules." Trez was sitting on one of the big armchairs to the side. The dog who had come in before dinner appeared again, and she called him over. "Buster, you'd blame Hugo too, wouldn't you?" She took its head in her hands and shook it for a "yes."

"Huge would never cheat on you, Trez. So that doesn't really count."

"But the other woman plays a part in it," Now Bella was talking, saying exactly what Nicola was thinking. "Odds are she knows he's taken, but she goes for him anyway. That's not exactly female solidarity."

"True." Juliet shrugged again. "What the hell do I know anyway? God." She stretched her arms over her head. "It's so good to be back in England."

"What's Hong Kong like?"

It wasn't the most scintillating of questions, but at least Bella had opened her mouth. Nicola was sitting there, mute, her mind whirling. Was that talk about jealousy a coded message? A *don't blame me if James ditches you for me* statement?

"Too many junks" was Juliet's response to Bella.

"Pardon?"

Nicola saw Juliet shoot Trez a quick look and smile.

"Junks. These boats they have in Hong Kong, which are enchanting and wonderful at first, but by the time you've had a million drunken lunches on them, you want to blow the whole bloody harbor up. I left before I blew up the harbor. So tell me, what's it like working at Boots? What's the part of the job you like the most?"

"Discounts."

"Thank God." Juliet smiled. "I thought you might say something like 'all those lovely customers.'"

"Believe me, I can count the lovely customers on one hand."

"Presumably Nigel was one of those fingers."

"Nigel stuck out like a sore thumb."

"That blond hair," Trez said. "He's always had it. I swear, though, that he gets blonder by the year."

"He was probably buying hair dye on the sly," Juliet said.

"It was deodorant, actually." Bella laughed. "But points to him for not trying to hide it."

Get me out of here. They're all having a great time, and I'm sitting here sweating and feeling paralyzed.

"You must think we're crazy, Nic."

There was that direct look again. The *we're partners; we understand each other* look.

"What?"

"I mean having men in one room, women in the other. I

bet they don't do that in the States."

"No. I mean, maybe, but not at any parties I've been to. But then I—"

"Exactly. Enough of this shit, right? Let's go in and join them. What do you say, Trez? Can we gate-crash?"

"Absolutely." Trez stood up. "God, we've missed you."

I was worried about his friends not liking me. If only I'd known. I would have faked being sick and made him turn around and go back to Kensington. Anything not to be staring at that lustrous black hair of Juliet's and that perfect dress, and those ballet slippers.

And now the three of us are following behind her as she leads the way back to the dining room like a fucking Pied Piper.

Chapter Five

"So, how did you like my friends?" They'd come upstairs, and were in the bedroom, undressing. James, she could tell, was slightly drunk, but he wasn't falling-down drunk.

"They're nice. I like Trez a lot. And Bella too. Although I guess she's not one of your friends because you've never met her before."

"Right." He sat down on the bed, took off his shoes, pulled off his trousers and socks.

"It must have been a surprise to see Juliet again. How long were you together?" She was about to take off her dress, but stopped. This wasn't a conversation she wanted to have naked.

"A few years. It was ages ago, as you've probably gathered. Back in my Cambridge days."

"So you were together for a few years, and what happened?"

"She went to Hong Kong. Nic, it's ancient history. Yes, I was surprised to see her. I didn't know she was back in

England, much less that she was coming here, but like I said: ancient history."

"Do you still have feelings for her?"

"Nic." He shook his head. "No, of course not. It ended years ago. End of story. Not worth talking about."

"Okay. It's just . . . I mean, she's captivating, you know. Everyone seems to love her."

"Everyone will love you when they spend more time with you."

"Not like that."

"Nic, honestly. You're being silly and it's been a long day and we're going to be shooting tomorrow and I've had too much to drink. All I want to do is sleep. Forget about Juliet and come join me."

If all he wanted to do was to sleep, this would be the first night as a couple that they'd spend without having sex.

But he was right, it *had* been a long day. Killing birds probably did demand alertness, a good night's sleep. She shouldn't make a big deal out of it. She watched as he went over to the sink, brushed his teeth, climbed into bed, pulling the hot water bottle in with him. Then he threw one arm over his eyes. Which is what he always did when he was going to sleep.

Finishing undressing, she went and brushed her teeth too, then walked over and turned off the light, got into bed beside him.

Was she being silly?

When they'd gate-crashed the mens' after-dinner discussions, Juliet had said: "What are you all talking about?"

"Boodles. Whites."

Were these more dog names?

"In case you didn't know, Nic—and really, why would you?" Juliet turned to her. "Those are all-male clubs. Where these young men here pretend to be their fathers—or grandfathers."

Right. Not dogs.

They then started straight in on the reminiscing James had promised wouldn't happen. Pubs in Cambridge. Weekends in Cambridge. Weekends away together. It was relentless. She and Bella sat silently.

In the middle of a story Badger was telling about some card game they all used to play, Juliet looked over at her, rolled her eyes, then said:

"Enough. This must be so very tedious for you and Bell, Nic. Time to go to bed. Actually, I'm surprised all this nostalgic talk hasn't put you to sleep already."

As they all got up and started to head out of the room, Trez said:

"It's been so nice meeting you, Nicola, and you too, Bella. What a lovely evening! The shoot will be brilliant. You'll be coming with us, Jules, right? Please don't say you're leaving tomorrow."

"I don't know. I don't want to barge in on you all again."

"Nonsense. You're not barging in on anything. We can find a gun for you. I'll tell Stewart tomorrow morning to arrange it all," Hugo stated.

"I have to confess. I brought my old gun with me just in case. Naughty, I know. Anyway, who is Stewart?"

"Ah—of course you wouldn't know him. He runs the shoots for me."

"He's flawless," James added. "Stewart is a real find."

"It should be a productive day tomorrow." Hugo was making his way out of the dining room. "This is all perfect. A reunion. Tomorrow night we'll have champagne, we'll have oysters . . ."

"We'll have hangovers," Juliet said, and they all laughed. Again.

Juliet should have been a stand-up comedienne.

Nicola looked down at James, now asleep, his arm still crooked over his eyes.

They'd all shared so much together. They didn't have to go to Whites or whatever the other one was called. They had their own club, the Cambridge Club. To which she didn't belong and never would.

James had said Juliet was ancient history: she had to believe him.

She was going to be the one by his side shooting the next day. She was the one going home with him to London. She was his present. Possibly his future.

Remember how you met him, Nic. Forget about Juliet and think about that plane trip.

* * *

SHE WASN'T A lucky person. She had never won a raffle. She always picked what turned out to be the slowest lane in a supermarket. So when she looked down the aisle and it seemed as if they were about to close the door of the plane, Nicola thought maybe this one time she'd hit paydirt. The seat next to her was empty. Not only that—it was a window seat. She could move over as soon as the doors were closed. The flight was a night flight, so there wouldn't be that much of a view taking off, but by the time they were nearing Paris in the morning she'd be able to look straight out her window and get her first sight of France.

Holding her breath, staring ahead, she watched as one large man trundled down the aisle, reached her row of seats, and kept trundling. He had to be the last person boarding. Except he wasn't. There was now another man heading down the aisle, checking the numbers above the seats until he came to her row.

"Sorry," he said as he stopped, then opened the compartment above and shoved a small carry-on bag in. "I hate people like me who come and rob me of an extra seat just as I'm getting my hopes up. I'm not usually late. Sorry."

"Don't worry, it's fine." She stood up, moved out of the way, and let him scoot past her into his window seat, then sat down again.

"Right. Okay. That's that, then. For a while there I thought I wouldn't make it. The taxi driver didn't know the way to JFK, can you believe it?"

"That's crazy."

"I thought so. I'm James." He put out his hand and she shook it.

"I'm Nicola."

She was surprised by his English accent and also by the fact that he didn't have a book or any magazines with him. Maybe he was good at sleeping on planes and would conk out as soon as they were in the sky.

"It's nice to meet you, Nicola. I like to talk to people on planes, but I'm aware other people might not like to chat. I have a friend, a crusty older man who is very English and very proper. He got on a plane once, in San Francisco, and straight off the bat he turned to the man sitting next to him and said: 'I have no desire to speak to you during this trip. I plan on reading, so please respect my wishes and stay silent until we land in Bogotá.'

"The man nodded and said nothing. About ten minutes later, when the plane was on the runway, queueing to take off, the captain came on and said: 'Welcome to our flight to Boston. Flying time will be five hours and the weather looks good en route.'

"My friend freaked out. 'Wait, wait, we're flying to Bogotá, not Boston,' he said to the man next to him, who replied: 'Well, I was going to say something to you about that mix-up while we were still at the gate, but you told me to respect your wishes and stay silent, so I did.'"

"You're kidding." Nicola found herself laughing. "Really? Did that really happen?"

"Good question. My friend does consider himself something of a raconteur. He may have invented it. On the other hand, it's possible. I can definitely imagine him telling someone not to speak to him. Anyway, don't feel obligated to talk to me. I'm fine with silence too."

"You're English. Why are you flying to Paris, not London?"

"Paris? We're not flying to Philadelphia? Shit! Why didn't you tell me?" He smiled. His face was remarkably open and friendly. He had brown hair, brown eyes, a great smile, and perfectly shaped ears. She'd never noticed anyone's ears before. But then she'd never had a conversation like this before.

"I'm flying to Paris because I'm headed for the South of France. The aged bats have a house there, and I offered to shut it up at the end of the season."

"Sorry—I don't understand. What bats?"

"The aged bats. My parents."

He'd pronounced aged as "age-ed."

"They live outside of London, in a county called Kent. And they have a house in a little French town called Saint-Maximin. What about your parents—where do they live?"

"In Maine. They run a garden center there. They're not aged bats, they're aged hippies."

Her parents always laughed about having such a responsible daughter. Which was no big surprise because they spent their lives laughing. That's what happens when you're high all the time. You laugh a lot. You giggle. You smoke dope and get stoned and eat a lot of ice cream and can't understand why your child isn't as laid-back as you are.

"Nic will take care of us in our old age," her father would say, and her mother would laugh and say: "She's taking care of us now, Don."

They managed to run the garden center successfully, yet when it came to anything to do with home life, they were feckless. Like little kids who keep putting off homework, they'd say: "Oh, the laundry can wait" or "There's nothing wrong in sleeping in the same sheets for weeks, is there? Really? Come on, Nic. Don't be so strict."

They weren't alcoholics, she kept reminding herself. They didn't do anything horrible. It was her choice to be so boringly sensible. She was the one who wanted rules and order, the one who hated it when her parents lit up in front of her.

"And now it's your turn to answer the inevitable sitting-beside-a-stranger-on-an-airplane question: why are you flying to Paris, Nicola?"

"I want to see the Eiffel Tower and the Arc de Triomphe and the Louvre, and I want to eat croissants with lots of butter."

"The greedy tourist."

"I guess so."

"But . . ." He narrowed his eyes. "What you really want is to find the out-of-the-way places no tourist has ever found before and soak in the culture. Am I right?"

"Yes. You're right. But I won't find them, will I? So I'll

settle for the fluffiest croissants I can get."

The doors went to manual, the captain made an announcement about flying time, the stewardesses took their seats, and after another five minutes the plane picked up speed as it went down the runway. She gripped her armrests.

"You hate takeoffs?"

"They make me nervous. I'm fine with everything else."

"Right, then. When the plane leaves the ground, count slowly to thirty-one. When you get to thirty-one, relax. We're safe."

"How do you know that?"

"My friend Badger told me."

"You have a friend named Badger?"

"English people love nicknames, Nicola. Okay, we're off. Time to count."

He started in on "one," and she counted with him until they reached thirty-one. They weren't that far off the ground—they were still rising at a steep angle—but she relaxed.

"Is Badger a pilot?"

"God, no. Badger doesn't do much of anything except hang around and read books. He does know random facts, though. Here's another one: at high altitude, your taste-buds stop working properly. Which is why they often serve things like curry on planes—spicy meals so airplane food doesn't taste as bland as it would otherwise."

"But if you're in first class, you get amazing food and

wine, don't you?"

"Exactly. I mean, you're supposed to. But I think you pretend to think it's amazing because of the expense."

This was crazy. She'd been on only four flights in her life: two with Greg to Florida for a winter break, the other two to Denver when Sue had spent a year there. On the outbound Denver flight, she'd been sitting beside an old man who never stopped coughing. On the homeward one, the woman next to her spent the whole time talking about her grandchildren. When she'd flown with Greg, he'd spent both flights reading magazines about cars.

It had never occurred to her that she'd be talking to an attractive, funny Englishman on his way to the South of France. She'd visualized the sights she was going to see; she'd bought a guidebook and a French phrase book in preparation. But she wasn't prepared to be having such a good time at the very start of this trip.

Don't do it, she told herself. But she did. She snuck a look at his left hand. He wasn't wearing a wedding ring.

Jesus, get a grip. It's been a half hour or so, and you're already acting like a teenager.

"Aha. The seat belt sign has pinged off." Unbuckling his seat belt, he shifted so that his back was against the window and he was at an angle to her. "So your parents live in Maine. Where do you live?"

"In Buffalo. Upstate New York."

"And what do you do in Buffalo?"

"I work—I mean, I used to work in the admissions department of a college there."

"But not anymore?"

"No."

"What happened?"

"It's boring."

"I want to hear."

He looked as if he really did want to hear, so she told him about Tony Kellow, how creepy he was, how she'd ended up hitting him. She kept the story as short as possible and skipped the part about Greg cheating on her.

"Jesus. Tony Kellow. What a wanker," he said when she'd finished.

"A what?"

"A wanker. Creep. Idiot. Useless excuse for a human being."

"You don't think I overreacted?"

"I think you *under*reacted. My friend Hugo runs a shoot. I should give him a call, arrange something." He must have seen the puzzled look on her face. "Hugo has a big house in the English countryside. A massive pile. He's going to be an earl someday, which is absolutely bonkers, but anyway, he invites people to his house to shoot pheasants. We should get that Kellow wanker over, paste a few feathers on him, and he can be one of the soon-to-be-dead pheasants."

She laughed. Again.

"He's going to be an earl? God. I didn't think I'd ever meet anyone who knew an earl, or someone who is going to be an earl."

"Hugo wasn't supposed to be one. His uncle is the oldest son, so he inherited the title when his father died. And he would have passed it on to his children, except he hasn't had any, and he says he's never going to, so it will all go to Hugo. Hugo's next in line because, sadly, *his* father died. I know." He shrugged. "The whole thing is crazy, but that's how it works."

"Does Hugo have a nickname?"

"Somebody used to . . . No, not really. But his wife has one. She's called Trez. Because that's what she is. The salt of the earth. A real treasure."

"Sounds like you have a lot of friends."

"I suppose I do." He pushed his hair back from his forehead. "Look—the drinks trolley is arriving. What do you think? Shall I get some champagne? We're going to France. It would be highly appropriate."

"Would we be able to taste it?"

"We'd feel the bubbles at the very least. It's worth a shot, don't you think?"

"I think it sounds perfect."

When her parents talked about people's auras and energy and "vibes," she'd think: *Where do you come up with this ridiculous stuff?* Now, sitting beside this stranger named James, she felt like calling them as soon as she landed and saying, *I get it. It took one person on a plane, but I get it. There really are people who give off amazing vibes.*

While they were drinking the champagne, James told

her all about his parents' house in Saint-Maximin, a little village up in the hills: The village had a bar and a square where the locals played a game called boules. It had four bedrooms and was near a medieval town called Uzès.

"They have a market in Uzès on Saturdays. All this amazing food, and you can sit in a café and eat oysters and little clams and drink wine, and it's blissful, I have to say."

"Are there lots of tourists there?"

"In the summer, but not now, not off-season."

"Right." She closed her eyes, trying to imagine it.

"You're smiling."

"Because you make it sound like heaven."

"I'm telling the truth. Not one exaggeration."

"Have Badger and Hugo and Trez been there?"

"Trez and Hugo but not Badger. You're good at remembering names. Why are all Americans good at remembering names?"

"Are we?"

"Yes, you are, Nicola."

"What were you doing in New York?"

"Some business. I'm involved in shipping. Insurance for shipping."

"'Involved'?"

"Unlike your story about work, mine really *is* boring. So tell me. Do you have siblings?"

"I did. I mean, I was born a twin, but my brother didn't live. He died about three minutes after he was born. Sometimes . . ."

"Sometimes what?" Again, the way he asked the question made her want to answer it.

"Sometimes I miss him. I know that might sound crazy, but I feel he was a part of me, you know? I think of what he might have been doing, how we would have had fun with each other. His name was Daniel. *Is* Daniel. I talk to him sometimes. Oh God. Shit. The champagne has gone to my head. I'm talking too much. I don't usually. Talk a lot, I mean. And I don't ever talk about him. I don't know why I told you that. You must think I'm nuts."

He sat back and was silent for long enough for her to wonder how she could have ever told him that. They were strangers. She wasn't in a confessional box; this wasn't the time to divulge childhood loss and angst. Much less how she had conversations with a dead sibling.

"Listen, Nic—and I'm going to call you 'Nic' because as I said, English people love nicknames and 'Nic' is exactly that, isn't it? A nickname? And that's a bad joke, but it could be worse—you should hear some of the jokes another friend of mine, Nigel, tells—they are embarrassingly bad—but the point is, I have an idea. Which might be considered a brilliant idea. Come with me to the house. I won't pounce on you, I promise. But I will get you on the flight to Marseilles with me when we land in Paris and you can see Uzès for yourself and you don't have to be an ordinary tourist. You can be part of France. I'll teach you how to play boules. You can leave whenever you want. That's another promise."

"You're *really* drunk." She laughed.

"Tell you what: Give me five good reasons why you won't come, and I'll forget all about it. But there have to be five. And they have to be good."

"Okay. One: I don't know you. Two: I don't know your last name."

"One and two are the same. I grant they qualify as a reason of sorts, but you still have four more to go."

"Two: I was supposed to go to Paris. I have the guide-book and everything. Oh God, that sounds tragic. Listen, they're all the same. All five reasons. I don't know you. You're a stranger; you might be dangerous."

"Nic." He shook his head. "My friend Nigel, the one who tells the awful jokes—he once said: 'I used to worry about you, James. But then I thought: *Well, the meek are supposed to inherit the earth, so I guess you'll be fine.* The point being, my friends, everyone who knows me, would be on the floor laughing if someone ever called me 'danger-ous.'"

"And my friends, everyone who knows me, would bet every cent they had that I wouldn't go with you. I'm a re-sponsible, sensible person."

"Really?" His eyebrows raised. "How responsible? How sensible?"

Her third-grade teacher had once called a boy named Bobby Tappan to the front of the classroom. He stood there blushing as the teacher then announced: "There is not a bad bone in Bobby Tappan's body." It was a truly bizarre moment, and the whole rest of the class laughed about it later, but the phrase had always stayed in her mind.

James looked like Bobby Tappan. They even had the same little bald spot at the backs of their heads.

"I really do want to see the Eiffel Tower. Don't ask me why. I just do."

"That's easy. We land early in the morning, the flight to Marseilles isn't until the afternoon. We can go to Paris, see the Eiffel Tower and the Arc de Triomphe, and get back to the airport in time to catch the Marseilles flight."

"You make it sound so . . . I don't know. I mean, it's all so crazy. You promise you won't kill me?"

"I'll do my best not to. I can't promise anything, though."

He made her laugh. A lot. But flying off with him?

This isn't you, Nic.

She could hear every voice in her head saying it.

There had been a girl in her seventh-grade class, Melinda, who used to invite her over for sleepovers a lot. Melinda lost her backpack one day, and Nicola remembered Melinda's parents, at the dinner table, sighing and saying, "She is *so* forgetful. Melinda forgets everything, loses everything. She's not like you, Nicola. She's hopeless."

Nicola had seen Melinda wince, then smile and say: "I know. I am. I'm hopeless."

The thing is, Nicola couldn't recall Melinda forgetting or losing anything at school except that backpack that one day. But as the years passed, she did. And every time she lost or forgot something, she'd smile and say: "I'm hopeless, aren't I?"

Maybe you grew into the labels you'd been given. And maybe those labels weren't accurate to begin with.

"Nic?" James nudged her with his elbow. "What's going on in that head of yours?"

"I'm thinking of people I used to know at school."

"Because?"

"Because you're like Bobby Tappan, and I don't want to be like Melinda."

"Would you care to elaborate on that? You've lost me."

"Does the village, does Saint-Maximin, have a place in it that sells croissants?"

"Absolutely. It has a little boulangerie that makes fluffy croissants. Fresh every morning."

"I think that sounds perfect."

Chapter Six

TREZ

"Tell me everything." Trez sat on the bed, her back against the pillows, while Juliet sat cross-legged opposite her, wrapped up in a blanket. "What was Hong Kong like? Why didn't you keep in touch? You stopped writing to me. And calling. Why?"

"It's a crazy city, Trez. And so busy, and I was run off my feet."

"Doing what?"

"Everything. So many parties, lots of travel. You can get to masses of exotic places easily from Hong Kong. It's blissful."

"But you came back."

"Well, there's no place like home, right?"

"How are your parents? Did you have a boyfriend in Hong Kong? How long are you back for?"

"Hang on." She put up her hands. "This feels like an interrogation. My parents are fine. I had a relationship, but that's over. And I'm back for good. Now can we talk about you? Badger told me all about you and Huge and the uncle who doesn't want to have children. You always said he would at some point. Is he gay?"

"Jonathon? Gay? No. I mean, I don't think so. It never occurred to me."

"So he buggers off, leaves you the house, and when he dies will leave you the title. Not bad. Where is he now?"

"In Mykonos. He likes the weather there."

"Of course he does."

"What does that mean?"

"God, Trez, you were always so naïve, bless you. He's gay. And God bless him, he hasn't married anyone and had an heir just to keep up the pretense. You know, you being in charge of this place is wonderful. You were always the best one at that god-awful secretarial college. You could run a company. You could run the world. Seriously, sweetheart. You're bloody brilliant."

She took a moment to let the compliment seep in, to bask in it.

"Thank you. But there are things I'm not good at."

"Such as?"

"Getting pregnant."

"Really? Well, that could be Huge's—"

"No, it's not his problem. We've checked that out. So it must be mine. I have an appointment with a specialist later in the month to take some tests."

She grabbed a pillow and hugged it. This was the first time she'd said it out loud. To anyone. Juliet sat quietly for a minute then said:

"Listen, you're still young. And it can take a while. You shouldn't worry about it. I'm sure Huge doesn't care."

"But he does care." Now she felt tears forming. "It means the world to him."

"Sweetheart, *you* mean the world to him. Besides, I'm sure it will happen."

"Are you? Because I'm not. You don't know what it's like. His family look at my stomach every time they see me to check if I have a bulge. All the people we see either avoid the topic in such an obvious way it's humiliating, or they actually dive right in and say something like: 'When's the sprog coming?' Or 'Feeling broody, Trez?'—I don't know which is worse. Every month—God, every single month, I'm full of hope, and every single month I'm in despair."

"Trez." Juliet got up from the bottom of the bed and came to lie beside her and put her arm around her. "Honestly, I'm sure it will work out."

"Please don't tell me to be patient." She buried her face in Juliet's shoulder.

"I wouldn't dream of it. I will tell you to cheer up, though. And when you do get pregnant, I know some great ayahs—nannies—in Hong Kong. I'm sure we could get one of them over for you."

"I don't think I would want anyone else to look after my

child if I had one."

"My God." Juliet laughed, hugged her. "That is a radical statement. Now—I have to get some sleep. I'm shattered. Which room am I in?"

"The one at the end of the hall on the right. On this floor. Your bag is there. I assumed you wouldn't want to share a room with Badger."

"If you hadn't assumed that, I'd be doubting your sanity right now." She gave Trez another hug then stood up. "Sweet dreams. And don't worry. Everything will be fine."

"We can have a talk again tomorrow by ourselves. After the shoot?"

"Absolutely."

"'I can't tell you how happy I am that you're back."

"And I'm happy too. Very happy. Jesus, Bella is something, isn't she? Those stiletto heels."

"And that blouse. She's such a switch for Nigel. He usually picks the demure English-rose type of girl. I was going to ask her where she's from, but then you arrived and surprised everyone. How did Badger get in touch with you, or did you get in touch with him?"

"I called him."

"You called Badger? Before calling me?"

"I didn't have your phone number, Trez. Badger was at his parents' house, the same number he's always had. Anyway, Bella's clearly from up north. Newcastle, Bolton? I don't know. Somewhere like that. Somewhere where they say 'pardon.'"

"God, we're terrible snobs. I hate myself for noticing those things."

"You can't help it. We learned not to use words like that from the time we started talking. It's ingrained. And I can't help it either. I'm looking forward to seeing what Bella wears tomorrow." Juliet slapped herself lightly. "Stop it! No more snobbery. I promise."

"I promise too. Jules? Did you get the wedding invitation I sent? You never replied."

"No. I moved flats a couple of times. It must have gone to the wrong one."

"I tried to call too."

"Shit. Must have been an old number as well. We'll make up for it, though. I want to see all the photos, hear all the gossip. But right now what I want most is sleep. Night, sweetheart, see you tomorrow."

Juliet left, trailing the scent of Fracas, the perfume she used to wear all those years ago when they'd met at secretarial school in Cambridge. The first day, they'd been assigned seats beside each other, and Juliet had frightened her, not only because she looked so stunning with her long, thick, black hair, her gorgeous paisley bell-bottoms, and her white linen shirt, but because she was terrifyingly proficient, typing at an incredible speed.

"Sorry if I'm being rude, but I don't understand why you're here," she'd had the courage to say when the day was finished, and they were getting their coats to go. "I couldn't help but notice. You're so good. You can't possibly need this course when you type as fast as that."

"You're not being rude at all. And you'd be right—I wouldn't need this course if I'd actually been typing properly instead of hitting random keys. I don't think I typed one intelligible word. It was fun." Juliet had brushed that black hair of hers away from her face and smiled. She was one of those females Trez had always envied, the type who was effortlessly chic and stunning.

"I'm Juliet. This is a horrible institution, so we have to be creative. Let's try to make it as much fun as possible, all right?"

"Absolutely." Trez had smiled back. "And I'm Jane."

"Really?" Juliet, one arm in her linen jacket, stopped and studied her. "Jane? Do you like that name?"

"No. The truth is, I've never particularly liked it."

Juliet was still studying her, staring at her, looking as if she were sizing her up for some important job.

"You're not a Jane, you're a find. I was worried I wouldn't meet anyone decent here, but here you are. And I didn't even have to hunt for you. You're a treasure. Which means that, as of now, you're Trez." She finished putting her jacket on. "Right. We're friends now, Trez. Officially. So we should start having fun together as soon as possible. How about a drink this evening?"

"Can I bring my boyfriend, Hugo?"

"Is he a new boyfriend or an old boyfriend?"

"We've been together since we were sixteen and seventeen."

"My God. And is he learning how to be a secretary too?"

"He's at Cambridge. I enrolled in this school so I could be near him."

"Well, then you have to bring him. Bring Hugo, bring anyone he knows, bring the mayor. Is there a mayor of Cambridge? There must be. I'll find him and bring him along too. Just don't tell me I'm crazy. I'm sick to death of being called crazy because I like to do things differently."

They settled on a time and a pub and said their good-byes.

When Trez then went to Hugo's room, James was there. The two had been friends since childhood, had gone to the same schools and now the same university.

"Listen, I've met this glorious girl at secretarial school. Her name is Juliet. She wants to have a drink later. She said to bring anyone I can, so you two have to come."

"A glorious girl? I'm coming," James said.

"She's given me a new name. I'm Trez now, short for Treasure."

"That was fast," James smiled. "One day and she's already rechristened you? Still, it suits you. Doesn't it, Hugo?"

"Trez? It's not a real name, is it?"

"I like it. A lot. It's better than Jane. Wait till you meet Juliet. She's different."

"*Gloriously* different?"

"Yes, James. You'll see."

The rest was history—the history of her and Juliet's

best friendship and Juliet and James's romance. Until three years later, when Juliet decided she'd had enough of England, enough of James, and had buggered off to Hong Kong.

Trez hadn't realized just how much she missed her until she saw her again.

She's back. She's going to bring me good luck, I know. Everything will be fine. The timing is right. Hugo should be back from walking Buster soon. Maybe tonight will be the night.

Chapter Seven

NICOLA

It hadn't been an easy night. Sleeping would have been difficult enough, thinking about Juliet's arrival, but the fact that the room was freezing cold meant she was lucky to have managed even a few hours.

She couldn't understand how Trez's mind worked. "It's so cold in here. Has the heat gone off? Should we say something?" she'd asked James when they'd first come in after dinner.

"No, Hugo and Trez aren't fans of central heating. And I should warn you they turn the hot water off during the night too. But we have hot water bottles. They'll keep us warm."

Hot water bottles were a sweet touch, maybe, but they made her think of being a little girl with a stomachache, and anyway, hot water bottles stayed hot for only so long.

She couldn't get up at two a.m. and refill hers from the sink in the corner of the room even if she'd wanted to, given this no-hot-water-at-night policy.

Having a sink in the bedroom was weird enough—not having hot water or heat was even weirder. There didn't seem to be any point to having all this money and all these people working for you if you couldn't keep yourself or your house warm in freezing temperatures.

She felt as if she'd had maybe two hours of sleep when James sprang out of bed, leaned over, kissed her, and said:

"I hate having a hangover when I'm shooting. I need to get a cup of coffee as soon as possible. How did you sleep?"

"Great."

"Not too cold?"

"No, fine. Is it okay for me to wear jeans and a sweater?"

"Yes. Some people dress in plus fours, but no one will expect you to. The German probably will. I'm not going to either."

"What are plus fours?"

"You'll see. God, I'm starving too. Why do hangovers make you so hungry? Let's get moving. Breakfast awaits."

When they entered the dining room, she saw that the breakfast was a buffet. All the food was laid out on the sideboard, in special dishes to keep it warm, so they could serve themselves. Trez, Hugo, Nigel, Bella, Badger, and a man she hadn't seen before were all sitting at the table with full plates of food in front of them.

"Good morning, Nicola. Hope you slept well." Trez

was dressed in blue-and-green plaid trousers and a blue sweater. The sweater had holes in it and was so big it had to be Hugo's.

At various points in her sleepless night, Nicola had replayed seeing Trez's tears of happiness when Juliet walked in. But she and Juliet had been great friends in the past, obviously. So it was natural for Trez to have been so happy to see her.

I have to be rational about all this. In the cold light of day, what's the big deal? An old girlfriend is an old girlfriend, not a new one.

"I slept really well, thanks."

"This is Stewart." Trez motioned to the unknown man, who stood up, came over, and shook her hand. "Stewart, this is Nicola."

He looked at her strangely for a second, then said: "It's nice to meet you, Nicola. And hello, Mr. Shuttleworth. It's good to see you again." He shook James's hand as well before going back to the table. He was good-looking; tall, with short dark hair, very blue eyes, and a long straight nose that suited his long face. She figured he was in his midthirties.

"Help yourselves to food and come sit down." Trez pointed at the buffet. "We've been discussing—"

"Did you know that oranges have been produced commercially in Florida since the mid-1800s?" Badger cut in.

"Badger, you interrupted Trez. And that really isn't an interesting fact." Hugo shook his head.

"I think it's interesting. I think it's fascinating, Badger."

"Thank you, James."

"Were you a cheerleader, Nicola?"

"What?"

"Aren't all cute blonde American girls cheerleaders, thrashing those pom-pom things around?"

"Hugo." James sighed. "Honestly. You are bloody hopeless."

"No," she said. "No. I didn't even try out to be one."

Really. Who is this man?

Juliet arrived then, sweeping in, going behind Hugo, putting her arms around his neck, saying, "Good morning Huge. And you." She moved over to Trez, ruffled her short hair. "It feels like the old days, doesn't it? Do you remember when I used to bring you a cold can of Coke when you were hungover?"

"A can of Coke and a chocolate bar. You'd always say: 'Sugar is underrated as a medicine.'"

Juliet was dressed in green corduroy trousers and a green sweater. She looked fresh, as if she'd slept soundly for twelve hours. The cold clearly suited her.

"Tell us about this German, Huge. Is he filthy rich?" Juliet asked as she went over to the sideboard and studied the food on display.

"Filthy."

Nicola, Juliet, and James helped themselves to food and sat down: Juliet was between Badger and Hugo, while Nicola was flanked by James and Nigel.

Turning toward Juliet, Nigel said: "Very interesting—the Fab Four are back together. I never thought it would happen."

"God—are the Beatles reuniting? I hadn't heard that."

"Unfortunately not. Or fortunately if you're not a fan. I never did like 'Yesterday.' So maudlin. No, I was referring to Hugo and Trez and Juliet and James. They were known as the Fab Four in Cambridge days. I think I gave them that name—or maybe Badger did. No, it was definitely me on one of the many drunken evenings. Anyway, when are you going back home?"

"Sorry?"

"When are you going back to the good old US of A, although the US of A is hardly old?"

"I don't know when I'm going back." Once again she felt herself blushing.

"Please—don't look so taken aback. I like to tease people. It's a bad habit of mine."

"Do you tease Bella?"

"As much as humanly possible. But Bella doesn't rise to the bait."

And I do. The Fab Four. Really? Rub it in, Nigel. Tell me more about how close everyone is, keep reminding me of what an outsider I am. Ask me again when I'm going back. The would-be cheerleader who has landed on her feet.

"Anyway, I think you'll enjoy the shooting. You've never been on a shoot before, have you?"

"No."

"Well, it's exciting. And Stewart says there'll be lots of birds today."

"Why didn't Stewart come to dinner last night?" Stewart was sitting away from them, at the far end of the table, looking uncomfortable.

"Stewart organizes the shoots."

"Okay. Right. And he didn't come to dinner last night because?"

"Because he's the one who organizes the shoots."

"So he's in a different caste?"

"We're not in India, Nicola."

"Could have fooled me." It slipped out before she could stop herself.

Nigel raised his eyebrows, gave her a quizzical look.

"You don't really think that, do you? We're not that bad. There are rules about these things, that's all. Unspoken rules."

"I was joking. Sort of. Anyway, I get it. There are rules. I just don't understand what the rules are. How long has Stewart been working for Hugo?"

"A while. Maybe three or four years. Stewart knows everything there is to know about hunting, fishing, and shooting. I remember once when we were shooting grouse in Scotland; he was there, and I asked him to take me salmon fishing with him in the morning before the shoot. As we were walking to the river, he turned to me and said, 'Quiet—I can tell there's a fish there,' and as we got to the riverbank he cast, midstride—and hooked a fucking whopper of a salmon."

"You mean he'd seen it there when you were walking?"

"We went just as dawn was breaking. It was still pretty dark out. He couldn't have seen it."

"So he sensed it?"

"Exactly. Stewart is a man of nature."

Hugo laughed loudly at something Juliet had said. Nigel looked over at them.

"Oh, Christ. He's still in love with her."

"What?"

"Hugo. He's always been in love with Jules. I shouldn't say that out loud. But as you know now, I say things no one else does."

"Does Trez... I mean, I don't understand. Are you teasing me again?"

"No. Everyone was in love with Jules in the Cambridge days. Now it's just a question of who still is, isn't it?"

"What are you two chatting about?" James, who had been talking to Bella, turned to them. "Nic, you look surprised. What's Nigel been saying to you?"

"We were talking about Stewart and his affinity to nature. That time I saw him catch a salmon."

"You always tell that story."

"True." Nigel nodded.

"That's completely mad," Hugo's voice boomed out. "Really, Jules, how do you come up with these wonderful things?"

"What things?" Trez asked. "What's mad?"

"I'll tell you later." Juliet laughed. "You're my perfect audience, Huge."

Badger started telling a story about some old friend of theirs he'd run into on the street in London while Nicola sat, eating her food, half listening.

There were nine people sitting at the table, and they didn't take up half of it. They might be laughing at parts of Badger's story, but it didn't feel as if they were adults enjoying themselves; it felt as if they were children waiting for the grown-ups to come in and tell them it was time to go to school. Or as if they were performing a play without an audience: she couldn't decide which.

No, she could. It *was* a play. And Juliet had the starring role.

Badger, as he was telling the story, was looking at Juliet. Trez, when she laughed, looked at Juliet. Both Bella and Nigel's eyes were on Juliet. Stewart's weren't, but then Stewart looked preoccupied. And James was staring at his plate of food. Was he frightened of looking at Juliet? Was it too painful for him?

"We should get going," Stewart suddenly announced, standing up. He had a sort of flat cap in his hands.

"Absolutely. Come on." Juliet rose as well. "Time to shoot a ton of birds. Let's show the filthy-rich German how to do it."

Of course. She should have guessed already. Juliet had to be an ace at shooting pheasants.

Everyone was in love with her. Now it's just a question of who still is, isn't it?

Chapter Eight

TREZ

Trez had woken up early, in an outstanding mood. She'd been right: Juliet had brought her good luck, and that good luck had brought her a huge amount of satisfaction. When he arrived back from walking the dog after dinner, Hugo had kissed her so passionately she stepped back in surprise.

"What's—"

Before she could say another word, he'd swept her up, laid her on the bed, undressed her, undressed himself, and proceeded to make love to her in the sort of way she'd almost forgotten was possible. Being together for so many years had already taken a toll on their sex life, and for the past two years the pressure of conceiving had made sex seem like a chore.

She'd laughed out loud afterward, and he'd asked,

"What's so funny?"

"It's not funny, it's glorious." She'd kissed him on his neck. "You're glorious."

"I suppose I have my moments."

She'd laughed again.

The weekend was going perfectly so far. Now that breakfast was finished, she made a move to the hallway off the kitchen to find a proper jacket and Wellington boots for Nicola. Normally, she'd stay behind and organize the shooting lunch, but Hugo had had a call earlier saying that a neighbor who was going to come to the shoot was sick and had to drop out, so Hugo had told Trez she could take the neighbor's place. Proud of the fact she was a decent shot, happy that she'd be shooting with Juliet, she hummed "Woman in Love" to herself and selected the boots and jacket.

"Where are you, Buster?" she heard Hugo call out.

Other women liked good-looking bad boys. She remembered one of Nigel's old girlfriends saying, "He's trouble, he's untrustworthy, he flirts for England, and I don't believe for a second he'll stick with me, but shit, he's attractive." Trez understood the concept; she'd read enough novels and seen enough TV to know women liked trouble if it came with a handsome enough face. So she understood, but she knew she wasn't that type of female.

He might not be the most attractive of men physically, but you couldn't have everything, and in the deepest part of her soul and heart she loved him to bits. He wasn't one for public displays of affection either, but he had a huge heart.

"There you are, old boy. We're going to have a good time today, aren't we?" The sweetness in his voice as he talked to Buster made her heart swell.

Ranger, Buster's predecessor, another black Labrador, had had to be put to sleep a few years before. In the vet's office, Hugo had sat holding him on his lap, cradling him as if Ranger were his last hope, as if Ranger would protect him from all the harm of the world. His eyes were dripping tears on top of Ranger's head, and he wouldn't let go of him even when it was over, not until, after almost half an hour, Trez had gently taken his elbow and said, "It's time, Hugo. It's time to go home."

"I can't bear it," he'd whispered. But then he'd relaxed his grip and let the vet take Ranger away.

He'll be like that if we have a baby, she thought. *He'll pretend to be strict, but he'll be soppy and let him or her get away with anything, I bet.*

If we have a baby.

If something isn't horribly wrong with me.

She couldn't think about it. When she did let herself think about it, she felt scared and sick and crazy. So crazy that lately she'd begun to bash herself on her thigh to stop the thoughts.

Belt up, Trez.

It was one of her father's favorite expressions. If she was sulking or feeling sorry for herself, he'd give her one of his stern, frightening looks and say, "Belt up."

Someone, at some dinner party, had said once that if you addressed yourself in the third person it helped to face down your fears and concerns.

These days everyone was talking about their children at dinner parties.

For God's sake, belt up, Trez.

Chapter Nine

NICOLA

Stepping outside and seeing the grounds in the light, Nicola said, "Wow," out loud, then turned around, looked at the house, and said, "Wow," again. What she hadn't seen in the dark was just how much of a mansion it was, stretching out for what seemed like the length of a football field. Made of russet brick and yellowing stone, it was three floors high with a tiled, gabled roof. The windows on the first two floors were tall and thin, while on the third floor, what must have been the attic, they were small and oval-shaped.

Then there were the columns at the front. How had she managed to miss seeing those the night before, even in the dark? Four fiercely imposing Greek columns, two on each side of the front door. She'd studied the difference between Ionic and Doric columns in school, but she couldn't remember which was which.

Resting above the columns was a balcony, like the balcony she'd seen at Buckingham Palace when she'd gone on her own one morning to the Trooping of the Guards. She could imagine Trez and Hugo coming out on it, waving to the minions below.

Buckingham Palace didn't have acres and acres of perfectly mown grass stretching in front of it, though, or the trees that lined that grass, creating a vast avenue, nature's equivalent to the Champs-Élysées and then some.

There were old amazing houses in New York too, but they were mostly museums. Once she and Greg had gone to visit Boldt Castle, a couple of hours' drive from Buffalo, on one of the Thousand Islands.

"The guy, I think he owned the Waldorf Astoria hotels or something—he built it for his wife, but she died before it was finished, so he just left it, and now they're fixing it up for tourists," Greg had informed her. *How incredibly romantic*, she'd thought, *and how sad*.

"See . . ." James was beside her, pointing down the avenue. "That patch of discolored grass there? That's the cricket pitch. They have matches in the summer. It would take me a century to explain the rules to you. All you really need to know is that you can play a match for five days and no one wins. You know, this place is a landmark. If you're on the right side of a plane coming into Gatwick, you can easily see it. Stunning, right?"

"What's behind that big hedge to the left?" she asked.

"A swimming pool. And there's a tennis court at the back of the house. A grass one."

"Like Wimbledon."

"Like Wimbledon. Why do all Americans put a 't' in the word and say 'Wimbleton'? I've never been able to work that out. Anyway, it is like Wimbledon"—he smiled—"but without the talent playing on it."

Did I say "Wimbleton"? Maybe I did. At least the others didn't hear that. How many more mistakes am I going to make?

"It's all amazing, beyond stunning."

Was it possible to overdose on beauty? Paris, the South of France, medieval towns, mews houses on Dickensian cobblestoned streets, and now this. She thought of how many hours she'd sat out on the stoop of her apartment, staring at the nondescript street in front of her. That was in the summer. Before she and Greg had been able to afford an air-conditioning unit. In the winter, she'd spend hours on the same stoop shoveling snow.

"James," Badger called out. He was standing beside a car that was parked in front of a huge garage to the right. It looked as if all the guests' cars were parked there, as well as a row of jeeps. With this many cars, there should have been a wedding happening or some major social extravaganza. "James, come here for a second," Badger called again.

"I'll be right back," he said, squeezing her elbow before he walked off.

Suddenly, Bella was at her side. "Have you counted the windows in this place? I mean, honestly, this is some pad."

"I know. I can't really believe it. And the idea that just two people live here. Or do the waiters and everyone live here too?"

"The servants, you mean. They may not use that word, but that's what they are. Nigel told me they only come in when there's a dinner party or some big do. They're from the villages around here, apparently. But I bet they used to have servants living here. The whole thing is from some other century when there were peasants or whatever.

"Christ—will you look at what Badger's got on? Those . . . what do you call them? I saw it in a book about shooting I got in a library. Something to do with addition. Plus fours. That's it. Plus fours. Those ridiculous-looking green plaid trousers that come down to just below his knees and balloon out. And those long wool socks covering his lower legs. With those little tassels sticking out. Who the fuck wears tassels? Oh my God. And the long jacket that matches the balloon-y trousers. He looks like a clown, especially with his red hair."

"I guess it's like some kind of uniform?"

"Sure. Like soldiers. At war with some poor little birds. Actually, they don't have to shoot them. If I were a bird and I saw these people dressed up like Badger, I'd drop down dead of fright."

"That's impressive—that you took out a book about shooting, I mean."

"I figured I might surprise Nigel with a few facts he wouldn't think I knew. Except I already almost forgot plus fours."

"How long have you and Nigel been together?"

"Three months. I played hard to get for a while there. Even though it's not easy to play hard to get when you're the girl who works behind the counter at Boots and he's a handsome flash git in the city making megabucks. But I managed. You know, if I took a picture of Badger now in that getup and showed it to my friends back home, they'd roll around on the floor laughing."

"Where's home?"

"Sheffield. Up north. It's a lot different in Sheffield, let me tell you."

"I think my friends in Buffalo would laugh too."

"Listen, love, we're the outsiders here. Northerners are like Americans, you know. We're friendly. And we speak our minds. That's one of the things Nigel likes about me. That I tell him when he's talking shite."

"Shite?"

"Shit." Bella laughed. "Shit. Like last night, I said: 'What's going on with these people? Why don't they turn on the central heating? It's not as if they can't afford it.' And he said, 'They're being careful, that's all. They don't like to waste money.' And I said, 'Really? That's why they have all the waiters and a cook and a lawn tennis court and a swimming pool and everything? They don't like wasting money? Well, I don't like getting pneumonia.' He thought that was a hoot."

The weather was cold, the skies dull gray. Nicola tried to imagine it here on a summer's day: People playing cricket however they played it on that patch of lawn. Then rushing back into the house to change into bathing suits—or tennis whites.

It would be a sight to behold, she knew. Yet now all she could think of was how big this place was, how two people were living in a house that should have held twenty; how Trez and Hugo must sit most nights by that roaring fire on their own, stranded in the immense living room, patting the dog.

Or maybe they would sit in a cozy kitchen. If the kitchen was cozy. She hadn't seen it. She hadn't seen the cook.

Juliet appeared from the house, went over to where all the cars were parked, and was talking with Badger and James as she pulled something out of the trunk of the car. A leather case. Nicola watched her lift out three pieces of what was clearly a gun, picking them out one by one and assembling them into a long rifle, which she then placed into a full-length type of sleeve cover.

At no point had she hesitated.

"I wouldn't touch one of those things, would you?" Bella waved toward Juliet and the rifle.

"No, never. I know there are a lot of guns in America, but I hate them, actually. Maybe *because* there are so many in America."

"I hope I don't faint when the first bird gets shot and

drops down dead as a dodo."

Juliet was talking to James. They were at an angle to her, so Nicola couldn't see their expressions, but she did see Juliet give James a playful little push. James raised his hands and it looked as if he was going to playfully push her back, but he then stepped back, away from her.

But he almost did. He almost playfully pushed her back.

They probably playfully pushed each other all the time when they were together.

James then went over to his car, opened the trunk, took his gun out, and put it together just as Juliet had.

"Here you go." Trez walked up to them and handed Nicola a green jacket and a pair of boots. "I think these wellies will fit you."

"Thanks so much." She stepped out of her loafers, tried them on. "They're perfect, thank you."

"Great. I have to go make sure the lunch is taken care of. I'll see you later."

"Wellies?" She turned to Bella.

"Wellington boots. Green wellies. Another part of the uniform." Bella shook her head. "Nigel bought me mine. And my green jacket, like the one you have now. Those are called Barbours. This whole shooting lark is bloody expensive. Ah—here comes your boyfriend. I better go find mine."

As Bella walked away, James came up. "Bella seems nice."

"She is. She says she's from the North and that it's different there. Is there a big difference?"

"Yes, more or less. I'll tell you about it later on."

"What did Badger want?"

"We were discussing guns."

And Juliet was playfully pushing you.

Can I say, Tell her to keep her fucking hands off you?

Hi, everyone, I'm Nicola. James hasn't introduced me properly. I'm a crazily jealous woman.

A silver BMW appeared, gliding down the drive and parking parallel to Badger's car.

"Safe bet that's the German," James stated. The engine switched off and a middle-aged bald man dressed in plus fours stepped out. "He looks bloody grim. And he's brought a loader with him."

Another man was getting out of the car.

"A loader?"

"He'll load the German's gun with more bullets for him when he needs them. That way he doesn't have to take any time out when he's shooting. Sort of like a page turner for a pianist."

"Right. Are they coming to dinner tonight?"

"God, no. They're here for the shoot only."

Hugo appeared and went to shake the German man's hand, then he looked at his watch, walked back to the front of the house, and clapped loudly.

"Come on, everyone: time to listen up."

They all walked over and formed a semicircle around him.

"Right." Hugo stood like a drill sergeant addressing the troops.

It is *like going into battle*, Nicola thought. *And now I guess we're waiting for our orders.*

"Firstly, good morning, all. We're running a little late, but we should be fine. Stewart here is in charge of our day, and he's going to tell you the order of play. So—over to Stewart."

Stewart had been standing to the left of Hugo, in back of him. Now he stepped forward and said:

"The day will run like this: We have four drives before lunch. We'll be starting with the kale drive adjoining Lynham Wood, then we will be going through in three drives. The first one is mainly blanking in for the next two. This is the first time through this year, and we expect two good drives, so don't stint on the cartridges you bring.

"After the fourth drive, we'll be stopping for lunch in the Gypsy Barn in the dell. At this stage of the season there may be some low birds. I know you'll let them go for safety reasons. There may still be some coveys of partridges, which we can shoot, but no ground game today. Now . . ." The older man who had served them the champagne the night before came out of the house bearing a tray with small glasses on it. "We're going to draw for our pegs. Mr. Langley likes to make drawing for your pegs enjoyable. So you'll find your number at the base of the little pewter shot glasses handed out. As Mr. Langley says: 'A little taste of sloe gin in the morning is good for the spirit.'"

Stewart was so serious. She wondered if he ever smiled, and what his face would look like if he did.

The tray was passed around and each man took a shot glass. As did Trez and Juliet. They downed them in one gulp then turned the shot glasses over and looked at the bottoms.

"What's a peg?" she asked James.

"A peg tells you where you stand when you're shooting, who stands beside whom in the line. You get numbers, then the number changes, so you switch positions in the line at each next drive."

"I see."

She didn't really understand, but she figured there would be a lot she didn't understand during the day ahead.

"All right, then, let's get going." Hugo clapped his hands again. "The Land Rovers await."

The Land Rovers were the jeeps, she realized, as they headed toward them. James and she ended up in the one on the far left, with Stewart, Bella, and Nigel.

Hugo and the German man with his "loader" climbed into the second one in line and Badger, Juliet, and Trez into the third.

She was between James and Nigel in the back, Bella was in the front, and Stewart was driving.

"What happens if, when we get there, no birds are flying?" Nicola asked as they set off down the driveway.

"They have beaters, love." Bella turned to face the back seat.

"Bella, Christ, how do you know about beaters?"

"I do my homework, Nigel. Not that I ever did when I was in school, but that's another story."

Nicola struggled to think of what beaters could be. Some kind of machines?

"The beaters' job is to flush out the birds, Nicola." Stewart's voice was like a patient teacher's. "Some are farm workers from the estate; some are from nearby villages. They walk in a line through the woods with sticks, and they crack sticks against the undergrowth and trees, and meanwhile they're whistling, encouraging the birds to move forward so that they'll eventually take off and fly over the guns."

"Do they get paid?"

"They do, yes. Some of them may do beating three or four days a week during the season, others just occasionally on estates where they know the owner or the keeper."

"Isn't that dangerous for them? What if—"

"The birds are in the sky, Nic," James cut in. "The beaters are on the ground. We shoot in the sky."

"Right. Of course. I get it."

"You ask a lot of questions, don't you?" Nigel sat forward a little, addressing her. "Whether Americans have a sense of irony or not, it would appear they have a sense of curiosity."

"Curiosity is an admirable trait." Stewart caught her eye in the rearview mirror and raised his eyebrows slightly. "It shows open-mindedness and a desire to learn."

"Stewart—a philosopher as well as a man of nature." Nigel sat back. "Who knew?" He said it softly, but Nicola saw Stewart's eyebrows rise again.

James and Nigel began to discuss something to do with insurance, which was even more unfathomable to her than the rules of shooting. She had thought they'd get to the first "drive" quickly, but that wasn't the case. Heading down a muddy road in convoy, all these jeeps, one by one, with their lights on, made her think of a funeral cortege. They drove through woods for at least ten minutes until they came to a halt on the side of a field.

As she followed James out of the jeep, she took a deep breath of the cold October air. The purity of the oxygen was so different from what she inhaled on the city streets. Trees breathe in what we breathe out: it was a partnership between man and nature she hadn't thought about since she'd been taught that phrase in junior high school.

Stewart, the man who could catch a salmon at dawn with one cast, was in the lead. They walked behind him across a field until they came to a stop, facing a forest. Nicola thought of Robin Hood and his Merry Men in Sherwood Forest. They had bows and arrows, not guns, and they preyed on the rich, but they must have killed animals as well. Friar Tuck couldn't have been so hefty if he hadn't eaten a lot of slaughtered meat.

She could see the pegs in the ground, set a long way apart from each other, a hundred feet or so. The trees sloped down from a hill, not a very large hill, but she was beginning to understand: the beaters were up at the top and would walk down through the woods with their sticks and their dogs, forcing the birds to fly toward the field they were standing in.

"The pegs are numbered one through seven from left to right," Stewart announced. "If you're not shooting, you stand a little behind your partner." He was looking at her when he said it. "Only for safety reasons."

He almost smiled.

"Here we go, Nic. We're at the far end." It was strange to see James set off toward the last peg on the left with a rifle slung over his shoulder. He could have been a hunter/gatherer—except she was by his side, not sitting in a cave, tending the fire.

Women were allowed to come see birds shot, and they could shoot the birds themselves, but they weren't allowed to sit in the same room as the men after dinner. The unspoken rules were crazy.

"The shooting won't begin for a while." They'd reached their peg. "A horn sounds when the drive begins and again when it ends. We can stand and chat until we hear it." He nudged her with his elbow. "So tell me what you really think of Badger—and Nigel."

"They're like you described them. At breakfast, Nigel asked me when I was going home."

James laughed.

"He doesn't mean it that way."

What way does he mean it?

Hugo and the others had gone to their pegs too. Nicola looked over and caught sight of Bella, who was with Nigel at the neighboring peg. She was applying a new layer of lipstick, while Juliet was at the farthest peg on the other end of the field, her hair tied up in a ponytail.

Trez was at the peg beside Juliet's.

When did Juliet learn how to shoot? Who taught her?

"Did you . . ." She stopped herself. "Never mind. I really am asking too many questions."

"No, Stewart was right. You should ask. Look. See behind us?" He took her by the shoulders and turned her around. There were three people, two men and one woman; the men both had two dogs with them, the woman had six—all ten of the dogs were black-and-white spaniels. "They're waiting and watching. At the end of the drive, they'll send their dogs to pick up the dead pheasants."

"So the dogs are trained to do that."

"Yes, they're hunting dogs."

"God, there are lot of people involved in all of this."

The sound of a horn blowing traveled over the air, and she was back in Sherwood Forest again, half expecting to see knights riding up on horses, ready to joust.

"Stand behind me," James said. "And be prepared. The guns make a hell of a racket."

A few minutes passed. Nothing happened. Maybe nothing was going to happen. Maybe the birds had gone somewhere else. Then she heard a shot; it came from the other end of the field, from Juliet or Trez. Another silence—and then James said:

"There."

He held his gun up in the air, and she saw it. A lone bird flying out of the woods toward them, its wings flapping. The noise of the shot, so loud it made her step back and cover her ears, blasted out. But she didn't take her eyes off the bird; she watched as the flapping wings stopped then started again, she watched as it flew past them, behind them, saw its flight beginning to falter, saw it beginning to drop, then pick up again. Then drop. Flying lower and lower to the ground.

"A runner," James said. "That's what we call the ones who don't die immediately. It will take a while for it to land, but the dogs will find it."

A puff of gunshot wafted back: a surprisingly soft smell of destruction.

And then they came in a rush; so many birds, like the geese she used to watch flying in formation. They filled the sky, dark and beautiful with their long, thin tails.

Boom. Boom. Boom. Boom. Boom.

One didn't make it as far as the field. It was shot just above the tree line and fell onto a branch, resting there like a child's lost kite.

Another, to the left of them, did a somersault, turning over then dropping down five feet beside her, landing with a dull thud. Feathers flew off it, floating onto the ground beside the body they once belonged to.

The bird had looked so beautiful in the sky, but now it

lay in an ungracious heap, its beak and eyes nasty, angry. Dead.

More and more pheasants were being cut out of the sky; She couldn't keep track of them all. There were some no one even aimed at. It took her a minute to realize they were the low-flying ones. The ones Stewart had said not to shoot at for safety reasons.

Boom. Boom. Relentless booms.

"Escape" she said to herself, looking up. "Fly low. All of you. Escape."

When she was ten, she'd been visiting a friend who had an older brother, Peter. He'd just been given a BB gun and was taking random shots with it. One of those shots actually hit a bird, a little robin that fell out of the sky, just like these pheasants. When he saw what he'd done, Peter burst into tears. Her friend told her afterward that Peter cried for the next two days.

"We eat them," James had said. "I know you eat meat, Nic."

Cows didn't fly. They weren't beautiful.

She didn't have to look at their dead bodies, see those dark, angry eyes.

And then the sky was empty. No sound of guns. Glancing over her shoulder, she saw a dog trotting about fifty feet behind her, a pheasant clenched in its jaw.

"Is it finished?" she asked James.

"No. Not yet."

Another boom rang out. Another bird dropped, to her

right, over Nigel and Bella.

She flinched as James raised his rifle again and fired.

"Good shot!" Was it Hugo or Nigel or Badger who had yelled that?

"Mine!" Another male voice, another shot.

She and Sue had laughed so hard one night, discussing the way people pretended to like doing what their new partner did. "You like to walk over burning coals? God, I love walking over burning coals!" or "You love marching bands—wow—they are my favorite things in the world." Lies that would inevitably catch them out, but not before they'd, as Sue had put it, "sealed the deal with the guy."

Was it cawing? Was that the sound they made as they flew? Like turkeys, almost. Or was it more like crows? Were they talking to each other? Or were those noises cries of fear?

Yet another bird dropped, this one falling straight down with no acrobatic spinning. Splat. Drop down dead.

Whistling and thrashing sounds were coming from the woods. The beaters were getting closer.

It had to be over soon. But this was just the "first" drive. There were more to come.

Boom.

The scream was high-pitched and piercing, a child's cry.

Seconds later a horn sounded, and Nicola saw movement in the trees, glimpses of bodies running, heading to the right-hand side of the field.

"Shit." James put his gun down. "Shit. I think something's . . . oh, fuck."

He was staring to the right, at the edge of the field where it met the woods.

"No. Fuck. No."

People were appearing from the trees. Now everyone had put down their guns and was running toward them. Nicola saw, as she and James got closer, a man carrying something in his arms.

The something was a boy. There was blood on the sleeve of his yellow jacket.

"I've got him," the man called out. "We need a car."

Stewart was the first to reach him. Pointing toward the Land Rover first in line, he ran by his side, then opened the back door. The man with the boy got in, Stewart shut the door, leapt into the driver's seat. The engine started, the jeep did a U-turn and raced off.

The rest of them—aside from the German man and his loader—gathered together in a group at the edge of the woods. "What the hell happened?" Hugo looked as if he'd been shot himself.

Stepping forward, Juliet said: "I shot him, Huge. God, I'm so sorry. He must have been walking down on the side and a bird flew over and I thought I'd aimed high enough, but shit. I'm so sorry."

"Jesus Christ." Hugo put his head in his hands. "Jesus."

The German man joined them; Hugo straightened up.

"I'm so sorry, Gunther. It was an accident. This has never happened before. Never."

"This is not right."

"No, of course it isn't. It's never happened before."

"I will not be shooting again with you."

"Gunther?" Juliet took a step closer to him. "It was my fault. Can I speak with you for a moment? Alone?"

She didn't wait for an answer. She took him by the arm, drew him away from the group, over to where her peg was.

"What's she saying, for Christ's sake?" Hugo shook his head. "I can't fucking believe this."

"Is he okay?"

"He's not okay, Nicola. He is furious. I don't blame him," Hugo spat out.

"I meant the boy."

No one said a word.

Juliet was gesturing, her hands waving in all directions as she spoke.

"She'll talk him round." Trez now put her hand on Hugo's arm. "She'll fix this."

"I don't think so." Nigel grimaced. "He's German, remember."

"But she's Juliet," Badger countered. "Juliet can fix anything. Never underestimate Juliet."

The other beaters had all come down from the woods and were walking past them on the edge of the field.

"Shouldn't someone go over and ask how the boy is? Or who he is? Something, anyway." Nicola turned to James.

"You're right. Hugo, you should go talk to them. Find out who the boy is at least."

Striding off, Hugo kept looking back over his shoulder at Juliet and Gunther.

"This is all pretty fucking terrifying. I hope he's okay."

"She was a long way away from him when she shot at the bird, Bella," Trez said, frowning. "I don't think he'll be badly hurt."

"A lot of those birds were a long way away, and they're fucking dead." Bella whispered it, but Nicola, right beside her, heard.

"Jesus Christ, they're laughing." It was Nigel again. Sounding uncharacteristically bewildered.

They were. Juliet and Gunther were laughing together.

"I told you, Nigel. Never underestimate Juliet."

Gunther walked over to the left where his peg had been and where his loader was still standing. Juliet came up to the group.

"Turns out I know a friend of Gunther's in Hong Kong. We had a laugh about how fat his friend is. Anyway, I'd told him it was all my fault, that I hadn't shot for a while but that I hadn't told Hugo that. He seemed to be all right. I don't know if he'll go ahead and bring people here, but he has definitely calmed down. God, what an idiot I was."

"The boy was probably too close." Trez went and put her arm around Juliet.

"It wasn't his fault, Trez. It was mine. I'm the one responsible."

"It's Matthew." Hugo arrived back. "He's Simon's son. Apparently, he's twelve years old. He loves going out with his father, being a beater. They think he was only clipped."

"Simon has a cottage near the estate," Trez explained. "I should have recognized him. Poor Matthew. Thank God he's not badly hurt."

"How was Gunther?"

"I did my best, Huge. It might be all right." Juliet shrugged.

"Well, if anyone can rescue this situation—"

"It's Juliet, as I keep saying, Hugo," Badger cut in. "Can you imagine if I'd been responsible? I dread to think. I know we'd end up talking about the war, you know. I suspect I may have had to point out the fact that we won."

A twelve-year-old boy had been shot. His scream had been wrenching. Was she the only one who thought this conversation was all wrong?

A pheasant appeared, waddling in a straight line in front of them, as if it had no care in the world, as if it were on the way to the tea party James had joked about.

The low-flying birds survived; the birds who walked on the ground survived: if Darwinism worked as it should, she thought, all pheasants would evolve into ones who were too fat to fly high, or who never got off the ground in the first place.

"What happens next?" Bella asked.

"No more shooting. We go back. We're one Land Rover short, so we'll all have to scrunch in to the others." Hugo took a deep breath in. "God, what a mess."

"I know." Juliet put her hand on his arm. "I know. I

couldn't be sorrier."

"Accidents happen."

"Don't try to make me feel better, Trez. It won't work."

"Matthew will be fine." Badger unbuckled the belt holding his cartridges from his waist. "Gunther will declare undying love to Juliet, and Hugo will get a plethora of filthy-rich Germans beating down the door to shoot here. There will be a happy ending."

When they got back to the house, James pulled her to one side and said: "Let's go to the village for lunch. There's a pub there. It would be good to get some time together, alone."

"That would be really nice," she said, wishing she didn't have to wonder whether he was worried about being back in the house and spending even more time with Juliet, whether that unremitting charm of hers was working on him.

She fucked up, though. She shot Matthew. She's not perfect. But how can I take pleasure in that when there's a wounded boy?

* * *

THE PUB WAS musty-smelling and claustrophobic. If it had old-world character, she couldn't see it. The patterned carpet on the floor showed wear, tear, and spills. What didn't smell of damp smelled of cigarette smoke. Almost all of the people in there were men, gathered together at the bar, speaking in loud voices, drinking pints of beer.

It may not have had much charm, but it was wonderful—because it wasn't Langley House. She was beginning to wish she didn't have to spend another night there, in the place with the creepy deer heads and the silent waiters and invisible cook and these people who shot birds and were so different.

And Juliet.

"I want you to know there's almost never an accident like that," James said as they settled at a table in a dark corner. "I guess Matthew walked a little farther down the hill than he should have."

"And Juliet said she was out of practice. Maybe she aimed a little too low."

"She used to be such a good shot. It's not like her."

"James? You may not want to talk about it, but I need to find out. What happened between you two? Don't say it's ancient history."

"But it is. I told you everything last night. We were together when I was at Cambridge. Then she went to Hong Kong, and I didn't."

"You didn't because you didn't want to or because she didn't want you to?"

"The latter."

"Right. Okay. She left, and you were heartbroken."

"I was hurt, Nic. I was young. I got over it."

"Was everyone in love with her back then?"

"No. I mean—why do you ask?"

"Nigel said Hugo was. He said everyone was."

"That's Nigel. He can be bloody idiotic at times. No, he must be talking about Badger. We all knew Badger fancied Juliet, but he would never have said anything. The thing is, Nigel loves to stir."

"Stir?"

"Stir the pot, cause trouble. Anyway, please, can we talk about something else? I told you I don't have feelings for her anymore, all right? Honestly. I've had enough of this."

It was the closest to angry she'd ever heard or seen him be.

"Okay." Tears were starting to form; she could feel them. *If you put your tongue up to the roof of your mouth and press really hard, you can stop yourself from crying.* She had no idea who had told her that, but it worked—occasionally.

"Nic . . ." James reached out and took her hand. "I'm sorry. I didn't mean to say that harshly. I want to get on with things, that's all—with us. I don't want to get bogged down because of some old relationship. I've never asked you about your exes, have I?"

"No. I've had only one serious—"

"Honestly, I don't want to hear. Not because I'm jealous, although I suppose I might be, but because he—any old romantic relationship on either side—is irrelevant. It's what we have now that counts."

"You're right." The waitress came, and they each ordered a ham-and-cheese sandwich. "I know, you're right."

She squeezed his hand. "I wasn't prepared, that's all—to see one of your ex-girlfriends."

"Neither was I."

"And then the whole shooting thing. It's so foreign to me."

"Did you hate it?"

"No, no. But the accident. That was horrific."

If they stayed together, would she tell him at some point that she loathed watching birds being slaughtered or would she keep pretending it was fine?

Or would she grow to like the gory spectacle?

"It was horrific. You're absolutely right. You know, I think I should try to take your mind off it. Because I'm sure Matthew will be fine, and we don't want to have a ghoulish pub lunch."

The smile that brought to her face made her feel a little guilty.

"I'll tell you some funny stories about how hopeless I was when I was made to take a part in a Shakespeare play in school. I had the part of King Lear, if you can believe that."

"You were King Lear? That's crazy. I played Portia in *The Merchant of Venice* when I was thirteen. I was beyond hopeless."

"I was beyond beyond hopeless. It was a shambles, to put it mildly. Should I tell you the details of just how shambolic it was?"

"That sounds perfect."

He'd tell stories in the self-deprecating, funny way he did, they'd laugh together, and she'd stop thinking about Matthew. And Juliet.

Right now, it was all about her and James.

Chapter Ten

When they got back to the house, they found Trez, Bella, and Nigel in the living room. Trez informed them that Juliet and Hugo had gone to visit Matthew in the hospital and that Badger was in the library reading. The library—of course there would be a library. James had told her at some point the night before that there was a ballroom too.

"How was the pub?" Nigel asked.

"Delicious ham-and-cheese sandwiches." James smiled.

"I bet. Gourmet all the way. Moldy bread and plastic-tasting cheese, right? Whereas we had the delicious steak-and-kidney pie we were going to have at the Gypsy Barn."

"Where are Hugo and Juliet?" Trez got up, looked at her watch. "They left for the hospital ages ago. God, I hope Matthew is okay."

"I'm sure he is." Nigel went and put his arm around her. "It will all be fine, and we'll have a slap-up dinner tonight. I, for one, can't wait."

Trez checked her watch again. "Oh God, I have to go talk to the staff about dinner."

"And I'm going to take a bath," Nigel announced.

"A bath sounds like a good idea." James walked over to Trez as well, put his arm around her so she was flanked. "And Nigel's right, for once. It will all be fine."

"Before I go bathward, what do you call a pissed-off German?"

"Oh God, Nigel, no." Bella sighed. "Please don't."

"A sauerkraut. So—are we taking separate baths, James, or should we pretend we're back in boarding school?"

"We're going to pretend you're a decent human being, that's what we're going to pretend."

Nigel pushed James in the chest, ran out of the room, James on his tail.

"Boys." Trez rolled her eyes.

"They're playing silly buggers." Bella laughed.

"Exactly. Anyway, you'll have to excuse me, but I really do need to go talk to the staff."

"Of course."

As soon as Trez exited, Bella put her hands up in the air and mouthed, *What the fuck?*

"I know. It's been a crazy day."

"You're not kidding. A boy who's been shot. And a woman our age who says: 'I have to go talk to the staff'? It doesn't get much crazier. Listen—I nicked a bottle of wine and some glasses before and hid them in our room. I was going to share it with Nigel, but sod him if he's taking a bath—he'll probably lie there for hours. Why don't you and me go outside and have a chat by the pool."

"The pool? It's cold, Bella."

"I know. But there are chairs there. And I need to get out of this mausoleum. Put on another jumper under your jacket. We'll be fine. Meet you there in five."

Up in the room, James was undressing.

"I'm going to meet Bella outside," she told him.

"Great." He put a towel around his waist. "Let's hope there's enough hot water for two baths."

"So you're not sharing with Nigel."

"Ha. Very funny."

"Well, going to separate rooms after dinner is pretty weird. And Bella said last night that Englishmen think that women spoil their fun."

"We have fun together, don't we?"

"You're different."

"No, what I am is freezing. I better get to the bath. Nigel's waiting." He smiled, gave her a quick kiss, and left.

She grabbed a sweater and went out to the pool.

Sitting on one of the sun loungers, waiting for Bella, she wondered how Matthew was, and what Juliet was saying to his parents.

Oops, I shot your son. But I'm Juliet. So no big deal, right?

The pool was covered with a blue plastic-looking sheet. Brown leaves were scattered on top of it.

If Juliet were there, she'd stand for a minute in her tastefully sexy bikini, then rip off the sheeting with one hand, do a perfect swan dive into the pool, and emerge, shaking that hair of hers. *Cold?* she'd say. *You call this cold?*

"Here we go." Bella was bearing an uncorked bottle of red wine and two glasses. Putting them down on the ground between them, she sat on the neighboring lounger.

"Let's toast to the outsiders." She poured some wine into the glasses, picked them up, handed one to Nicola, and clinked her glass.

"I've been feeling so out of it it's making me a little paranoid, I think. But are you really one? I mean, you're English. You can't be that much of an outsider."

"You're wrong there. This . . ." She made a sweeping gesture. "This pool, this house, these people—they're foreign to me. I grew up in a council house on an ugly street. My father and mother both work—my mother at a dry cleaner's, my father in a toy shop. I went to a state school. I left at sixteen to start working myself. I'm twenty-eight now, and I work at Boots, which is a chain store, a chemist. I think they're called drugstores in the States, which is pretty funny when you think about it. Oh, and we speak differently up north. I *used* to speak differently."

"What do you mean?"

"We leave out 'the' in sentences. We say: 'I'm going round corner to shop'—not *the* corner, or *the* shop. We call dinner 'tea.' I've been teaching myself ways to fit in, you know. But look at me last night. I wore the wrong clothes. And bloody Nigel didn't tell me I was wearing the fucking wrong clothes."

Taking a swig of wine, she shook her head. "He's going to ditch me. It's just a matter of when. And the worst thing about that? I thought: *Well, this will be fun, to date a rich git,* but now I've bloody fallen in love with the sod. He tells shite jokes, and he comes across as arrogant and even sneaky at times, the way he teases people, you know, to get under their skin, but he's different when we're alone. He drops that bullshit. He's actually kind and funny and, I know you won't believe it, but sweet. I'll really miss him when tells me to piss off, it's time for him to go back to his kind."

"He's not going to ditch you. You're smart and beautiful and you're his equal, Bella. However you speak or whatever school you went to."

"That's the Yank in you talking. Equality. It doesn't work like that here." She waved her arm round again. "Anyway, how are you doing? With James and with Juliet being here. She's something else, isn't she?"

"Yes. But—"

"But what?"

"I shouldn't say this. But I was pleased that she made a mistake. Not that I wanted her to shoot someone. That's awful. I mean, I'd never—"

"I know. But you're human and you're chuffed she fucked up. If she were Nigel's ex I'd probably want her to have killed the poor wee boy. No . . ." She laughed. "I'm not that bad. But Jesus, she's really perfect. Isn't she?"

"Nigel said this morning that Hugo was in love with her. And still is. And James told me at lunch that Badger fancied her."

"I'd say they all were in love with her. She's one of those—what do you call them? Fem something?"

"Femme fatale."

"Right. That's it. But she's not one of those women who ignore other women. There are even times, when she looks at me with that look of hers, drawing me in, like I'm the only person in the room that counts, like we understand each other—those times, I think I could fall in love with her too. Not that I'm inclined in that way."

"I know what you mean. She looks at me that way too some times. As if we're conspiring together."

"Trez loves her, that's for certain. But maybe Hugo won't love her so much now that she's messed up his precious shoot."

"Maybe."

It had been so long since she'd had a conversation like this with a female friend, a woman she could confide in. If Sue were here—Sue before marriage and babies—they could have spent all day talking about everyone and analyzing them, but ever since she'd boarded that plane, Nicola had been with James, only James. There were things you couldn't discuss with men, even with a man like James. She couldn't picture sitting with him like this by a covered swimming pool on a cold autumn day, drinking wine and talking about femmes fatales.

Bella took another swig of wine. "The thing is, they all went to the same type of schools, the same types of parties. So it kind of makes sense that they fall in love with the same types of people. I mean, they want to interbreed, keep the bloodlines socially acceptable. All that crap."

"But it's 1980."

"I know, love. But do *they* know? I went to the toilet downstairs this morning—you know, the one beside the room they call the library room. Oh, fuck, Nigel told me I'm supposed to say 'loo,' not 'toilet,' but screw that. Anyway, I checked this house out, you know. If you go past the library and to the right, there's a fucking ballroom. Can you believe it? A ballroom? Anyway, you know what they have hanging up on the wall in the toilet? School photographs. I'm sitting there, and there are these boys in their uniforms peering at me. From the age of seven or something like that to teenage boys, standing in lines looking like they own the world or they're about to own the world. Who puts school photos in a toilet except people who want you to know what posh school they went to?

"The point is, that's what I'm hoping too. That the tribe will realize that it's time to figure out what century we're in, for you and me both. I need some good luck when it comes to romance, believe me. My last boyfriend—oh, shit—I can't even think about it."

"Tell me. Come on." Now Nicola took a large sip from her glass and leaned forward. "I'll tell you about *my* last boyfriend. I was with him for six years; we were living together—he dumped me for an older woman, a divorcée. I had no idea he was sleeping with someone else. It was so humiliating."

"Okay, not good, granted, but I've got you beat, Nic. My last boyfriend—his name was Mark—we were together two years—and I know not as long as you and the divorcée-screwing douchebag, but listen to this—Mark and I were out to dinner together. He almost never took me out, never to a smart restaurant, but this night he did, so it was a big deal. After we finished eating, he said: 'Bella—do you picture us walking down the aisle together?' And Jesus Christ, there it was—I was being proposed to and I was loving every second of it and waiting for the ring, thinking how nice a diamond would look on my finger. So I said, with this huge grin on my face: 'Yes, I do, Mark, I do picture us walking down the aisle together.' You know what he said? He said: 'Well, I don't.' That's what he said: 'Well, I don't.'"

"Jesus. That's unbelievably cruel. It's brutal. God—what did you do?"

"I walked out. Never saw him again. Which is what he wanted, obviously. He was—uh-oh . . . I hear a car. Juliet and Hugo must be coming back. I don't want them to see us. I feel like Juliet has superpowers, that she'd be able to see us through the hedge, knocking back the booze I stole. Let's go. I know the way to the back door, where we can stash the bottle and glasses. Follow me."

Bella grabbed the bottle, Nicola grabbed the glasses,

and they rushed out of the swimming pool area, heading around the house and into a door at the back, giggling together.

Like little kids hiding from their parents, she thought.

Thank God for Bella. She might stop me from losing my mind and saying or doing something really, really wrong.

Chapter Eleven

TREZ

Hugo had been quiet when he got back after the visit to the hospital.

"Matthew will be fine," he'd announced when he'd come into their bedroom. "They're letting him out of hospital later tonight apparently. The shot winged him, so there was no real damage."

"That's a relief."

"It is."

"What a shame that had to happen. Juliet must feel awful. I should go to her now."

"Juliet's fine too. I'd leave it."

"But—"

"Leave it, will you, Jane."

"Jane?"

He was standing at the window, opening and closing the

curtains.

"You only call me 'Jane' when you're upset with me. What have I done?"

"Nothing. I'm going out for a walk. You must have things to do."

"I've already dealt with the dinner arrangements. Hugo?"

"I'll see you later." He strode out, and for a second she thought he was going to slam the door behind him, but he left it open.

He was upset, obviously. The accident had ruined the day and possibly his connection with Gunther, however much Juliet had tried to make it right. It made sense that he was tense. But not that he was so short with her.

Knowing Hugo, though, he'd perk up at dinner. He'd take his walk and come back in a better mood. He didn't hold on to a bad mood for long. He'd shake it off like a dog shakes off water after a swim and get back to himself.

She went straight to Juliet's room and knocked on the door.

"Jules? Can I come in?"

"I'm exhausted, Trez. I need to take a quick nap."

"I only wanted to tell you—you shouldn't feel badly. Accidents happen."

"I know accidents happen. You already told me that. And believe it or not, I knew that anyway. We'll talk later."

"Okay. Sleep well."

She stayed standing outside the bedroom door, confused. They'd barely spoken to each other—only that one quick chat the night before. There was so much to catch up on, so many stories she wanted to hear, and to tell herself. Hugo had been short with her, and now Juliet had turned her away with an annoyed tone.

She'd been watching out of the bedroom window before for Hugo and Juliet's return. When she saw the car coming down the drive, she also saw Bella and Nicola running out from the pool area, carrying a bottle of wine and glasses. Laughing.

That's what she and Juliet should have been doing. Drinking wine and laughing.

It will all be fine. Matthew is going to be fine. Hugo will cheer up; Juliet will get some sleep and she'll cheer up too. When the others leave tomorrow, I'll get Juliet to stay behind, and we'll drink plenty of wine and laugh like we used to.

This sense of foreboding I suddenly have will disappear.

Chapter Twelve

NICOLA

After they'd snuck in the back door, which led to a little pantry, Bella put the wine bottle and glasses on one of the shelves, then took Nicola by the hand and dragged her back outside and back around the house then through the front door.

"Whew. No one saw us!" She did a little jig in the hallway. "Time to go and be proper people again. I'm going up stairs to room." She smiled. "Up *the* stairs to *the* room. Come on."

They ran up the stairs. Bella disappeared into her room, and Nicola went down the hall to hers.

"Hey . . ." James was sitting on the bed. "Nice walk? You look flushed."

"I am a little. Bella and I went and had a drink by the pool, not a walk." Sitting down beside him, she took his hand. "We were being naughty teenagers. The outsiders. I mean, she's from the North and I'm from America, so that's what she thinks. That we're the outsiders. She's great, by the way. I really like her. She thinks Nigel is going to ditch her because she's from a different kind of background. He wouldn't do that, would he?"

"I hope not. But I know his parents, and he might have a hard time introducing her to them."

"Why? Because she's from the North of England? Seriously?"

"Because they are very socially conscious."

"What? They'd disapprove of her because she comes from a different part of the country?"

"She comes from a different part of the country, and it's obvious that she comes from the working class."

"You mean she and her parents actually have jobs? And that's not respectable? To have a job?"

"It depends on what job you have."

"Jesus. But it's fine for Badger to have *no* job?"

"Nic, we can get into a long discussion about the English class system and its absurdities, but right now I'm wondering—you said that you two were acting like naughty teenagers, but exactly how naughty?"

Now wasn't the time to have a conversation about the English class system—he was right. They'd have it at some point. He'd said "its absurdities," so he wasn't like Nigel's parents—and she hoped his parents weren't like them either.

"Pretty naughty." She kissed him on the neck. "We didn't finish the bottle, but we made a pretty hefty dent in it."

"Right. Well, I wouldn't be averse to a little naughtiness at the moment. Sorry—that was a really cheesy thing to say."

"It was. But I wouldn't be averse either."

"Then we won't be averse together."

She forgot about absurd class distinctions and Juliet and dead birds and blood on a boy's jacket.

Being with James was being happy: it was as simple as that. He'd always make her laugh at times when they made love; he was playful and fun, but then he could be serious and thoughtful too. They were still discovering each other—in life and in bed—and it felt as if they might never stop discovering, that there was an infinite source of mutual wonder they shared.

This is what's real, she thought as she lay in his arms afterward. *This is what love is. I could tell him I love him now. The man doesn't have to say it first, not anymore.*

But it could be too much too soon. It could go so horribly wrong. What if he said nothing, or worse, what if he were like Bella's Mark and said: *Well, I don't love you?*

She sat up, knocked her forehead with the palm of her hand. "I can't believe I haven't asked. I hope Matthew is all right. We should get up and go find—"

"Relax, he's fine."

"How do you know?"

"Juliet stopped by when she came back—she told me he'll be out of hospital tonight."

Juliet must have come straight to their room from the car, but she couldn't have stayed for more than a few seconds, just long enough to tell James the news.

"That's great news. Juliet must be relieved."

"Yes."

"She must have been so worried."

"Yes. Right—actually, maybe we should get up and start getting ready for dinner."

"Okay."

Even the mention of Juliet's name had broken the magic ease of the connection they had.

"What time are we leaving tomorrow?"

"After breakfast. If we leave before lunch, we'll avoid any potential traffic."

"That makes sense."

Thank God. Only two more meals with Juliet—dinner and breakfast.

Then she'd be back in London with James, and this hellish weekend would be over. She'd been lucky on that plane trip; maybe she'd be lucky after they left. Maybe she'd never have to see Juliet again.

* * *

DINNER WAS CLOSE to an instant replay of the previous night. Although the tone of the evening was more subdued—at the beginning, anyway. Everyone was talking in quieter voices, and no one mentioned the shooting. Not even Nigel, which surprised her a little. They had drinks in the living room, and she stayed standing beside James, who was talking to Badger and Nigel about playing boules in Saint-Maximin and where they all might be able to play boules in London.

Bella wandered over, champagne glass in hand, and pulled her aside.

"I keep wondering. Do women dress for men or for other women or for themselves? Anyway, look, I've learned. I'm dressed suitably tonight." She was wearing black velvet trousers and a thin black cashmere sweater.

"Very chic."

"Thanks. I got the jumper in a charity shop. Still—I'm not as chic as Juliet."

Juliet had on flowing white silk trousers and a red silk jacket. She was wearing the black ballet slippers again and a big, wide red silk sash for a belt.

"Those clothes seem tailor-made for her. I guess there's a lot of silk in Hong Kong."

"And a lot of wool in England." Bella tilted her head toward Trez.

The poodle skirt was gone, and in its place was another voluminous wool skirt, a green one, and a blouse—also green, but a shade that clashed with the skirt.

"That's not bitchy of me, is it? I actually admire Trez for not caring, you know. I'm just trying hard to picture her being a countess, at countess-type parties. I suppose countesses don't have to care about what they wear. I wish I didn't care."

"You'd look great in anything, Bella."

"Except a see-through blouse." She made a pained face. "You should have seen the looks I got from Hugo and Trez when I came into this room last night."

The gong sounded, and they trooped off to the dining room. Nicola sat between Badger and Bella and tried to be calm about the fact that Trez had seated James between herself and Juliet.

She found herself staring at them, trying to read any body language but not succeeding.

"I've seen a few famous people," Bella was telling Badger. "I had a Page Three Girl in my Boots the other day."

"Really?" Badger looked intrigued. "Which one?"

"How would I know her actual name?" Bella laughed. "I recognized her because she gets a lot of press, but it's not like I study Page Three Girls, writing down their names every day."

"What's a Page Three Girl?"

"Nicola wants to know what a Page Three Girl is." Badger said it so loudly, the rest of them stopped talking. "Nicola." He turned to face her. "There is a national newspaper here called the *Sun*. Every day they run a picture of a topless girl on page three. Hence the name 'Page Three Girl.'"

"A topless photograph?"

"Yes, indeed."

"In a national newspaper? I mean, is it a paper like the scandal sheet we have in America, like the *National Enquirer*?"

"It's supposed to be a proper paper, Nic. It's antediluvian." Juliet shook her head in seeming dismay. "You're learning what a sexist society it is here. It's shameful."

"Jules—you're overreacting." Nigel sighed.

"That's what men always say to women to try to shut us up. *You're overreacting.* Or *You're being hysterical.*"

"Because half the time you are." Nigel said it with a smile in his voice which might have tempered the accusation, but then again, might not have.

"It *is* shameful," James stated. "And it's *not* an overreaction."

"I think you're making a big deal out of nothing," Trez spoke up. "Who cares, really? It doesn't hurt anyone."

"Trez? Really?" Juliet's eyebrows were raised. She shot one of her *we're in this together* looks at Nicola. "So Jimmy and I and Nic agree. What about you, Bella? Where are you on the subject of Page Three Girls?"

"I think men will always want to look at tits. I think there will still be Page Three Girls in the twenty-first century. I don't know if it's right or wrong. The girls are getting paid. They're not forced into doing it."

"They're being dehumanized, objectified." Leaning forward, Juliet put her elbows on the table, her head on top of her hands.

Juliet would have faced down Tony Kellow in one second. She would have put him in his place and had him apologizing for even daring to make a sexist comment.

"They might be being objectified, but at least they're not being shot at. Except by a camera. Sorry, Jules, bad joke." Nigel shrugged.

"For fuck's sake. She *didn't* bloody shoot anyone." The words burst from Hugo, who had been sitting silently. His ruddy face was glowering.

"Huge, don't—"

"No, I will, Jules. I know I told you I'd keep it a secret, but I can't. I won't let you take the blame for something you didn't do."

"What's going on?" Trez looked from Hugo to Juliet and back again. "What do you mean she didn't shoot anyone? It was an accident, I know, but—"

"But *you* shot him, Trez. Jules covered for you because she knew it would look worse for us if you were the one responsible. She knew she could say she hadn't been shooting for a long time, that she could talk Gunther down."

"Me? I . . . didn't . . . I don't understand. Jules?"

"Oh, Christ. This wasn't supposed to happen." Leaning back in her chair, Juliet crossed her arms. "Look, we were shooting at the same bird at the same time, that's all. I could see you aimed too low, that it was your shot that winged Matthew, but I knew it was better if I took the blame. Huge never should have said anything. He promised me he wouldn't. Jesus, Huge . . . Anyway, it's all silly and Matthew's fine and no real harm done, so let's not talk about it anymore."

"I didn't really. Did I? I didn't think . . . God, it was me? I'm so sorry. I can't believe I'd do that."

"Seriously, sweetheart. No harm done. Let's change the subject. Where were we? Page Three Girls. Honestly, what if it were Page Three Boys, with young men showing their dicks? How would everyone feel about that?"

Silence. Within a few seconds it became such an uncomfortable silence that Nicola was about to break it with some ridiculous observation about the weather or something, but then she saw Bella drive an elbow into Badger's side. At which point, Badger sat up straight and said:

"I doubt that pictures of dicks every day would drive down circulation. Right now the *Sun* is read by three million, seven hundred and forty-one thousand people. Amazing, isn't it?"

"How many of those three million–odd are men, Badger?" Nigel had rowed in to help. He kept rowing as he and Badger began to discuss the politics of the *Sun* and Margaret Thatcher.

Despite their efforts, the unease around the table was palpable. Hugo was silent, and still, Nicola could see, angry. Trez seemed on the verge of tears, biting her lip, frowning, probably trying to recall the moment that she'd pulled the trigger. James did what he'd done at breakfast: he stared at his food, as if his plate of roasted pheasant, roasted potatoes, and brussels sprouts in front of him were a work of art.

"I'm sorry." Trez rose from her seat. "I'm not feeling well. I have to excuse myself. Go on without me, everyone. I just need a quick lie-down." She fled from the room, and Juliet turned to Hugo. "Go after her, will you?"

"She'll be fine. Let her rest for a while."

"Then I'm going." She tossed her napkin down on the table and marched out.

"Oh dear," Bella spoke. "I hope she'll be all right."

"Juliet will fix her," Nigel stated. "That's part of Juliet's MO, as Badger said before. She can fix anything."

Nicola winced when she saw James look up from his food and nod his head.

Juliet hasn't made a mistake. Trez made the mistake.
Juliet's never going to make a mistake.

Chapter Thirteen

TREZ

She'd shot Matthew? How had that happened? She was always so careful with guns. How could she have gone wrong like that?

Now she understood why Hugo had been so ill-tempered with her. It wasn't as if she knew she'd shot the boy, though. She hadn't been hiding anything.

She would have come out and admitted her mistake right away if she'd known. There had been that moment of confusion when they'd realized what had happened and everyone had looked down the line and then when they'd all huddled together, Juliet had stepped out and said, "It was me."

I didn't know I shot him. She wanted to go downstairs and scream it to all of them. *I didn't know.*

Throwing herself down on the bed, she buried her head

in the pillows.

"Trez . . ."

A hand was rubbing her back.

"Trez, come on." Juliet pulled her so she turned over, then pulled on her arms to get her to sit up. "Don't cry, silly. I keep telling you, it's not a problem. Matthew's fine. Gunther's fine. Come back down."

"I didn't know. Honestly, Jules. I didn't know I did it."

"No one thinks you did know."

"But Hugo's so cross with me. He was cross when he came back. He was furious at dinner."

"I told him not to say anything. I didn't want anyone to find out. I knew you'd be upset. But I fucked up. We were chatting away in the car and he said how you'd been distracted lately and I said, 'That's probably why she . . .' and then I stopped, realizing what I'd said. He kept pushing me and I kept telling him to drop it, but he wouldn't, so I told him. My fault. I'd tried so hard to cover for you, and then I blew it. Sorry."

"But I haven't been distracted. Why would he say that? Oh God, what an idiot I am. You remember how clumsy I always was. I thought I was better. Really. I thought I'd changed, Jules."

She felt as if a part of her had disappeared—the part that had carefully built some sense of self-confidence.

"I still don't understand. You stopped writing and ringing me. Why?"

"I told you last night. Life was so hectic. I was traveling

a lot. I got swept away."

"With other friends."

"I did have friends there, Trez. It's allowed, you know."

"I know." It was pathetic, this need she had for Juliet to see her as capable and in control. She would never be capable. Or in control of anything. She was doomed to be always the teenage girl who tripped over things and wasn't pretty and the woman who shot a beater and ran out of her own dinner party in tears.

"Sweetheart . . ." Juliet put her arm around her, pulled her to her. "You'll always be my best friend, you know that. God knows how miserable my life would have been if I hadn't found you in that gruesome secretarial school."

"You'd have been fine."

"Trez. Seriously. Now *I* have to say that *you're* over-reacting."

"Am I?"

"Yes. Matthew will be able to tell his story to all the kids in school. He'll be a hero, and I promise Gunther will bring hordes of other filthy-rich Germans to shoot here and you'll give tons of glittering parties and there'll be photographs of them in *Tatler* and you'll be the countess extraordinaire, who might just deign to invite her oldest, bestest friend to some of those bashes."

"I would never not invite you." She rubbed the tears off her face. "I've missed you so much. Nothing exciting happens when you're not here."

"Like no one gets shot?"

"That's not funny."

"I know. Sorry. Nigel's horrible sense of humor can be catching. You know I've missed you too. Really. A lot. Tons. Oceans-ful of missing."

Juliet drew her closer to her and kissed the top of her head. That "oceans-ful" comment had made her remember just how quickly Juliet could make her feel better. One perfect comment, the right compliment or the right appeal to her sense of humor: somehow she could reach the sad, depressed part, the area inside her heart that felt off center and neglected, and like a chiropractor with a fierce yank, could straighten it with a snap.

"I knew you'd cheer me up. You always did, whenever I was sad. When Hugo forgot my birthday or didn't forget it and bought me a terrible present. God"—she paused, remembering the look on his face in the dining room—"he was angry at me today. He even called me 'Jane' this afternoon. I don't really understand why. He wasn't as angry at you when he thought you were the one responsible."

"I'm a guest. That's different."

"I guess so."

"Maybe he wasn't really angry about that. Maybe he was angry or upset about . . ." Juliet stopped.

"Angry or upset about what?"

"Nothing." She drew away, got off the bed. "Let's go back downstairs. Let's have some fun."

"Angry or upset about what, Jules?"

"Forget it." Juliet grabbed her by the wrist, was trying

to pull her off the bed, but Trez resisted.

"Angry or upset about me not being able to get pregnant. That's what you were going to say, wasn't it?"

"I have no idea what I was going to say. Which is why I stopped saying anything." She tugged at Trez's arm again. "It's going to look like you're pouting if you stay up here. What did your father and mother used to say? 'Sulking is for weak people.' Something like that—I remember you telling me."

"He always said, 'Belt up.'"

"That's it. Exactly. So belt up, sweetheart. Come on, your guests are waiting. Hugo really will be cross if you stay hiding up here."

He would be; she knew Juliet was right.

This day, which had started so brilliantly, had turned into a mess. And she was the cause of all that mess.

She got up and smoothed down her clothes.

"I've got a good idea for an after-dinner game tonight. It will chase away these blues of yours."

Juliet linked their arms together the way she used to whenever they were going out together. Then said what she always used to say as they set off for any event: "Time to boogie."

And then they laughed the way they had always laughed.

Except Trez hadn't hated herself quite so much then.

Chapter Fourteen

NICOLA

After dinner had finished, Juliet announced the name of a game they could play. "It's called Lava. You'll all love it."

Lava—was it going to be a quiz on the names of volcanoes around the world? If so, the only person who might be able to play well was Badger.

As it turned out, Lava was a gymnastic form of athleticism. The idea was to circumnavigate the living room without touching the floor, the floor representing the molten heap of "lava": if anyone fell or touched the floor in any way, they were out of the game and, effectively, dead.

Juliet went first, stepping on the sofa, walking across the top of it, dropping down onto the armchair, then stretching out as far as she could to find the middle shelf of the bookcase. At the end of the bookcase, she stopped.

"There's no other way, is there? Let's hope the glass table will hold me."

"Jules—you could hurt yourself. Don't use that table."

"Don't be a wimp, Badger. There's no way of doing this without using the table. Come on, what are the rest of you doing? You're supposed to be playing this too. And we all have to yell 'Lava' if anyone screws up." She stretched across the gulf between the bookcase and the glass table, and made the transition safely.

"Your go, Huge. I'll make my next move after you start."

Hugo got up on the sofa first, went to shift down to the armchair as Juliet had, and slipped, falling between the two.

"Lava!" they all cried out as Hugo picked himself up.

"No way, Huge—if you fall, if you touch the lava, you stay sitting on the floor," Juliet commanded.

I thought she was sophisticated. I pictured her in a salon entertaining French philosophers, Russian novelists. Instead, she's treating this house like a playground and yelling as if it were a game of Red Rover.

Hugo sat down again.

"I want another go."

"Can't have one, Huge. The rules are the rules. Right, so where next for me?" Nicola saw her eyeing up the next chair, but it was a long jump away from the table, and she wouldn't get much purchase with a standing jump.

The white silk and red belt swished in the air; for a moment it looked like she wouldn't make it, but she just did, tumbling over the back of the chair into the seat of it, managing to keep her feet above the floor.

"Bravo!" Hugo clapped. "Magnificent!"

"Jesus, Jules. You're a fucking acrobat!" Badger exclaimed. He had followed Hugo and managed to make it as far as the bookcase. But he was tottering, and the tottering turned into a fall.

"Lava!" they all screamed at once. Badger went to join Hugo on the floor.

"Too much wine," he stated. "I could do it easily if I were sober."

Juliet had made the easy step from the armchair to the top of the piano bench, then another easy one from the piano to another armchair.

Nigel was next in line. He got as far as the bookcase. "No way am I going on that glass table, but . . ." He looked around for another route, and ended up flinging himself at the curtains beside the table. Catching hold of one of them, he then slid down to the ground with a thump.

"Lava!"

"Good work you didn't pull the curtain down with you." James laughed. "There was no way in hell you could have made it to the chair from the curtains anyway."

Juliet quickly completed the circuit of the room and took a bow, to the sound of claps and whistles.

"Okay, my turn!" Bella did a dance on the top of the sofa, then jumped straight to the ground, yelling, "Bloody fucking lava!" as she did.

"I'm the hostess here, so I can bow out too." Trez sat down in the middle of the floor with the rest. "I'm happy to sit in the lava."

"Come on, Jimmy. See if you can do it. I know how competitive you are. Bet you can't make it all the way and join me."

The challenge was there. Juliet had thrown down the gauntlet. Nicola saw, she saw so clearly, that James was going to rise to it.

He rubbed his hands together, climbed on top of the sofa, began the course. Nicola watched as he made his way around, following the moves Juliet had made.

Before, in that field, she had willed the birds to fly low and escape. Now she was praying that James would fail.

When it came to jumping on the glass table, he did it so quickly he barely touched the glass before leaping to the chair, then onto the piano, then completing the game as easily as Juliet had.

He too received a round of applause and whistles. Juliet took his arm and held it up in triumph. "We're the winners."

And that was it. There they were, standing together—the only ones who could do it. The magnificent, acrobatic, perfect, radiant, happy couple.

"Wait a second. I haven't tried yet."

"Of course. Nic." Juliet's tone was apologetic. "Sorry, we got swept away. Your turn. We didn't mean to leave you out."

She hadn't been a star athlete at school, but she wasn't hopeless either. She could run. She could jump.

It had to be possible.

I think I can. I think I can, I know I can. The Little Engine That Could. *I'll be the little engine. I'll break up that perfect couple.*

Moving from the sofa to the bookcase was easy. So was negotiating traveling along the shelf of the bookcase. It was getting from the bookcase to the glass table and from there onto the armchair. That was the hard part. James had done it in one fell swoop. Juliet hadn't. She'd lingered on the glass table before that balletic leap of hers. She wasn't that much heavier than Juliet—maybe a few pounds—which meant the glass table shouldn't have a problem holding her weight. But then again, it might.

"Come on, Nic." She heard Bella's voice.

She made the decision: she'd do it James's way. Holding her breath, she jumped onto the glass table, ready to leap straight off again.

The table collapsed with an explosive noise, like breaking ice. She hit the ground, somehow managing to land in a sitting position. Shards of glass surrounded her.

"Nic! Jesus!"

I know I can't. I know I can't.

They were all gathered round her, outside the circle of shattered pieces of glass.

"Is she bleeding? Is she cut?"

"I don't see any blood."

"Nic? Nic?"

She reached out, began to pick up pieces of the glass.

"Nicola, stop it, you'll hurt yourself."

Who said that? Was it Trez?

"I'm fine." She kept gathering glass. "I'm so sorry. I've ruined your table. I'm so sorry."

"Stop picking up the glass!" It *was* Trez, commanding her. "Really. You'll hurt yourself. We'll get someone to clean it up. Are *you* all right? Have you cut yourself? God, you poor thing."

"It was my fault. I'm sorry. Your table. I wrecked your table."

"Don't be silly. It was an old table. I don't see any blood. It's a miracle you weren't badly hurt. Now stay sitting there while we pick up the glass. We'll move inward, until we get to you. Stay still."

"I said it was bloody dangerous." She heard Badger's voice.

But Juliet did it.

Juliet and James did it.

The winners.

They were all around her, bending over, gathering the glass bit by bit, then putting it in a heap by the side. They were making their way toward her.

Another child's game: Let's pick up the glass! See who picks up the most glass first!

Juliet will win.

If I picked up a piece of glass and stabbed her in the

heart with it, would she look surprised?
  No, nothing surprises Juliet.
  I want her dead. I want her gone forever.
  No.
  No, no, no.
  How can I even have that thought?
  It's not me. I'm not like this.
  What the hell has happened?

Chapter Fifteen

November

NICOLA

It was a huge mistake. She should have known, as soon as she found the two photo albums in his cupboard, that looking at them wasn't a good idea. He had a history here that didn't include her. She had no history in London. No one she could call and say, *Remember when we went to the Tate Museum?* or *Remember when we got drunk at that bar?* She had one suitcase, and it didn't contain any photos of friends or family. When she'd fled Buffalo, her escape to Europe was supposed to last two weeks only.

But there was a limit to discovering a new city, going out every single day when James worked and finding a new museum or art gallery, or even, as she'd done a couple of times now, going to a movie in the afternoon on her own. Besides, it was expensive. And it was raining. Really hard.

"It's pouring with rain," James had said when he left that morning.

"That's such a strange phrase. No one ever says: *It's swirling with snowflakes* or *It's booming with thunder*."

"You're right." He laughed. "What are you going to do today?"

"I'm not sure yet."

"Well, don't get soaked."

"I'll try not to."

The shooting weekend had taken place two weeks before. Since that time neither of them had mentioned Juliet's name. Nor had they discussed future plans.

"When are you going home?" That question of Nigel's would often fly into her brain, creating anxiety.

Her money had almost run out. She'd been so careful and responsible saving money when she was working. She didn't go to fancy hairdressers or buy expensive clothes, so she had enough for the trip she'd planned. The two-week trip.

Christmas was looming in the not-so-distant future.

The visa she had for her stay in England would expire after three months.

Greg had paid three months' rent for the apartment when he'd moved out. After that she was on her own.

In a different country with no job, not much money, and a boyfriend who hadn't told her he loved her.

She'd push all those facts out of her mind, sweep them into a corner of her brain labeled "Romantic Bliss: nothing else matters," but they'd creep out and assail her late at night while James slept and she lay awake, thinking that she might have changed course, become more spontaneous and carefree, but she could never stop worrying.

The humiliation of breaking the table in her desperate bid to equal Juliet had abated slightly, but it lingered. They'd all been solicitous and kind. James kept telling her it wasn't a problem, that the only thing that mattered was that she had escaped unharmed.

That night he'd made love to her with a special tenderness. Which would have been wonderful and reassuring if she hadn't been thinking of Juliet the whole time, replaying the vision of her white and red silk flying through the air. That had been two weeks ago, though. As soon as they'd returned to London, the world had been righted on its axis and they'd been as happy as they had been before the shoot.

She decided not to go out and brave the rain. Instead, she'd stay in and read one of James's history books and learn something fascinating they could talk about at dinner that night. Scanning the bookshelf, she found one on the Enlightenment, read it for a while, made herself some lunch, read some more, turned on the television, couldn't find anything she wanted to watch, wandered around the house, came back to the living room, and opened the cupboard underneath the bookshelf. Two photo albums were in it.

She made herself a cup of coffee and sat down on the sofa with the albums in front of her. The first one contained photos of his childhood—baby and little-boy snapshots that made her smile, and pictures of his parents. There was a photo of his parents framed on the mantelpiece of the living room, so she had studied them already: they were both tall and serious-looking. In the photo album they were younger and looked more relaxed and approachable, which made her less anxious about meeting them the next night.

They were going to the opera together. She'd met Greg's parents in their house in New Jersey. They'd had dinner together, watched some TV, and managed to jump the first-meeting-of-parents hurdle easily. A few weeks later, when Greg visited her parents' house, he'd smoked a joint with them and all was hunky-dory.

In a way, meeting at an event like an opera was a good idea. James's parents wouldn't have much time to grill her—dinner was apparently in the opera house at intermission, so it couldn't take long. All she really had to do was sit and be polite and listen to music and applaud.

When James had first told her about his parents and the opera date, she'd immediately wondered how Juliet had first met them, whether they loved Juliet too, even whether Juliet had been in touch with them since she'd returned. It was instinctive now, the way she compared everything to Juliet. And she was sick of it. Sick to death of her own insecurity. It was her fault, not James's, for making everything about Juliet.

Meeting parents was a huge step forward in a relationship. She looked at another photograph of them—it was the last one in the album; it must have been taken at a party when they were in their twenties. They were sitting on a couch, looking at each other. James's father had a cigarette in his hand; his mother was holding a martini glass and was looking at him the way Nicola knew she herself looked at James.

Closing that album, she picked up the second one, opened it, and saw Juliet standing between a younger Hugo and Trez. They were outside a pub, and all three of them looked sickeningly happy. On the page opposite was a series of pictures taken in front of a circle of huge stone slabs. Juliet, in jeans and a paisley shirt, was doing cartwheels in the sun. You could see her bare flat stomach, and that long black hair was flying all over the place.

Nicola closed the album.

She shifted to the other side of the sofa, picked up the phone from the table, and dialed. As soon as she heard "Hello," she dived in.

"Sue—it's me, and I'm freaking out."

"Nic? God—hold on one second." She could hear a door close. "All right. The twins are in their cribs. I can't guarantee anything, but we should have ten minutes. Where the hell are you? I got that postcard from France and then nothing. Have you been kidnapped? Do I need to find ransom money?"

In much the same way she'd recited the story of Tony Kellow to James on the plane, Nicola told Sue what had happened as quickly as possible.

"The thing is, I love him. But his old girlfriend is back from Hong Kong, where she's been for the last eight years. Juliet. And she's amazing. She jumps on tables and she does cartwheels."

"What?"

"Cartwheels. Anyway, the point is I think he may be in love with her still, which makes sense, really, because everyone is in love with her. You kind of can't not be. And she's single. He says she is ancient history, but you should meet her, Sue. She can shoot."

"Shoot? What the hell are you talking about?"

"It would take too long to explain. She can do anything. That's what I'm trying to say. I've never met anyone so charismatic."

"You've met me. I'm phenomenally charismatic."

"It's not funny. I wish I could laugh, but I can't."

"He's with you. Right? You said you're staying at his house. If he wanted to go back to her, he would have."

"I'm not sure about that."

"I am. Men do the easy thing all the time. It would have been simple for him to say: 'Sorry, Nic, but my old love is back in town and I want to be with her.' What's *not* easy is having you living with him when he's in love with someone else."

"Okay, but I wish you could meet her, that's all. You'd understand why it's so hard."

"I do understand that it's hard. Ex-girlfriends are always a bummer. Do you have to see her again? Is she hanging around?"

"No, but she's friends with all his friends."

"That's not fun. I get it. You'll just have to rise above it."

"Okay." She took a deep breath. "I shouldn't look at old pictures of them together, should I?"

"Oh, definitely do that, Nic. And while you're at it, sign up for a torture session."

"Thanks for making me laugh. I needed that. I'm sorry—I haven't asked you anything about your life."

"There's nothing to tell. Baby milestones. Very little sleep."

"I miss you. If it weren't so expensive, I'd call all the time."

"I miss you too. Don't waste your money on the telephone, though. Go get some ravishing clothes to put that woman in her place."

"That's not possible."

"Uh-oh—I have to go. Happy crib time has ended. Tell the gorgeous, rich English guy to pay for your phone calls. And some designer clothes. And stop worrying about the Cartwheel Woman. Here's a good idea: forget about rising above it—next time you see her, kill her."

After she'd hung up, she felt better—for about thirty seconds. She put the photo album away, but those pictures of Juliet refused to disappear from her brain. Juliet and James. Juliet and *Jimmy*. Juliet in her silk outfit flying over the furniture with ease. Juliet, who clearly came from the same "class," who was in the Cambridge Club, who knew all those unspoken rules.

Jesus, Nic. You're the one who's obsessed with her. Think about what you have with James. Think about France.

* * *

SHE'D BOARDED THAT plane in New York and landed in Oz. James had managed it all. He'd found where to leave their bags in the airport, taken her by cab into the heart of Paris, discovered a lovely café near the Eiffel Tower for their breakfast. After a short walk around the city, they headed back to the airport, where he arranged for her ticket on the flight to Marseilles.

The house in Saint-Maximin was just as he had described, except he hadn't told her about the tall windows with the beautiful blue shutters or the terra-cotta planters of lavender beneath those windows, or the gorgeous terrace with more flowering plants. Or the view. Or the pool.

"Welcome," he said as he opened the door with a big iron key. "This is where I kill you. Would you prefer to be murdered upstairs or downstairs?"

"In the kitchen, I think."

"I think that sounds perfect."

I think that sounds perfect had become a running phrase between them—already. And the prospect of him killing her was a running joke; in the space of twenty-four hours they were more in sync than she'd imagined possible.

"Here, let me take your bag." He grabbed it and started walking up the stairs. "Your room is on the right—here." He opened a door off the corridor. "It's all pretty basic."

The bed was made of whitewashed wood, the sheets a pattern of blue and yellow flowers that matched the curtains. And there was a small desk in front of the window.

"It's beautiful."

"Mine's nicer." He grinned. "And yes, we have separate bedrooms. I'm an English gentleman, Nic. Nigel gives me shit about that. Even though he's one too."

"I have to say, Nigel doesn't sound very nice."

"Nigel's cool. He likes to tease people, that's all. We all tease one another. It's our way of showing affection because English men aren't big on being emotional."

"What are they big on?"

"Giving each other a hard time in a funny way. And football, which translates as soccer to you. And cricket. The closest translation to cricket is baseball. I'll put my things away and meet you downstairs. That little bar in the village does food, so we can eat there, and tomorrow we can go in town and get food to cook here." He walked up to her, gave her a kiss on the cheek. Then walked out.

Sitting on the bed, she grabbed a pillow, hugged it.

"You know, people's lives can change like that," her

mother had once said, snapping her fingers. "One little thing can turn your whole life around. Like this . . ." She snapped her fingers again. "Presto!"

Nicola couldn't remember if her mother had been stoned when she said it.

One little thing. A seat assignment on an airplane.

Closing her eyes, she snapped her fingers.

When she opened her eyes, she was still on the bed. In the South of France.

The air smelled of lavender. She took a deep breath.

Presto.

They were there for five days. Each morning they'd have breakfast sitting on an old wooden bench by a table in front of the pool, drinking strong coffee and eating warm, fluffy croissants from the village boulangerie. If she looked toward the house, she saw those windows, the blue shutters, the lavender plants; if she turned away from the house, she gazed out on vineyards stretching to the horizon.

After breakfast they'd meander down to the tiny square and James would give her lessons in playing the French game boules. Then they'd take on the locals for a few games every morning and invariably lose.

In the afternoons they'd go into Uzès, eat oysters, drink wine, and wander around town. Or else take a walk in the countryside.

Every bit of her life could have been a postcard: the older Frenchmen in berets and striped shirts playing boules with cigarettes hanging out of their mouths; the table with the coffee press, mugs that looked more like bowls; the oysters in circles on a platter; the bottle of red wine resting on a checkerboard tablecloth.

It didn't just sound perfect—it was perfect. A dream, a fairy tale.

A disaster.

She'd fled from the mess of her life and ended up walking into a swamp of future despair. Not a walk into a swamp, actually—more like a headlong march into quicksand.

It could have been all right. She could have gone back to Buffalo and replayed the memories, bought herself croissants for breakfast, run and rerun scenes from this dream time in France, while she tried to figure out what the hell she was going to do next. It wouldn't have been easy, but she could have managed it.

If she hadn't fallen in love. Or raced into love or jumped into it or whatever it was you did that ended up with you being out of control and hanging on to every second you were with that person because the clock was ticking down and pretty soon you'd never see him again and your whole life would be spent reminiscing about five fucking days.

They'd arrived on Tuesday, and he was flying back to London at some point on Sunday.

On Wednesday morning, when she'd made a good shot in the boules game, he'd hugged her. At which point she tried to turn herself into an instant boules pro, concentrating as if she were in the Olympics, desperate for another good shot, which might mean another hug, and ending up playing hopeless shots because she was so tense.

She was stupidly proud when she made him laugh.

That night she insisted on cooking dinner. When he took a mouthful of the chicken casserole, he'd said, "Wow. That's delicious." Which felt like getting an A-plus in every subject she'd ever taken.

The ferocity of these feelings was new to her.

If that divorcée hadn't come along, the odds are I would have married Greg. I'd never have known what it's like to feel like this. I was in love with him, yes. But it was as if I were a kid in a baby pool, splashing away happily enough, wading up to my knees. Now I'm in an adult pool, with water deep enough to dive into, a whole different kind of love. A you-could-drown-any-second kind of love. What will happen when this is over? It's the old Is it better to have loved and lost than never loved at all? *question. Which I can't answer—at least not until I've felt the "lost" part.*

After that dinner Wednesday night, James had found a big spare blanket and they'd gone outside to sit on the bench by the pool. He'd lit two candles, placed them on the table in front of the bench, and she'd thought: *This is it. This is when he makes a move.*

"Tell me about your hippie parents," he'd said.

She told him a few stories, how they weren't like any other parents she knew. They never looked at her report cards, they never made any rules. "They'd make jokes a lot. They'd say, 'If you don't skip up the stairs to bed and dream about waterfalls, we'll ground you for a month.' That kind of thing. My friends adored them."

"That's an unusual method of parenting."

"It was." She was holding on tightly to her wineglass. "I felt as if . . . I don't know. I felt guilty."

"Why guilty?"

"Because I was there and Daniel wasn't. Because I think they looked at me and thought of Daniel and they couldn't be normal with me because they wanted to be normal with him too."

"I don't think I understand."

"Every time they looked at me, they must have thought about him. I did. I mean, every time I looked in a mirror, I'd think of him. And I'd wonder: *Why him and not me?* I always thought I should do something special, be someone special, to make it okay. I thought I should live his life for him too, but I didn't know how to do that. And then I started talking to him. So that he was alive. So that he'd be my friend, instead of this missing presence that made me feel guilty, if that makes any sense." She finished her wine, reached out and poured herself more. "And now, well, he *is* my friend, my brother. I love him. But he's my secret, you know. I've never told anyone except you. I feel as if, if I told people, then he'd disappear. He really would die. I can't explain it, James."

"But you've told me, and he's still alive for you."

"Yes." She nodded. "He's fine with me telling you. Oh God, you must think I'm completely crazy."

"No. Not at all. I think you're the very special person you wanted to be."

He didn't then move toward her and kiss her or even hold her hand. They stayed on the bench, staring at the sky in silence for a while. Until he said, "Damn, it's getting cold," and they retired back into the house, and he kissed her on the cheek, as he had on the first night, saying, "Sleep well, Nic."

The next morning, at breakfast, he was buttering his croissant when he asked: "What were your plans? I mean what were your plans for this trip before I so rudely interrupted them?"

"I was going to stay in Paris for a week, then go to Rome and spend a week there, then fly home."

"Rome, right." He nodded, took a bite of the croissant. "So—you want to immerse yourself in the culture while you're here? Well, I happen to have studied French history. So I will instruct you. And decide later whether to set you an exam."

Thursday and Friday raced by in a haze of James instructing her on French history, boules games, a quick expedition to the Pont d'Avignon, and boom, just like that it was Saturday and they were in Uzès at a table outside the café they liked. He hadn't kissed her, he hadn't even held her hand. Did he have anything but friendly feelings for her?

He was picking up the bottle of wine on the table when he said: "You know, my parents sent me to boarding school. When I was seven."

"What?"

"My parents sent me away to school when I was seven." He poured her and himself a glass.

"Seven? Seven years old?"

"Yes." He nodded. "It was something of a shock. What I mean to say is, I didn't really understand that when they left me there that they were actually *leaving* me there. I kept thinking they'd come back. The next day. Or the one after that. I cried every night. For God knows how long."

"How could they have done that?" She leaned forward, wishing she had the courage to grab his hand.

"Everybody did it." He said it dismissively. "Everybody we knew, I mean. Hugo went the same time I did to the same school. I remember him saying, 'Gosh, James, won't this be fun!' the first night. The next night he was crying too. One of the matrons had taken his stuffed animal away when she caught him whispering to me after lights out. I remember him saying, 'I can't bear it,' over and over again through his sobs. Some boys were fine with it, though. In fact, Hugo was in his element after a couple of weeks."

"I think it would have been impossible to be fine with it. I can't imagine how painful that must have been. Jesus. Seven years old. That's unbelievable."

"You learn to deal with it." He reached out for his glass, took another sip of wine. "I don't talk about it. I've told you. We English aren't big on talking about emotions. Except . . ." He put the glass back down on the table, then looked up to the sky. "It feels like that again. I mean you leaving tomorrow. It feels like you're sending me back to school on my own."

"James?"

He was still looking up at the sky.

"James?" This time she did grab his hand. "What do you mean? Tell me what you mean."

"I know you were planning to go to Rome for a week and then back to New York, but I don't want you to leave." He looked at her, looked away. "I want you to come to London with me. But I don't know . . . I mean, you have your plans. Except . . ."

"Except what?"

"Except Rome. Who wants to go to Rome? No history. No culture."

How did that happen? He had been close to tears, she could tell. And now he was joking. But was this his whole English way of joking when things got serious? In which case, should she follow his lead?

"You're so right. Rome has zero history, zero culture, and zero art."

"Don't forget the lousy food."

"Rome's really a dump, isn't it?" She laughed.

"Such a dump. Whereas London, Nic, London . . ."

"I think London sounds perfect."

They didn't kiss until they got back to the house.

Now she couldn't imagine a time when they hadn't kissed.

Chapter Sixteen

It was around five thirty when the doorbell rang. She wasn't expecting anyone and felt a little odd as she went to see who was there because it wasn't her house.

"Hello, Nicola."

It was Stewart, standing in front of her. He didn't have a raincoat on, yet he didn't seem fazed by the fact raindrops were running down his face.

"Stewart. God, you're wet. Come in."

"Sorry." He stepped inside. "I don't use umbrellas. I don't like macs either. Mackintoshes—raincoats." He smiled that almost smile of his, one that didn't change the serious demeanor he seemed to own.

"Here. Wait, I'll get you a towel."

She ran upstairs to the bathroom, grabbed a towel, ran back down, and handed it to him. He wiped himself off, handed it back.

"I was supposed to meet Mr. Shuttleworth here at six—I'm early, I know. Sorry."

"I didn't know you were meeting him. Hold on." Once again she ran up the stairs then stashed the towel in the laundry basket. When she came down, she said: "Stewart, really, his name is James. 'Mr. Shuttleworth' makes him sound as if he's your fourth-grade teacher. Would you like some tea? Coffee? Sit down." She pointed to the kitchen table, which functioned as the living room table as well.

"No thank you. Very much. I don't need anything to drink. I'm fine." He sat, his back ramrod straight.

"Tell me." She took a chair opposite him. "How's Matthew?"

"Healthy as a horse." The same semi-smile. "I'm here to discuss another shooting weekend—not at Langley House but in Scotland. Grouse shooting. In early December. I should be able to arrange it, but Mr. Langley told me Mr. Shuttleworth might know—sorry, I really can't call him 'James'—that he might know of a lodge we could rent for the weekend."

"Is grouse shooting like pheasant shooting?"

"Grouse fly faster. They're smaller, much harder to shoot. And you shoot up in the moors, not in the woods."

"I'm so glad Matthew wasn't hurt badly. You were great. I mean, taking them to the car and the hospital."

"Thank you."

She tried for a second to picture Stewart having fun, laughing, saying more than one sentence at a time.

"I know how sorry Trez was that she shot him."

"Not in my opinion."

"What?"

"In my opinion, Mrs. Langley didn't shoot Matthew."

"That doesn't . . . Who did? I don't understand."

"The woman with the ponytail."

"Juliet? She was shooting beside Trez at the far end of the field."

"Yes, her." He nodded.

"Then why did Juliet say she hadn't? It doesn't make sense. She said she did to begin with, then said she'd been covering for Trez."

"I might be wrong. I was watching, and that's what I thought I saw. I might be wrong." He shrugged.

"Did you tell Hugo—Mr. Langley?"

"It's none of my business. As I said, I could have it wrong."

Nicola sat back, amazed. Why would Juliet say she had and then take it back? Especially as she'd told Hugo to keep it a secret.

She'd told *Hugo* to keep it a secret.

Hugo wasn't the type to keep a secret.

"Are you homesick?" he asked. That question was out of the blue.

"Yes, I mean, a little, maybe, but I haven't been here that long yet."

"It's an interesting word, isn't it? When you're carsick or seasick, you're physically sick to your stomach. When you're homesick, you're yearning for home to make you feel better."

"You're right. I've never—"

"Hi! Nic, Stewart. You're here already." She hadn't noticed the sound of the key in the lock. James took off his raincoat, hung it up, put his umbrella in the umbrella stand by the door. "I thought we were meeting at six? I'm sorry if I'm late."

"No, I apologize." Stewart stood up. "I'm early."

"Sit down, please. Have you had a cup of tea? Coffee? Do you want a drink? We have plenty of half-decent wine."

"No thank you. I'm fine."

"I'm afraid I checked out that lodge I told you about for the grouse shooting, but it won't be possible to rent it. You're on your own finding one. I should have rung you. I'm sorry you came here for nothing. You should stay for dinner."

"I can't, but thank you for the invitation. And it shouldn't be a problem finding a lodge. Don't worry."

Nicola took another step into the quicksand of love. James didn't care about those unspoken rules. He'd invited Stewart for dinner.

He belonged to the Club, but he wasn't one of them, not really.

Thank God for that.

Chapter Seventeen

TREZ

Nothing seemed right. Trez couldn't put her finger on what exactly was wrong, but there it was: wrongness, floating in the air between Hugo and her. She couldn't remember a time when they'd been so off-kilter. He said he'd forgiven her for shooting Matthew, and she believed he had. Whatever was wrong, it wasn't Matthew—whom she'd invited to the house, along with his parents, for a delicious lunch. She'd given him a Rubik's Cube for a present, and he'd seemed delighted with it.

Hugo wasn't angry; he was, as he'd claimed she was to Juliet, distracted. He took more walks; at meals, when he spoke to her, he wasn't concentrating. And he'd taken two trips to London without her, saying he had business there.

"There are a few people who are interested in hiring the shoot," he'd explained. "You don't need to be there."

"You never go to London unless it's absolutely necessary."

"Well, this is. Absolutely necessary."

Distracted and distant.

Juliet was distant too. She'd left with Badger that Sunday morning of the shoot, saying she couldn't stay on because she'd only just returned from Hong Kong and there were tons of things she had to sort out.

"Don't worry—I'm around now, for good. We'll have plenty of time together as soon as I've dealt with the whole process of moving back here."

There couldn't be *that* much for her to do to "sort things out." Two weeks had passed, and Juliet hadn't even called. Until this morning, when she'd rung, all bright and breezy, saying, "What's up, Trez?"

"Nothing."

"Really? That's ineffably boring."

"Sorry."

"Trez? Why that tone of voice? What's going on?"

"I don't know." She sighed. "No, I do know. It's Hugo. He's been off with me lately. Distant. He's gone to London twice now, and he's gone today too. He hates going to London. He says he's meeting people to hire the shoot, but it makes me uncomfortable. The way he's acting . . ."

"I'm sure it's nothing. But listen. I have to rush off now, but would you like me to talk to him? I'm in London. I could see him when he's here, find out if there's anything you should know."

"Would you? That would be wonderful. And I'll see you soon, won't I?"

"Absolutely. As soon as possible. ASAP. We have a lot of talking to do. Just not right now."

Didn't you ring me? You're making me feel as I rang you.

"Thanks, Jules."

"My pleasure. Now cheer the fuck up."

After she had hung up, Trez wandered around the house aimlessly. She'd hoped for years that Juliet would return, and Juliet *had* returned, yet she felt more ill at ease than she had been for ages. In the drawing room, she stopped, stared at the new glass table she'd bought. Nicola may have been embarrassed when she broke the old one playing Lava, but Trez had already been embarrassed and ashamed because she was sitting on the floor, doing nothing, opting out of the game altogether.

It had been her party, in her house, yet Lava was an impossible game for her to play. She wouldn't have been able to get up on top of the sofa without bumbling in some way, much less take a step away from it. It reminded her of her youth, not being chosen for any sports teams, being laughed at when she tripped or bumped into something. The little girl with the glasses who wasn't part of any group, who had yearned for acceptance. She hadn't been bullied. She'd been ignored.

"You're going to be a countess, Trez," she said to herself as she walked out and continued wandering. "Remember that.

"You'll get tables at restaurants when no one else can. You'll give those glittering parties.

"People will wish they were you."

What the hell did any of that matter, though, if Hugo was unhappy with her? If Juliet was pretty much ignoring her?

If she was never going to have a child?

This huge house could be emptier than all those people who admired it would ever believe.

Chapter Eighteen

NICOLA

The night at the opera with James's parents had gone well: they'd been polite, she'd been polite, they hadn't blinked when she told them she'd never been to an opera before. James's father, Graham, simply said: "I hope you enjoy it, Nicola. But don't feel obligated to. It's not to everyone's taste, I know."

She had enjoyed it, she'd enjoyed the whole experience: The Royal Opera House in Covent Garden was a stunning building with beautiful, plush red seats. They'd been in a box there, with a perfect view of the stage. The story of the opera, *Madama Butterfly*, was a sad one, but it was sung beautifully, and she'd been moved, even close to tears. At dinner in the interval, she'd asked for stories about James as a boy, and they'd both been happy to tell them, especially James's mother, Daphne, who clearly adored her only child.

At one point during dinner, Nicola had to stop herself from laughing out loud when she imagined James's parents meeting her parents. They were so straightforwardly conservative; her parents were so wildly not.

She'd met his friends; she'd met his parents. Two hurdles had been leapt, but she still wasn't sure if there was a race to be run. The tenuous nature of their relationship was agonizing. She was effectively sitting twiddling her thumbs while he was leading his normal life: the balance was off, yet she had no idea how to level things out.

She sat on his sofa, in his house, pondering.

She'd spent way too much time sitting on his sofa, pondering.

When the doorbell rang, she leapt up, grateful for any kind of interruption. Grateful until she opened the door and saw Juliet standing on the threshold.

"You don't mind, do you, Nic? I was in the area and thought I'd drop by. Badger gave me the address."

"No, I don't mind at all. Come in. Sit down. Can I get you something?"

Juliet walked straight past her to the sofa.

"You don't need to get me anything, thanks. I'm so pleased I found you in. Come, sit down."

So now Juliet was telling her what to do—and she did it. Because that's what you did when Juliet gave an order. You obeyed it. She sat down on a chair at an angle to the sofa. Juliet had on jeans, riding boots, and a black leather jacket. She threw one arm over the top of the sofa.

"I have to admit, this isn't a random visit. I have a purpose in coming here. I want to clear a few things up. It's funny. I feel as if I were a man and the father of a girl I was dating has asked me what my intentions were."

"I'm sorry, I don't understand."

"I wanted to tell you I have no intentions. That's what I mean. I have no intentions toward Jimmy. And before you get upset, let me say, even if I *had* had intentions, I know he wouldn't reciprocate. He obviously adores you. I'm so happy for you both."

"Thank you." Was that what she was supposed to say? She couldn't think of any other way to respond and felt as stymied as she so often had when Tony Kellow would aim one of his lewd comments at her.

"I bet you went to university, Nic."

"I went to college—university—yes."

"You're so lucky. I wish I'd gone. I *should* have gone. It was the biggest mistake I ever made. I followed the path expected of me—you know that poem 'The Road Less Taken'?"

"Robert Frost, yes." She wasn't going to correct her and say: "*The Road Not Taken*."

"Well, I took the road *more* taken, and that *has* made all the difference."

"You weren't expected to go to university?"

"Nic. I'm a girl." She snorted. "Girls like me went to secretarial school. Or got married young. In either case, the whole idea was to get married. And to marry the most suitable boy or man possible. I wanted . . . well, I wanted more."

"Did you find more in Hong Kong? Sorry, that was a stupid question. If you had, you wouldn't be here."

"That is a sadly true statement."

For a few moments neither of them spoke.

"You know what they called us? The girls my age who went out to Hong Kong?"

"There was a name for you?"

"Yes. We were called the Fishing Fleet."

"What? Why?"

"We were going to Hong Kong to fish for a rich husband. There were masses of Englishmen there, bankers and financiers who were good catches. And we were there to hook them. If anyone came back without a catch, well, it was empty cargo."

"God. That's crazy. It's so insulting."

"The thing is, in some cases it was true. But not in my case, Nic. I was looking for adventure, excitement, something *different*. What actually happened? I ended up as a secretary in an ad agency. A big ad agency. Nothing was the way I had imagined it might be."

"I'm really sorry."

She was. It had taken only a few sentences, and she had started not to hate Juliet. Bella hadn't been to college, Trez hadn't, Juliet hadn't. And she had to guess, neither had Stewart. Who did go? Upper-class boys, apparently, and very smart people from the middle classes? She couldn't figure it out. College wasn't necessarily the answer to life, but it was a place where you could learn—not only learn but start to find out who you were and what you wanted.

"Did you have a job you liked in America?"

"I did. Until my boss began to make all these suggestive comments. I ended up punching him."

"You didn't! That is brilliant, Nic. That's the best thing I've ever heard."

"It wasn't brilliant, not really. I lost my job, obviously. And I didn't even hurt him."

"Come on—you punched the asshole; that's all that matters. I wish I'd been there to witness it. God, I see why Jimmy's so enamored. Forget seven hours on a plane—I'd be inviting you to come stay with me after ten minutes."

"That's . . . that's really nice of you to say."

"Remember, I told you we'd be good friends. Now . . ." She rose. "I would love to stay, but I'm meeting a friend for lunch. It's been wonderful talking to you. I'm glad we got the chance."

"So am I."

Did she mean that? she wondered, after Juliet had disappeared. Juliet in person had an effect, a kind of magic it was hard to not fall for. As soon as she'd gone, though, Nicola thought of the way she'd assumed so much. Assuming she'd be in, in the first place, assuming she needed to hear that Juliet had no designs on James, assuming that Nicola would even want her to stay to chat further. All

these assumptions. It was Juliet, not Trez, you felt you had
to curtsey to. Even if she felt she'd lost out by not going to
college, even if she'd been unhappy in Hong Kong, Juliet
still had that regal bearing.

But . . . but she'd been friendly and complimentary and
seemingly sincere.

The Fishing Fleet. Who had come up with that expression?

Juliet hadn't hooked anyone, and no one had hooked
her.

Empty cargo.

Was she sincere?

Could Juliet ever be sincere?

She could stay in the house, asking herself questions
about Juliet, driving herself crazy, or she could get out and
do something. She'd been to the Tate museum, but she could
go again. And visit the National Portrait Gallery again as
well. It was noon, so she could grab a little lunch—do both
and get back in time to do some food shopping and think
of something to cook for James.

It was a plan. Which was what she needed. Distraction.

* * *

BY FOUR O'CLOCK she was fed up, not with the art she'd
seen, but with being a foreigner. The homesickness Stewart
talked about had suddenly ambushed her, hitting her heart
with a vengeance. Walking through the Tate museum, she

heard American accents and headed straight for them, standing behind two women who were discussing a painting. All she wanted was to hear them talk. So she eavesdropped until one of them turned around and gave her a look, at which point she scurried away like a guilty stalker.

Then she remembered. On the Sunday of the shooting weekend, at breakfast, Badger had made a comment about the Savoy hotel—how that was the only place in England where, when you turned into the entrance, you drove on the right. "And it has the American Bar too," he'd said. "A very posh one with very good, very strong martinis."

Fuck it. I'm going to be an American. And I'm going to have a martini. A very good, very strong one. I don't care how much it costs.

Jumping in a taxi, she said "The Savoy hotel, please."

"Great hotel. You Yanks love it. The wife and I went to Florida last year. We'll go back soon. They have those cheap flights now."

The driver kept talking. He was a big fan of the Everglades.

"Ever been there?" he asked.

"Sadly not."

The short driveway into the Savoy did indeed force him to drive on the right—for about two seconds. They came to a stop behind another taxi.

"Would you look at that? Honeymooners? Or is she his bit on the side?"

A couple were standing in front of the hotel entrance,

entwined in a passionate kiss. When they broke it off, the man opened the door of the taxi in front of them, ushered the woman in, then went in himself and shut the door.

The woman was wearing a black leather jacket and riding boots.

The man was wearing bright pink trousers.

She had seen their faces.

Hugo and Juliet.

Juliet and Hugo.

Jesus Christ.

* * *

"Nic? Are you all right?"

He'd come home and found her lying on the bed, staring at the ceiling.

"I'm okay. It's just . . ." She sat up.

"Just what?" James sat down beside her. "Tell me. You look as if you might be getting a bug. Do you feel feverish?"

"No. I saw something this afternoon. I saw . . ."

Her hands began to claw at the bedcover.

"What did you see?"

"I went to the Savoy hotel. I was going to have a drink in the American Bar, and I . . . and I saw them outside the entrance. Hugo. Hugo and Juliet. They were . . ."

"Go on. They were what?"

"Kissing."

He burst out laughing.

"They were, James. They were kissing. The taxi driver thought they were honeymooners or something about a side bit, whatever that is. I didn't know what he was saying—I guess an affair. They're having an affair. She came here to visit me and then she said she had to meet a friend for lunch and that must have been Hugo and they were at a hotel and they're having an affair."

"Oh, Nic, you've got it so wrong." He put his arm around her, gave her a squeeze. "Juliet's tactile; she's a tactile person. I'm sure they were having a nice long lunch, a nice chat, and she kissed him. Affectionately. They're old friends."

"It was more than a friendly kiss."

"You were in a taxi? You probably couldn't see properly."

"I was close enough, James. I promise. My taxi driver saw it too. He didn't think it was just friendly."

"Listen, Nic. I get that you think you saw that, but there's just no way in hell. I know Hugo. And Juliet. Hugo would never kiss another woman in anything but a fond, friendly way. And Juliet? There isn't a chance she'd kiss him. It's not like she's ever fancied him. Or ever would."

"Maybe things have changed since the old days."

"Not on that score, believe me."

She'd replayed that scene enough times in her head to know she wasn't wrong.

"I don't know if I should say something to Trez."

"Nic." He stood up. "Seriously. I love you, but this is madness."

"What?"

"I said, 'I love you, but this is madness.'"

There it was. What she'd been waiting for. In the absolutely wrong context, but still, who cared?

"I love you too."

"Well, that's a relief." He sat back down. "Good to get that out of the way, isn't it?" He gave her a little nudge. "Possibly not the most romantic way of saying it, though, right?"

"Possibly not." She laughed.

"It might be more romantic if we got under the duvet in this bed now."

"It would be—definitely."

There was no way in hell she could have misinterpreted that kiss. Still—it wasn't her business. It wasn't her place to tell Trez. They hardly knew each other. And Trez wouldn't believe her either. The only thing that mattered was what James had said.

"You really love me?"

"I *really* love you. Let's get something straight, though. This doesn't mean I'm not going to murder you."

Chapter Nineteen

TREZ

You visited Nicola? You visited her and you haven't visited me?"

"Oh, please. I talked to Nic for a few minutes. How old are you, sweetheart? You're sounding like a pissed-off toddler."

"That's because I don't understand. You ring me and tell me you've visited Nicola and had a chat, and you haven't visited me or had any kind of long chat with me. I think I have a right to be upset. I'm supposed to be your best friend."

"You think Hugo isn't paying enough attention to you, you think I'm not paying enough attention to you. Are you all right, Trez? Seriously. I'm worried about you. What's really wrong?"

"Nothing."

"Jesus, you're crying."

"I'm not feeling well. I'm tired. That's all."

"Listen, sweetheart. I saw Huge in London, and honestly, you're imagining things. He's fine, he's happy. All is well. You're creating problems where they don't exist."

"Okay. I'm sorry. I haven't been myself lately. But why did you visit her? I have to ask. Did you come back for James?"

"That's why I went to see Nic. I wanted to tell her that I have no plans to break up their little dalliance."

"You think it's just a dalliance?"

"It may not be a dalliance. It might be the real thing. I have no clue. Christ. You know, there are some times when I miss Hong Kong." She sighed.

"Did you love someone there? Were you heartbroken?"

"Life can be disappointing—that's all I'll say."

Juliet was disappointed in life? She'd never expected to hear that. Thinking about it, though, it made sense. Jules had flown off to Hong Kong looking for adventure. She might have traveled to fabulous places, but she'd come back, and come back on her own. Whereas she, the one who had been Juliet's sidekick, was happily married and living in an incredible house. The only disappointment in her life could well be fixed when she saw the specialist in a few weeks.

Juliet was right. She'd been creating problems where they didn't exist. Now her anger had vanished completely. If she felt any negative emotion, it was embarrassment for being so self-absorbed.

"Are you very disappointed, Jules? That's awful."

"Oh, shit, I have to run now. I almost forgot, I have a dentist's appointment. Sorry. But don't worry about me, sweetheart. I'll be fine. I'll be just tickety-boo."

* * *

"TREZ, I'M TIRED," he stated. "It took me ages to get back here from London. The traffic was appalling. And I just took Buster for a long walk. I'm worn out."

They were sitting in the drawing room. She'd suggested they go upstairs to bed immediately, which was one of their ways of asking each other to have sex.

It had been weeks since they'd made love: the last time had been that first night of the shooting party weekend. Still—maybe he was sick to death of trying to get her pregnant. That was understandable.

"Right, well. We'll stay here, then. What news do I have for you? Juliet rang. Apparently, she went and saw Nicola yesterday. To tell her she has no designs on James. I know that's nice for Nicola, but there was a huge part of me that hoped Jules and James would get back together."

"That was over a long time ago."

"I know. I was only hoping. Although that wouldn't be nice for Nicola."

"I think Nicola and James make a good couple."

"Really? I didn't—"

"What else did Jules say?"

"She said life could be disappointing, Hugo. Hearing that made me sad."

"Some things work out for the best in the long term."

"What does that mean?"

She saw a sudden sadness in his eyes.

"Is anything wrong? You look miserable."

"Nothing's wrong." His expression shifted. "Everything is tickety-boo."

"Tickety-boo? Juliet said that too. She said everything would be fine for her, that it would be tickety-boo. God, you both sound a hundred years old."

"I'm a spring chicken."

"Well, that makes me a spring chicken too. Are you sure you don't want to go upstairs immediately and be spring chickens together?"

"Another time, Trez. I'm sorry. You're a good sport. You've always been a good sport."

A good sport? It wasn't what she would have liked to be called by her husband, but she knew it was his idea of a compliment.

James had told her about those first days in boarding school, and her heart wept thinking of Hugo, a little boy deprived of his stuffed animal. His parents. His home. He'd adjusted: James claimed he'd adjusted a lot faster than he himself had, but that didn't mean he had been happy.

He didn't talk about those days, and she didn't push him to. Hugo worked at his own speed. He'd never complained about her not getting pregnant. He'd never been anything but kind; perhaps not always thoughtful, but kind.

I'll take it. A good sport is high praise in Hugo's world. I understand that. I understand him.

I'm so lucky. I'm not disappointed in life. Poor Juliet. I never thought I'd feel sorry for her, but I do.

Chapter Twenty

NICOLA

Jesus, Nic. He's told you he loves you?"

Bella had called her early in the morning, saying she was going to take a day off work, pretend to be sick, and that they should go shopping together. They'd trawled through various charity shops Bella knew and bought a dress each, then taken the bus back to Bella's tiny, one-room flat in West London.

"I know. It was a shock. A wonderful shock."

"Sorry, love, but with news like that I have to have a fag."

"You smoke?"

"I do, but Nigel hates it, so never in front of him. It's not as if he comes to this flat, though. I always go to his. So I won't get caught if you don't tell."

"I won't."

"So—that's big news. I wonder what Juliet—*Jules*—will think of that?"

"She came to see me, to tell me she had no designs on James."

"No shit."

"She was being friendly. In that Juliet way she has. She also said that she wished she'd gone to college—university."

"Then why didn't she?"

"I think no one expected her to?"

"No one expected me to either, but for different reasons. It bothers me, you know. When rich people moan. The arrogance of them all."

"I don't think James is arrogant."

"Hey, I'm not saying he's *arrogant* arrogant, just that the way he was brought up, the way they all were, well, they almost can't help being arrogant. That's all. No one I know, no one my age, owns a house, much less these kinds of houses."

"No one I know does either. Everyone rents. Except maybe my ex-boyfriend's divorced lover. I bet she does."

"See—we're still the outsiders." She smiled, lit the cigarette, and inhaled. "When I forget and say 'toilet' instead of 'loo,' Nigel winces. He actually looks pained. Same goes for 'couch' and 'sofa.'"

"Wait, which one is the right one?"

"Sofa. And listen, I'm in deep shit if I say 'pardon.' He told me that a couple of days ago. I can say 'excuse me,' or even 'what,' but not 'pardon.' So I said, 'Fuck me. What kind of bullshit is that? Oh no, pardon my French.' He laughed. I have to give him some credit. He has a sense of humor."

Nicola thought about telling Bella how she'd seen Hugo and Juliet together, but then she'd probably tell Nigel and he'd say something to someone, maybe even Trez, and it would get back to James, and he'd know it came from her originally. That wouldn't be good.

"I'm saying all the wrong things too. I pronounced 'Wimbledon' wrong. I say 'couch' and 'toilet' all the time. So I'm in seriously deep shit."

"Listen, you're American. Americans don't count. No one expects Americans to say the right thing, if you know what I mean. So even though you're an outsider, you're actually less of one than I am."

"That's insane."

"That . . ." Bella shook her head. "Is England."

Chapter Twenty-One

TREZ

Jesus, Trez. Where the fuck are you?"

"Jules?"

"I'm sitting here at the salon waiting, and I had to ask them to use their phone. You're supposed to be here. Paul is waiting."

"Paul?"

"The hairdresser we booked. For today. You were supposed to be here half an hour ago."

"We booked a hairdresser? I don't . . ."

"Remember? At breakfast on that Sunday of the shoot. We were talking about hair, and you said you wished you could do something about yours, something different, and I said I knew someone."

"Yes, but you didn't say you'd make a booking. Did you?"

"I did. And then I said I'd book for the two of us today at eleven. And you said you'd put it in your diary."

"I don't . . . Really? Oh God, I'm sorry. I don't think I heard you say that about the booking. And you didn't mention it when you rang last time."

"I didn't think I had to. My plan was that we'd get our hair done and then go out to lunch."

"That would have been brilliant. Just what I need. God, could we do it another time? Tomorrow?"

"I'm already getting my hair done today. You know I'm having dinner with Huge tonight."

"You are?"

"Yes. Why don't you join us? We're going to Sale e Pepe. That great Italian restaurant near Sloane Square. You could catch a ride into town with him."

"He took the car to London an hour ago."

"Shit. Bad luck."

"Maybe I could come on the train."

"Absolutely. And you two can stay at that club of his, and then he can drive you home tomorrow. I'll make a reservation at eight thirty."

"Okay. See you there. And Jules, I'm sorry about forgetting the booking. Really."

"Don't worry, sweetheart. You always were forgetful."

Was I? she wondered after they'd said their goodbyes and she'd hung up. *Uncoordinated, yes.* "You get so many bruises tripping and bumping into things, Trez, you should give a Black and Blue Ball," Juliet had once remarked.

I said stupid things at times too, but I don't remember being forgetful.

Well, you wouldn't remember being forgetful, would you?

She smiled.

Perhaps she'd accidentally-on-purpose forgotten the hair appointment. Any trip to the hairdresser's was depressing. Each time she'd walk in hoping for a miracle, but her hair was miracle-proof.

As was the rest of her physical appearance. It didn't matter what clothes she bought. She could have dressed herself head to toe in Givenchy and she'd still end up looking silly.

She'd have to go search in her closet for something reasonable to put on for the dinner tonight. It had been ages since she'd been out to a restaurant.

Hugo hadn't mentioned having dinner with Juliet, but he'd been in a rush to get out that morning, saying his meeting in London was scheduled for ten a.m. and he was running late. Yet another trip to London. But that meant he was getting a lot of business for the shoot, so that was good news.

Buster appeared in the study, wagging his tail, looking hopeful.

"All right, silly. I'll take you for a walk and then I'll go ransack my closet."

She got down on the floor, kissed him on his forehead, hugged him fiercely.

"You don't care what I look like, do you, Buster? You're

always happy to see me in whatever clothes I wear, however my hair looks. You're the best dog in the world."

She kissed him again. And again.

She had no idea why she was crying.

* * *

SHE'D NEVER BEEN to Sale e Pepe before, but it was, as Juliet had said, off Sloane Square and easy to find. When she went in, she could see that it was full. Waiters were weaving in and out of the kitchen, cutlery was clanking, voices were loud. She spotted Juliet and Hugo at a table at the far end of the room.

"Oh," she said when she arrived at it. "You've started already."

Plates of parma ham and melon sat in front of both of them.

"The reservation was at eight," Hugo said.

"Jules, you said eight thirty, didn't you?"

"No, eight. It doesn't matter, though. Sit down, sweetheart, join us. We ordered three glasses of champagne—the bubbles have died a little, but yours should still be cold."

She sat, took a sip of the flat, warm champagne.

"Well, this is fun. We haven't been out to a restaurant in ages, have we, Hugo?"

"No. Jules said you forgot your hair appointment today."

"I know. Silly of me." She'd chosen a blue maxi dress

with long sleeves. Juliet was wearing black trousers with a black top. The top was sparkly and had COKE: THE REAL THING written across it in red cursive letters.

"I love that top, Jules."

"Thanks."

Juliet's hair was even shinier than usual and blow-dried so that it curled at the bottom. She was wearing a gold bracelet, which rested flat against her wrist; little rubies were scattered over the clasp.

"And that bracelet—wow! I've never seen you wear any jewelry. Did you get it in Hong Kong?"

"You wouldn't believe the jewelry you can get in Hong Kong. It's a shopper's paradise. Anyway, far more interesting: Huge and I were talking about Nic and Jimmy. Isn't it perfect that we all think they make such a good couple? It would have been dreadful if she were a bitch."

"He's dated a few bitches."

"Hasn't everyone, Huge?" Juliet laughed.

"I never dated anyone—except Trez."

A waiter with a mound of floppy black hair arrived. Trez said she'd skip the first course and join in on the main one.

"The spaghetti *vongole* is delicious here. That's what I'm having." Juliet handed the waiter the menu.

"I'll have that too, please," Hugo said.

"Make it three. Why not?" Trez smiled. "That makes things easy."

"And a bottle of Valpolicella," Hugo added.

"Huge, your birthday is coming up soon, isn't it? We

should have a party."

"I already suggested that to him a month ago, Jules. But Hugo hates parties. You know that. He's always hated them."

"You won't hate this one, Huge. Annabel's. That's where we should have it. Annabel's. Trez, you can arrange that, can't you?"

"Yes, but—"

"Huge, come on." Juliet put her hand on his arm. "Your birthday should be celebrated. What else are you going to do? Sit by the fire reading the *Times*?"

"You have a point."

Hugo always did end up following Juliet's instructions— they all did. If Juliet wanted to go for a walk, they went. If she said she would like to take a trip to Blackpool to see if it was as grim and depressing as she imagined it was, off they'd troop to Blackpool. Trez thought: *Yes, Jules does have a point*. Annabel's, the private club in Mayfair, was the perfect place to celebrate. She hadn't been there in ages either.

It felt as if they hadn't been anywhere aside from Langley Hall. They'd effectively shut themselves up there. The occasional dinner party or lunch party with people from the surrounding area, the occasional visit to her parents' or her brothers', but otherwise they stayed put.

Was that her fault? Was she the one keeping him in? That thought had never occurred to her before.

There was a sudden clanging: the mop-headed waiter

was running through the center of the restaurant, yelling, "Mouse! A mouse!" All the waiters were running, holding their trays high up in the air, yelling, "A mouse!" One came out of the kitchen wielding a broom like a weapon.

"Jesus." Trez jumped up, but Juliet grabbed her hand, pulled her back down.

"It's an act, Trez. They do this every night."

"What?"

"They pretend there's a mouse."

"Why?"

"To frighten people like you, I suppose."

"I hate mice. I have a phobia about them. Sorry."

She reached out to get a sip of water, knocked over her wineglass. Red wine spread over the white tablecloth.

"Trez." Hugo said it in that tone she hated. As if she were a small child he was scolding.

"I'm sorry."

"Don't worry." Juliet threw her napkin over the wine stain. "Now no one will see it. So, what do you say? A party at Annabel's? A dinner? Then dancing? Doesn't that sound like a great idea?"

"Yes, yes, it does." Hugo sounded so enthusiastic.

Had she been the one keeping him at home?

"Do you remember that party we went to in Cambridge? The one when we all ended up walking by the river at five a.m., singing and dancing? Until the police showed up?"

"And that policeman fancied you." Trez smiled. "You

invited him to have breakfast with us. I don't think James was too pleased."

"He was too drunk to notice. He passed out, remember? On the riverbank."

"He wanted to swim. We were all about to swim. Which was crazy. We could have drowned, easily."

"We were having fun. I miss that. But we'll have fun at Annabel's."

"We will." Trez sat back.

What's wrong with me? Why did I believe there was a real mouse? Why did I knock over that glass?

The spaghetti arrived. Hugo and Juliet were reminiscing; she sat, listening, nodding her head, trying to understand why she wasn't enjoying the conversation. She'd loved those old days. So many times she'd yearned to have them back. Now all she wanted was to be sitting on the living room sofa at Langley Hall with Buster curled up between her and Hugo, both of them taking turns patting him as they talked about mundane things.

There was no need for her to be at this table. If she disappeared suddenly, went to the loo and didn't return, would it make any difference?

I'm unnecessary. Superfluous.

Grabbing her thigh, she squeezed—hard enough to hurt.

Get a grip. This is exactly what you wanted. A night out on the town with Hugo and Jules. The two people you love.

She squeezed harder.

Belt up, Trez. Pull yourself together. You're being an idiot.

Chapter Twenty-Two

NICOLA

The crunch was coming. She had just enough money to last maybe a week before she'd start to get in debt. She could have called her parents and asked for a loan, but they weren't the types to have saved anything. The *Nic will take care of us in our old age* comment might have been said in a joking manner, but it did mean that they didn't expect to take care of her in her twenties.

She'd already phoned them twice, filling them in briefly on what was happening in her life. On the first call, they'd been intrigued. Passing the phone back and forth to each other, asking questions about "The Brits," oohing and aahing. On the second they'd talked about what was happening in Maine, at the garden center, telling stories that ate up expensive phone time until she finally managed to say goodbye without being rude.

She could sublet her apartment, but how could she do that at the same time as keeping it available if she had to go back and live there? "I love you," he'd said, but that was a long way away from saying, *And I want to marry you.* She was in limbo: unwilling to go back; even more unwilling to say to James, *Um, what should I do now? What kind of job can I get here?* That would be presupposing he wanted her to stay for a long time.

That night all the Cambridge friends would be together again, at a nightclub called Annabel's. For Hugo's birthday. She knew she'd be keeping an eye on Hugo and Juliet, watching them closely, scouting for signs of romantic feelings between them. She hadn't broached the subject of the kiss with James again. He'd been so adamant about it not having happened, she knew that the only way he'd believe her was if she found that taxi driver to back her up. Fat chance of that.

What am I doing sitting around thinking about stolen kisses and what I should wear to a party at a swanky nightclub?

I'd worked in the admissions department in a small American college in Upstate New York. How would I translate that to a job here?

Hey, guys. Can you pull some of those strings of yours and get me a job at the University of Cambridge? Then I could talk about all the great pubs there too.

I'll find something to do here, okay, Daniel? I'll get my act together. I'm not a fucking fisherwoman. I'm not someone who's landed on her feet.

That comment really got to you, didn't it?

Yeah, well, at least Juliet didn't say it.

But you know she thinks it.

* * *

ANNABEL'S WAS ON Berkeley Square in Mayfair, one of the most desirable addresses in London, or so Nicola had been told. There was a dark canopy above iron steps leading down to the basement level. When they went through the door, James was greeted by a man standing at a desk on the side. "Good evening, Mr. Shuttleworth. It's wonderful to see you again."

"Hello, Dick, it's great to be back."

As they were handing their coats to another unsmiling man, Nicola heard Dick saying to someone who had arrived just behind them, "No, Mr. Farley isn't in. He may be your host, but you cannot go in until he arrives."

More rules for the rich.

The nightclub was like a house. Which made sense because it must have been a house at some point, and this was the basement. They walked down a passageway. To the right there was a room with sofas and stools, the walls of which were covered with photographs of glamorous people. She could see all the tables were full, all the people filling them dressed up, waiting to see and be seen. On the left there was a small bar. A man stood behind it, shaking and throwing a cocktail shaker into the air.

"That's Albert, the bar chief," James said. "And behind that bar is a cool little room called the Buddha Room. It has a Buddha statue in a prosperity pose."

What the hell is a prosperity pose? she wondered. It was probably the same pose of confidence everyone in this place seemed to have.

They kept walking, through swinging doors, and she saw they'd reached the dining room. The lighting was very dim, the atmosphere rich and romantic. More beautifully dressed people sat, as if they were posing for a painting.

It screamed "well-off" by whispering "well-off," she thought. When they reached their table at the far end, she wasn't surprised to see two large crystal bowls of caviar sitting at each end and two bottles of champagne in the middle. One side of the table was a banquette where Bella, Nigel, and Badger were sitting.

"The birthday boy hasn't arrived yet." Nigel motioned for them to take the seats across from him. "I took the liberty of ordering caviar. And champagne. That's my present sewn up. I couldn't think of anything thoughtful or touching."

"We couldn't either. Nic and I bought him a jersey." James put the gift-wrapped present he'd been carrying on the table.

"Trez will end up wearing it."

"You're right for once, Nigel." Badger reached out for a bottle of champagne. "I'm starting already. I'm thirsty."

Just as he'd uncorked it, Juliet appeared, looking as captivating as always, dressed in a beautiful white silk dress with black buttons down the front. Buttons that were there to be unbuttoned. Before, Juliet had been extremely striking. In that dress she was supremely sexy.

"I'm sitting beside Nic," she announced. "I assume Huge and Trez will be at the ends of the table."

"Makes sense to me. What did you get for Hugo?" Nigel asked.

"A lead. A dog's lead. And before you say it, Nigel, it's fetching." She laughed.

"Nice one, Jules. I wonder, where are our hosts?"

"They weren't far behind me. I think I heard Dick greeting Huge in that obsequious way he has."

"It's his job, Jules." Nigel raised his eyebrows. "No need to be snide."

"I'm not being—"

Hugo and Trez arrived, breaking off Juliet's defense.

"This is so exciting." Trez went to the chair at the end beside Nigel, while Hugo took his place at the other end. "It's perfect to have you all here, to celebrate."

"We wouldn't miss Huge's birthday. It's an event."

"Thanks, Jules. Thank you so much for thinking of this. It was a brilliant idea." When Hugo put his hand on Juliet's arm, Nicola went on full alert. "I see we have champagne and caviar already. This is going to be a night to remember."

"It definitely will be." Trez was smiling. Clearly, she

wasn't feeling threatened or anxious. Nicola thought she looked almost as happy as she had when Juliet had first arrived at that shooting dinner. She was wearing her poodle skirt again, with a white blouse. The opposite of sexy. Could someone who was the salt of the earth ever be sexy? She wondered. Did being nice and kind automatically rule you out from being an object of lust?

"Hang on," Nigel said, turning to her. "It's almost Thanksgiving in America, isn't it?"

"Yes, next Thursday."

"You know what day the British Thanksgiving is?"

"I didn't know you had one."

"We do indeed. It's July Fourth."

"When we got rid of you Yanks." Hugo laughed. "Brilliant, Nigel. I hadn't heard that before."

We *got rid of* you! she wanted to scream. Before coming to England, she'd never felt particularly patriotic. Now, if someone gave her an American flag, she'd wave it in all their faces and sing the National Anthem.

"Right, well, before we order, seeing as how we have the champagne here, fill your glasses—those of you who haven't already." Hugo shot a look at Badger, whose glass was half-empty. "I want to make a toast."

"No. *I* want to make a toast." Trez stood up. "Sit down, Hugo. It's my turn first. Now, everyone, pour yourselves some champagne. And Badger, pour yourself some more." He did just that, then passed the bottle around and opened the second.

Looking flummoxed, Hugo sat back down.

"Trez, it's Huge's—"

"I know it's his birthday, Jules, but I'm in charge right now."

Juliet looked as flummoxed as Hugo had.

"We're waiting, Trez," James put in. "Our glasses are full, and we're desperate to drink."

"First of all, I want to toast my husband. Hugo, you may not always be the most romantic of husbands . . ." The men at the table laughed. "But you have always been the best husband. In the world. In all the galaxies. I can't imagine anyone who could make me happier, or anyone who deserves happiness more than you. The fact that you don't always show your feelings doesn't mean you don't have them.

"You know—you all know—I wouldn't normally practice a speech like this or even make one, but tonight is special. So I did practice. For ages."

"You're doing beautifully," James said.

"There is one big hiccup, though. I want to toast you, Hugo, but I can't."

Juliet was sitting beside her, and Nicola felt, like some electric shock, Juliet's body tensing. She sat up straight, as if she were bracing herself.

Trez stood silently for a few seconds, then wiped her eyes.

Shit. Shit, shit, shit. She's crying. She knows. She knows about Juliet and Hugo.

She grabbed James's hand under the table.

"I can't toast you because I can't drink this champagne. Or any champagne. Or any alcohol. I did a test today. I'm pregnant."

"Oh my God, congratulations!" Bella was the one who said it first, then there were other voices saying, "Congratulations," but Nicola didn't hear Hugo's voice in the mix. Juliet slumped, but only slightly and only for a few seconds, before she sprang up, walked over to Trez, and hugged her.

"God, sweetheart. That is amazing news! That is wonderful!"

"Hugo?" Trez called over to him after Juliet's embrace had finished. "I know I sprang this on you, but aren't you going to say anything?"

"I'm speechless," he finally said. "God. Why didn't you tell me?"

"I wanted it to be a surprise. The best birthday present possible."

"It is." He nodded. "It is."

Nicola knew she was the only one who would notice that he looked at Juliet after the second time he said "It is," that Juliet gave her head the tiniest of shakes. That when Hugo then walked over to Trez and hugged her, his shoulders were hunched.

"How pregnant are you?" Bella asked. "When is it going to be born? I need to know what sign it will be."

"Jesus, Bell."

"Shut up." She elbowed Nigel. "It's important."

"I know when I got pregnant. Sit down, everyone. No more hugs. I'll start crying again." Trez shooed Hugo back to his seat. "I got pregnant over the weekend of the shoot. Maybe that's why I made that terrible mistake. Something crazy was happening to my body. I didn't think I was . . . until a few days ago. Anyway, July. That's when it's due."

"Cancer—a homebody." Bella nodded. "Or if it's late, a Leo. A lot more fiery, Leos."

"Oh, for Christ's sake." Nigel grabbed the mother-of-pearl spoon out of the crystal bowl, heaped it with caviar, and shoved it into Bella's mouth. "That should stop all this nonsense."

"Hugo, you look shell-shocked." Badger clapped him on the shoulder. "A father. You're going to be a father. That really is something."

"Wow." Back in her seat, Juliet grabbed her glass of champagne and drank it in one fell swoop. "This is incredible. I'm so pleased I suggested a party. What a perfect way to tell everyone, Trez. We're all delighted. I can't wait to hit the dance floor."

Trez was sitting happily, oblivious. The one being cheated on was so often the last one to know. Because they didn't want to know. Or because they were too trusting. It would have taken seeing Juliet and Hugo in bed together, actually doing it, for Trez to believe it could happen, Nicola decided. Not only was Hugo cheating on her, but he was cheating on her with her best friend. That couldn't happen, not in a nice person's world.

Now Trez would never know. That little nod Juliet had given Hugo was the signal that it had ended. Nicola was certain of it.

They were all talking excitedly around the table. Continually congratulating Trez, and teasing Hugo. Juliet was joining in—of course she was; she had to.

Another bottle of champagne was ordered. People ate the caviar and ordered food. Yet another bottle of champagne was ordered. Trez continued to sit happily, smiling, laughing, full of joy.

They waited for their food to arrive, they ate their food, and she sat listening to talk that ranged from tales of the past, to what school the boy or girl would attend, to what was happening in the mining industry, to which university the child would attend, to who would win the FA Cup, to whether the baby would look more like Trez or Hugo. However often they switched from the topic of Trez's pregnancy, within minutes one of them would come back to it.

"You're being very quiet." James leaned over to her at one point.

"Are you okay?"

"I'm great, thanks. I like listening, that's all."

Nigel made a drunken toast saying he'd never thought Hugo had it in him. Badger then toasted Hugo saying that he himself would be responsible for what books the child would read, as Hugo was not to be trusted, and that by the way, his birthday present to Hugo was a pair of reading glasses, which Hugo would need in his rapidly advancing old age.

James made a sweet speech about Hugo having been by his side from the age of seven and how proud and privileged he was to have him as a friend for life.

"We bought you a jersey for your birthday, Hugo. It's for you *and* Trez." He paused for the laughter—which came quickly. "If we'd only known, we would have bought a silver spoon—to add to your massive collection." More laughter.

James sat down, Juliet stood up.

"All I can say is how happy I am for both of you." She swept her hand through her hair. "I won't make any jokes because this is serious. Wonderfully serious. I do have one demand, however. I insist on being made godmother of the brat."

"Absolutely!" Trez exclaimed. "Of course, Jules. We wouldn't have it any other way."

People were on the dance floor, which was lit by tiny ceiling bulbs that pulsed. The music was getting louder. Nigel took Bella for a spin, Badger went up and bowed to Trez, then they joined the others.

"Do you want to see what a god-awful dancer I am?" James asked.

"I do. Definitely."

As they danced to Donna Summer singing "No More Tears," Nicola looked over toward the table, where Hugo and Juliet sat on their own. They were sitting beside each other, and Juliet seemed to be the one doing all the talking. Until the song was over and the next one began, at which point Juliet took Hugo by the hand, led him to Trez and Badger, then took Badger's hand and pulled him away, leaving Hugo to dance with his pregnant wife.

Nice move, she thought, thinking back to her conversation with Juliet, the one when she said she had no intentions toward James. She had intentions toward Hugo, though. What those were exactly, Nicola couldn't figure out. James had been right on one thing: Juliet couldn't really be attracted to Hugo. No way. Which meant she wanted more from him than sex. Had she really believed Hugo would divorce Trez and marry her?

She must have. But now that Trez was pregnant, she'd have to change those plans.

I'm beginning to grasp some of these rules. You don't divorce your wife when she's about to have your baby. Especially not if that baby might be a boy and the heir to a title. English society wouldn't countenance that.

It's not done.

"Am I really *that* bad?" James was beside her, shouting so he could be heard over the music. "You look truly distraught."

"We're both lousy dancers," she shouted back.

"But I'm a good murderer. I'm biding my time to kill you, you know. That's crafty of me."

"True. You're a highly proficient murderer-in-waiting."

And I'm a highly proficient spy.

* * *

JAMES WAS DRUNKER than she'd ever seen him, to the point that he was weaving as he walked, and he was finding it difficult to negotiate climbing the stairs to the bedroom.

"Careful," she said as he bumped into the banister, then ricocheted against the side wall. "James—watch out, you'll hurt yourself."

"You need to come up to bed."

"I know. We both do."

"You *really* need to."

"Okay, well, that's where we're going, and we're almost there." She was behind him, worrying what would transpire if he fell down on top of her. She'd break his fall, but they'd both probably break some bones.

"I have something. For you."

"Great. Let's just get up to bed."

He managed to make it to the bedroom, then flopped onto the bed, lying on his back, his arms spread out. "Here." His right hand was reaching for something, making swipes. "Where the fuck is it?"

"What?"

"It's somewhere." He kept swiping.

Then she saw it. Perched on the pillow. A black velvet box. The kind of box that has a ring inside it.

Going to the side of the bed, she picked it up.

"Is this what you're looking for?"

He sat halfway up, looked at it, crashed back down.

"Yes. It's for you. Open it."

Shit.

What if it wasn't a ring?

What if it was a pair of earrings? Or something else?

She sat down on the bed, hesitated.

"Open it. Fuck, it wasn't supposed to be like this. Open it."

Diamonds surrounded a huge, gorgeously green emerald.

"Will you marry me, Nic?" he asked.

She said, "Yes."

He passed out.

PART TWO

They were always comfortable. If something went wrong, they'd find a way to fix it—easily. Ninety-nine percent of the time, they'd find someone to fix it for them.

Generally, however, things didn't go wrong—not for them. They skated along, knowing the ice beneath them was thick. They had their money, they had their social standing, they had their tribe of well-to-do upper-class friends and relations, and they didn't stray off the reservation. Except sometimes for "fun." When a man would go visit a hooker or a woman would have a naughty afternoon with a plumber, or someone would decide to play a game of darts at the pub with the locals. They'd dally, but then they'd always go back to their own.

If you asked them, they'd say they were entirely free of prejudice. They'd forget all the little remarks they made to each other. The He's not one of us or She's not our class, dear—comments often shared over brandy or port. Port that had to be passed to the left down the table, not to the right. They lived in their bubble, and that bubble cared very much about which way to pass a bottle of port.

Because they took so much for granted, they didn't pay attention. They were blind to possible threats, to all that comfort of theirs. Or, if they did sense any threats, they dismissed them. They didn't understand that when there is an "us" there is a "them." And that those thems might just be waiting their turn, biding their time, getting ready to take that bottle of port and smash it over those privileged heads.

Chapter Twenty-Three

NICOLA

It was funny, the things you missed. As soon as she got back to America, she took James to a Dunkin' Donuts. A glazed donut and a cup of Dunkin' Donuts coffee: one bite, one sip, and she felt right at home.

They'd booked their flights two days after the proposal and flown the day after Thanksgiving.

"I need to ask your father for his permission to marry you," he'd said.

"You do not. All you need is my permission, and you have it."

"It's how I was brought up, Nic. Whether it's old-fashioned and sexist or not, I'm doing it."

She knew she shouldn't have liked that he was asking her father for her hand, but there was a little-girl-who-loved-Disney-movies part of her that was pleased.

They'd landed in JFK, then flown to Buffalo, where James helped her deal with her landlord and negotiate the end of her lease. He met Sue and her husband and the twins too, and she watched as he charmed them all. Even the babies were responsive to him. He would put his finger in his mouth, make a popping sound, and they'd both gaze up, with what looked like—to her, at least—intrigue and excitement. She didn't even have to try to show him off. He asked Sue lots of questions, joked with Sue's husband, Steve, about the difference between football and soccer, left them all wanting more of his company, she could tell.

"Jesus, Nic." Sue had taken her to the side on the way out of the house. "You've hit the fucking jackpot."

It was a variation on *You've hooked a good one*, but Nicola didn't mind, not anymore. However anyone wanted to put it, the fact was that she was going to marry the man she adored.

The drive from Buffalo to Bangor took eight hours, so they set off early in the morning and stopped in a small New Hampshire town for lunch.

"Christ, we'd be in Scotland by now, the end of the country. Meanwhile we've only gone through three of your fifty states."

She had missed that too—the sense of space. She hadn't done much traveling, but there was always that possibility in America: get in a car, drive for days, go to California. Or Alaska. Across fields of corn and prairie land, the wide open country. She thought of all those hedges as they drove to Langley Hall. You were pinned down in a small country, on a small island.

"England has so many hedges."

"Hedges?"

"Yes."

"I've never thought about that. But you'll see when we go to Scotland, it's a lot more open. The moors are beautiful. Think of *Wuthering Heights*."

She did, and when she did she saw Stewart as Heathcliff. Heathcliff without a Cathy. Maybe Stewart had a Cathy, though. If he did, he'd keep quiet about it.

They were sitting in her parents' two-bedroom house in Portland, Maine. Her mother and father were on the couch, holding hands. She and James were in chairs on either side of them. A plate of Oreo cookies rested on the coffee table in front of the couch, beside a huge ashtray.

"This is a trip," her father said. "You didn't have to ask my permission, for fuck's sake, James. We're glad to get rid of her. That's a joke, you know that, right?"

"Right." James smiled. "Of course."

Her father was wearing blue jeans and a sweatshirt with THE GRATEFUL DEAD written on it. Her mother was in jeans too, with a plain brown sweatshirt. Nicola flashed back to the meeting with James's parents to tell them about the engagement. They lived in a beautiful house in Kent—obviously. Not on the scale of Langley Hall, but then there wouldn't be many houses on the scale of Langley Hall.

James's father had been in a suit. His mother had worn

a pale blue dress. And pearls. And high heels.

"When Nic told us about visiting an earl, we couldn't fucking believe it," her father said. "And what's the deal with this shooting business, James? That's a little rough on the poor birds, right?"

"I know. Can you forgive me?"

"Sure, what the hell. Fuck 'em if they can't take a joke."

James actually laughed. Nicola squirmed.

"If it's all right with you, we thought we'd get married in May. In the South of France. My parents have a house there. I know that's not traditional, that the wedding should take place here, in the bride's—"

"I'd love to go to the South of France." Her mother perked up. She had been sitting quietly, shifting her hands from her lap to her knees, then back again. "The Cannes film festival. I've always wanted to go to that."

"Since when, Mom?" She couldn't stop herself. Her mother had never talked about traveling anywhere— except to Woodstock for the music festival. The Cannes film festival? How had she come up with that one?

"Since always. Your father will tell you."

"She has. We both have."

Really?

"I think a wedding there sounds very romantic, James. Absolutely lovely."

Her mother had said "absolutely lovely" in an English accent, or what she must have thought would sound like an English accent. It came out as half Scandinavian, half from somewhere from the South—Alabama or Mississippi.

I'm being too hard on her, on them both. They're quirky and odd, but they have good hearts. I shouldn't be embarrassed by them. Or by the house.

She'd never really noticed before how cheesy the paintings on the walls were—woodland scenes that could have been done by numbers. The worst, though, was the big picture of a lobster hanging over the fireplace. It had a white fluffy hat on its head, its antennae sticking out of the top, with the caption LOBSTACLAUSE. She'd seen it a million times and had become so used to it, it hadn't bothered her—until now.

"Well, I hope it's romantic and lovely. My proposal wasn't. Did Nic tell you? I passed out a second after asking her to marry me."

"That's hysterical." Her father reached over, patted James on the knee. "You're a stitch, aren't you?"

"I guess I am. My friend Nigel, who makes terrible jokes, as Nic will testify to, would say I'm trying to sew things up here."

Her father laughed again.

"You're going to live in England. That's so far away. But I guess you can do all these neat things. You can ride all those big double-decker buses. And see Windsor Castle." Thankfully her mother's accent was back to normal.

"Bobbies on bicycles two by two," her father suddenly sang.

"Dad?"

"It was a popular song here in the sixties. By Roger Miller. The guy who sang 'King of the Road.' You know that one, right, James?"

James looked at her, squinted quizzically, then said, "I've heard of it. Yes."

They were trying so hard it pained her. Trying to be convivial and funny and welcoming, but she could sense something beneath all that effort. It had lurked in the way her mother had said, "That's so far away."

She'd always thought of them as too-old-to-be hippies who played at being adults, who loved each other so much they didn't need anyone else, not even their only child.

I didn't think of their loss enough, Daniel. I thought about my own loss, about not having a brother. If Trez were to lose her baby . . . if any parent lost a child, they'd be scarred and desolate. Maybe one way of covering grief is hiding it in clouds of marijuana smoke.

Then I took off as soon as I could to go to college in New York. They have each other, but they never really had either of us. And now I'm effectively gone for good.

"You'll love it in Saint-Maximin, I know you will. Dad, you can learn how to play boules. It's a great game." Weirdly enough, she actually could see them fitting right in there. All her friends had loved her parents; the Club doubtless would as well. She had been the one who had had a problem with them.

It was a problem that could be fixed, though. Because of James. Being with him had freed her from negative thoughts and feelings. It was impossible to be downbeat when you were with someone who radiated cheerfulness ninety-nine percent of the time. Whenever she called him at work, he'd answer the phone mid-laughter, as if someone had just told a funny joke or story. Every morning when they woke up, they'd stay in bed talking together, saying what they thought the day would be like—and it was always going to be a good day.

"I'm sure we will love that place however you pronounce it. Nic, you should take a walk with James, show him around."

Her first reaction was: *Okay, Dad, you want us out so you can light up.* But it was followed closely by: *So what? It's not a big deal, not anymore.*

Their house was on Shore Road, not on the water, but not far from it.

"I'll take you through Fort Williams Park and then to see the Portland Head Light," she told James when they went outside.

"We're going to see a car headlight?"

"It's a lighthouse. I love lighthouses."

"Who doesn't?"

He grabbed her hand.

"I think that went well, don't you?"

"Yes. They love you. And I know they will love France. Even if they miss the film festival."

"I have no clue when that's on, but maybe it jibes, maybe I could find some way to—"

"James, that was . . . I don't know what it was, but I think they were trying to sound sophisticated or something."

"They don't have to do that."

"I know. But they're not used to someone like you."

"Someone like me?" He stopped. Let go of her hand. Did a little twirl on the sidewalk. "A great ballet dancer? Is that what you're saying?"

"That's why I first fell in love with you on the plane, you know. Because you made me laugh."

"I'm supremely witty, aren't I?"

"You're ridiculously witty. With the emphasis on 'ridiculously.' When did you first fall in love with me?"

"I don't think I can pinpoint the exact time. Love snuck up on me, but it was a quick sneak. It didn't take long."

Did you fall in love with Juliet at first sight? Or did she sneak up on you too? No, it would have been instantaneous.

He put his arm around her, drew him to her. The wind was blowing fiercely behind them, pushing them forward.

"The waves will be huge at the Head Light. I used to go there when I was a kid, sit and watch them come crashing in."

"Big waves like that scare me a little."

"Sometimes I think huge waves or storms, tornadoes, all those types of things are nature's way of reminding us."

"Reminding us of what?"

"Human beings cut down trees, we kill animals, we

build dams, we think we run the earth, but we don't really. If nature decided to release all its power at the same time? We'd all be dead. Crashing waves are a way of nature saying, *Watch out. I can do a lot worse*."

"I'm not sure I want to go to that lighthouse anymore. Now you're scaring me—a lot."

"I could never scare you."

"You certainly could. But . . . let's get on to unscary topics. I was thinking that when we get back I'll tell Hugo that I'd like him to be my best man. How does that sound?"

"Great."

"Who do you want for your maid—or matron of honor? I know Sue said she and the family can't make it, so who is your second choice? I was hoping maybe Trez?"

"Trez? I don't really know her, James. We've never really talked. I hadn't thought beyond Sue, but I guess if I have anyone, it would be Bella."

"Ah."

"Is that a problem?"

"No. It would have been cool to have Hugo and Trez, but obviously you should have whoever you want. Jesus, it's windy—and it's cold here too."

"But at least we have heat at home. And look, you can see it now—over there . . ." She pointed to the left. "The lighthouse is incredible, isn't it? It looks so noble standing there."

"A bulwark against the sea."

"You're my bulwark, James."

"Against what?"

"The bad things in life. Things going wrong. Everything."

"Well, being your bulwark will be an easy job." He hugged her again. "Nothing's going to go wrong or be bad, Nic. Not with us."

They walked as close to the lighthouse as they could get, then stood, watching the waves hurl themselves against the concrete. She wondered if they'd come from England, or would it have been Spain? Geography hadn't been one of her better subjects.

Seagulls were riding the air streams, crying out against the wind.

"Don't go shooting anymore."

"What?"

"Nothing."

"No, really, I couldn't hear that. What?"

"I said I hope my parents aren't stoned when we get back."

"I kind of hope they are." He laughed. "I think they're great. I thought Sue and her husband were great. And you get on really well with my friends and parents now. So . . . give me your left hand."

She did and he took her engagement ring off her finger.

"James? What the—"

"Look." He knelt. "I did it really badly last time." He was shouting the words. "I had it all planned out for after the party and, as I said, I hadn't factored in that I'd be so drunk when we got back. I'm sober now. And this is a much better setting than my bedroom. If I promise to be your bulwark, Nic, will you marry me?"

"Yes."

"What?"

"I said yes," she screamed.

A wave broke over the wall, splashing them both. Standing up, James wiped his face, placed the ring back on her finger. His kiss was salty.

"Let's go back now. Last time I proposed, I passed out. I'd prefer not to get swept out to sea and drown this time."

Chapter Twenty-Four

TREZ

Juliet was sitting on the sofa, her legs curled up beneath her, sipping a cup of tea. Seeing her like that and inhaling the sweet smell of burning wood made Trez, in her comfy jersey—the one James and Nicola had given Hugo for his birthday—feel more at peace than she could remember being in ages.

"They're in America, are they?" Juliet asked. "I forget where she comes from—which state."

"Maine—that's where her parents live. He wanted to ask her father's permission. That's sweet, isn't it?"

"I suppose, although he'd already popped the question and she'd already said yes, so it seems pointless to me. What would he do if her father said no? Not that her father would ever say no to James."

"No father could say no to James. If this baby is a girl,

I'd want her to marry someone like James."

"I fucked up, didn't I?"

"What?"

"I fucked up. I never should have gone to Hong Kong. I never should have come back hoping."

"Hoping for what? You told me you didn't have feelings for him anymore."

"I lied, sweetheart. I came back because I finally realized I love James and I always will. But I walked into this room and I saw Nicola and I saw how great they are together and that was that. I was too late. Crazy, isn't it? If I'd come back a month earlier . . . but I didn't." She put her cup of tea down on the table. "More fool me."

"Jesus, Jules. I'm so sorry." She roused herself from the armchair and went to sit beside her. "Are you sure it's too late? I do like Nic, but if . . ."

"They're engaged, Trez. So . . ." She shook her head as if she were trying hard to wake herself from a deep sleep. "I am going to be a good person. I'd like to help them, you know. To have the perfect wedding—even if I'm not invited."

"I'm sure they'll invite you."

"I hope so, but it doesn't matter. What matters is that Jimmy is happy. I screwed up when I left, and I hurt him badly. I'd like to help make that up to him—and Nic—now. I've been thinking that you could invite Jimmy down here for a day or night. I'd be here with you, and we could tell him all the things a woman really wants when she gets married. He's clueless, really, when it comes to things like that. Most men are."

"That's true. Hugo certainly is. I haven't told you about how he proposed to me yet. We were in this field and stopped to look at cows. He proposed and then we kept walking."

"Typical Huge. Right, so you and I can give James some guidance. Without Nic, so it will be a surprise for her. I'm sure you can arrange for him to come without her. You can arrange anything."

"But . . ." She reached out, put her hand on Juliet's. "Won't that be hard for you? Seeing him and talking about his wedding?"

"I don't get jealous, remember? It's funny. In the old days, there was that time when Nigel was dating some girl who was crazily jealous of him. She used to follow him around and spy on him? What was her name?"

"Olivia. I remember."

"Yes! Olivia. Anyway, Jimmy said back then that he hated seeing jealous people. That jealousy is the ugliest of emotions. And he told me he knew I'd never have reason to be jealous of him. Which I wasn't. I'm not jealous of Nic now either. I had my chance, and I blew it. I'd like to help him out—both of them. They deserve a happy life."

"You're a better person than I am." Trez frowned. "I wouldn't be able to behave like that."

"You never know—not until it happens to you. Which it won't. Where's Huge, by the way?" Juliet stretched her legs out, so they rested on Trez's lap. She had this way of lounging alluringly, a way Trez knew she'd never be able to pull off herself. Her legs were way too short to begin with, and she would probably fall off any sofa anyway in the attempt.

"He has business in Portsmouth. I'm not sure what it is, but he said he was sorry to miss your visit."

"Bummer. I'm sorry to miss him. That was some birthday party. I was pleased to see Annabel's never changes."

"I doubt it ever will. As long as there's enough money around. The other day I remembered you telling me ages ago how your parents were so profligate. Are they still?"

"No, they're fine now. We're all fine, aren't we? Badger has just enough so he'll never have to work—if he doesn't get married, that is, and we all know he's not likely to. Nigel does all right in the city—Badger told me that. His family doesn't have as much as you might think, but he's earning well. You and Huge don't have any worries. Obviously. And Jimmy—he has a lot of family money, *and* he makes a lot in shipping. A lot more than Nigel." She moved her feet in circles. "So everyone will be able to keep their membership at Annabel's."

"Are we really all that shallow?"

"Absolutely." Juliet laughed, prodded Trez with her foot. "Shallow as glass. Now—will you rub my feet the way you used to way back when, when we were young things, discussing life and who was involved with whom and what we'd be like when we were ancient, while we now discuss when to get James down here so we can tell him how to be the perfect groom?"

"Gladly. You never cease to amaze me, Jules."

"I often cease to amaze myself."

Juliet wasn't spending the night. "I borrowed Badger's car, and I want to keep borrowing it, so I should be good and get it back to him tonight," she'd announced when she'd arrived. After she left, Trez stayed sitting by the fire, with Buster, thinking.

In the past, Juliet had been the one who was going to have the amazing life, but Fate, or whatever it was that guided a person's life, had turned that upside down. Trez was having the amazing life. Married to Hugo, pregnant, living in this incredible house, not far away from becoming a countess. While Juliet was on her own, still in love with James, doing the "good" thing by not interfering with his marriage to Nicola. With no man in sight. She didn't even have her own car.

"People come into their own, they peak at different times," she remembered Nigel saying to her once. "I figure I'll peak at around thirty-three, Badger will peak at ninety years old, if he makes it that far. I wonder occasionally whether Juliet is at her peak now, if after we leave Cambridge, that peak will dwindle."

Jules will never dwindle. That's what Trez had thought then. And she hadn't, not really. She was still Juliet in all her glory. She'd admitted to being disappointed by life, though, and that was even before James had announced his engagement.

I'll find someone for her. Christmas is coming up fairly soon. There will be lots of parties. I'll make sure she's invited to all of them. There has to be someone who can keep up with her, who can make her happy. That's my new job. Matchmaker. It will be difficult, but it will be fun.

It was time to get to work. She needed to get to her desk, get out her diary and address book, and start figuring out how to be a successful Cupid.

Chapter Twenty-Five

December

NICOLA

Bella had convinced her to look for wedding dresses, telling her they had to go to Harrods "just to check some out," that she'd take her lunch hour at work and come with her. "It's easy to get a bus from Piccadilly down to Knightsbridge. Meet me at Boots and I'll try to stretch my hour too, so we can have proper time there."

The prospect of seeing wedding dresses excited her, but she felt a little guilty too. Her mother should have been with her. Finding a perfect wedding dress in such a short time in Maine, however, wouldn't have been easy. She didn't even know what type of dress she wanted. They were getting married in May, so the weather in Saint-Maximin might be lovely, or, as James informed her, there could be a big wind: the mistral might hit them.

It wouldn't be a real wedding either. The legal ceremony would take place at a registry office in Kensington two weeks before. The ceremony in France would be more like the kind of weddings in America, with a minister and vows and friends and families, but the deed would already have been done. They would arrive in France as Mr. and Mrs. James Shuttleworth.

She still got a thrill riding a red double-decker bus and wondered when that would wear off for good. This time, though, she wasn't alone on one. Bella was beside her, talking away about the lousy morning she'd had. "I wish I worked in Harrods. You've been there, haven't you?"

"No."

"It's brilliant. You'll love it. I could spend hours walking around that place, looking."

The night before, Badger had stopped by for an impromptu drink. When Nicola told him she was going to meet Bella at Harrods the next day, he'd said: "Did you know Harrods used to sell wild animals? They gave a baby elephant to Ronald Reagan when he was governor of California back in the sixties. People say Noël Coward bought an alligator there. And then, of course, there was Christian the lion."

"A lion? You're making this up." She was incredulous.

"He isn't making it up," James chimed in. "Two backpackers bought Christian the lion from Harrods and kept him in their flat in Chelsea."

"They took him to Africa and set him free eventually. But Harrods stopped selling wild animals. So you and Bella can't buy a giraffe for fun." Badger smiled.

"Jesus, Badger, you know how to ruin my day."

Badger and James both laughed. It wasn't that funny, but she didn't care. They had laughed. She was fitting in. Bella was definitely her friend now, she was developing a soft spot for Badger, and now that she wasn't worried about Trez and Hugo's marriage, she thought she'd soon be on good terms with them too.

"What type of dress are you looking for, Nic?"

"I don't know. I'm only looking to get ideas. I can't afford anything here. James will chip in, I know, but I don't want him to spend too much. I think the best idea would be to wear something really simple. It's going to be a small wedding. There's no point in spending a fortune on a dress."

"There's always a point on spending a fortune on a dress, love. Wake up. You're going to marry a rich man, but he's not going to be an earl, so you can't get away with dressing like Trez."

"If I tell you something, do you promise not to tell anyone? Not even Nigel?"

"Definitely. I love secrets. I won't tell anyone, especially not Nigel."

"I saw Juliet and Hugo kissing outside the Savoy hotel. They didn't see me—I was in a taxi. James says I misinterpreted it, that it would have been a friendly kiss, but it wasn't. I promise."

"Shit. Juliet and Hugo? How is that even possible?"

"Exactly. That's what I thought."

"Juliet and Hugo?"

"Juliet and Hugo."

The bus came to a stop; Bella grabbed her. "This is us." After they'd made their way to the back and stepped off, Bella said: "Hang on for a second. I need a fag.

"I don't understand." She pulled out her pack of cigarettes and a lighter from her bag, lit up. "Juliet is Trez's best friend. Hugo is . . . well, not the sort of bloke you'd fancy the pants off. Unless you were Trez."

They were standing on the sidewalk across from the entrance to Harrods.

"I have to think about this. What the fuck is she—"

"Nic! Bella! Great, I found you here. I was going to go to the bridal section to catch up with you, but now we can all go together."

"Juliet? What are you—"

"I was in Mayfair, so I dropped by Jimmy's office to congratulate him. You two took off to the States so quickly I didn't get the chance before. He told me you and Bella were coming here to look at dresses at lunchtime, so I thought I'd take the chance of meeting you and join in on the fun. I hope that's okay. Is it, Nic?"

"Yes, of course."

She'd dropped by "Jimmy's" office. To congratulate him.

"And oh my God, look at that ring." Juliet took her left hand in hers, studied the engagement ring. "I adore emeralds. And it matches those greenish eyes of yours. They are green . . ." She looked up, stared at Nicola. "Aren't they?"

"Hazel. So sort of green."

"Won't this be a blast? Throw away that fag, Bell. Let's get going and see some gorgeous dresses. Jimmy said I'd be a good help."

"Nic isn't buying anything here. She's just looking."

"That's wonderful." Juliet maneuvered herself so she was between them, linked arms with both of them. "And afterward we'll go have a glass of champagne."

"I have to get back to work." Bella sounded disappointed.

"Don't be ridiculous. You'll have time for one glass, Bell. Who turns down champagne?"

"Good point."

Harrods was like a huge Aladdin's Cave. Nicola was assaulted by the array of silk scarves, designer watches, designer clothes, by floor after floor of every conceivable gift or item. Money hung in the air like the expensive scents lingering as women wearing furs passed them by.

Juliet knew exactly where the wedding dresses were. She knew how to navigate the huge, unbelievably upmarket department store that was Harrods. She knew how to talk to the saleswoman on the wedding dress floor, how to tell her that they wanted to be left alone, that they'd come back when they had an idea of which dress was "the dress," but meanwhile they wanted only to browse.

She kept up a running commentary as she pulled dress after dress from the racks and held them up against Nicola.

"See, Bell." The three of them were facing a large mirror. "This looks great on her, doesn't it? Nic, this would be perfect in Saint-Max. It *looks* French, doesn't it?"

"It suits you, Nic." Bella nodded. "But I'm not sure. Maybe the waist is too high?"

"Oh God, yes, you're right." Juliet swept the dress away, hung it back up, flicked through the hangers, grabbed another one. "Here we go. Simple. Classic. Not too high a waist. Chic. This is *the one*."

The problem was that the dress was the one. She could tell, even without trying it on, that it would be perfect. No frills, but with a subtle lace embroidered V neckline, a beaded white belt, and buttons down the back.

"Don't you love the buttons?"

She did. She loved the buttons, she loved the dress. The dress Juliet had chosen.

"It's beautiful." She couldn't help it, she couldn't stop looking in the mirror and admiring it. "But I can't afford it. It's fun looking at dresses here, but I can't afford any of them. Maybe we should stop now."

"Fuck. It really is the perfect one for you." Bella sighed. She reached over, pulled the price tag out of the back of the dress, and looked at it. "Jesus H. Christ. I was going to say you should try it on just for the hell of it, but if it looked as good as I think it would, you'll be so depressed."

"Not necessarily." Juliet sounded thoughtful. "I know people in Hong Kong; actually, I know a seamstress who could knock up a dress just like this for almost nothing. All we have to do is take a photo of it. There should be plenty of time for them to make it and send it back once we've sent the photo and your measurements, Nic."

"Really?"

"Absolutely. First I'll persuade one of these women working here to take your measurements." Within three minutes, Juliet had done just that. "Okay, that's done. I'll come back here tomorrow morning with my camera, distract the saleswoman somehow, make her leave, so I can take a picture without her going berserk, and then Bob's your uncle."

"What?"

"It's an English phrase," Bella explained. "It means, basically, problem solved. That's genius, Juliet. A really, really brilliant idea. Try it on, Nic. Go ahead."

She did. She stood in the changing room in Harrods, looking at herself in the mirror, imagining herself in the French countryside, standing beside James.

"I dropped by Jimmy's office to congratulate him."

"Jimmy said I'd be a good help."

"Saint-Max." How many times had she been there?

Nic, stop this lunacy. The woman is helping you get a wedding dress you wouldn't be able to afford otherwise. She told you she stopped by James's—she isn't hiding anything. She's been to Saint-Maximin a lot of times, and she

*shortens everything and everybody's name anyway. Grow
the fuck up.*

*Okay, don't get so mad, Daniel. Only she's so good at
so many things.*

*Except she wasn't any good at loving James, was she?
That's what counts. She wasn't, and you are.*

When she came out of the dressing room, both Bella
and Juliet told her how amazing she looked in it, that she
absolutely had to have it.

"I'll come back tomorrow and sneak a photo," Juliet
whispered. And then said, in a normal voice, "I assume
this means I get to come to the wedding too, Nic. I won't
do a thing for you unless I'm invited."

"You're bold as brass, aren't you?" Bella said, looking at
Juliet with what Nicola recognized as admiration. "You're
funny too. What's the story, Juliet? Why aren't you with
some handsome billionaire on your yacht anchored off
your private island in Greece?"

"Good question. If I knew the answer to that, believe
me, I would be. Sitting on the deck sipping a cocktail, getting a foot massage."

Bella laughed.

"Get out of the dress, Nic," Juliet commanded. "We
need to get a glass of champagne as soon as possible."

Back in the changing room, Nicola looked at herself in
the dress again and tried not to cry. Juliet had hijacked the
day and was going to continue hijacking it. There was no
way she could complain about it, not with the Hong Kong

seamstress in the wings and the glass of champagne waiting.

Bella was being drawn to Juliet's side, as if there were a tug-of-war game going on and Juliet was winning. But there wasn't any tug-of-war game. They weren't children in the playground; they were adult women, and she shouldn't mind so much that Bella admired Juliet or thought she was funny. *I was friends with Bella first* was what she felt like saying. *I need a friend a lot more than you do!*

"Get out of the dress, Nic," Juliet had commanded. She was giving orders again. But what was she supposed to do? Say, *I'm not going to get out of the dress now. I don't want any of your fucking champagne. I know you kissed Hugo. What's the story, Juliet? What do you really want?*

Keep it civilized, she told herself. *Don't freak out. She's being helpful.*

After leaving Harrods, Juliet took them on a short walk to the Motcombe Street Wine Bar, telling Bella as they went that she'd get a cab for her after the one glass and send her back to work in time.

"My treat, Bell," she stated. "We girls need to treat ourselves if men won't treat us."

"James treats me." As she said it, she knew she was simultaneously showing off and staking a claim. "He buys me flowers a lot. He takes me to really nice restaurants."

"That's a relief." Juliet found them a table to the left of the bar. They'd all taken a seat, Bella beside Nicola, facing Juliet. A waiter approached, and Juliet ordered three glasses of champagne.

"In my experience, Jimmy was piss-poor at romantic gestures, so I'm glad to hear he's changed. But he told me about passing out after proposing. Jesus. That's even worse than when he proposed to me."

"He proposed to you?" Bella asked. Nicola thought she might never be able to speak again.

"Oh God, that was yonks ago. Eons ago. It didn't count, Nic, believe me. He was drunk; we both were. We were punting on the Cam. Oh dear, that sentence must sound so foreign to you, Nic. I'll translate for you. The Cam is a river in Cambridge. And a punt is a kind of boat you push along with a pole. Anyway, we were punting and we were drunk and it was sunset. I mean, if he hadn't proposed, it would have been criminal. Against the rules of romance. It was that kind of sunset. In any case, he tried to get down on one knee, and of course you can't do that when you're in a punt on a river, so the boat almost tipped over and we were both so pissed we would probably have drowned. We ended up laughing about the whole fiasco—for months."

Bella gave her knee a little squeeze under the table, but that didn't help. James had proposed to Juliet. He'd actually proposed to her. Did he have a ring? She couldn't bear to ask.

"Well, no one has bloody proposed to me. You've known Nigel for a long time, Juliet. Do you think he'll propose?

Ever? To any girl?"

"If Nigel proposes to anyone, Bell, it will be you."

"Thanks. That's nice of you to say."

If only she could be back in Maine, sitting in her parents' house, looking at that stupid lobster. This wasn't death by a thousand cuts; this was like people taking turns with a chain saw, cutting off slabs of her flesh.

"Shit." She made a show of looking at her watch. "I have to get back."

"What's the rush?"

"People are coming to talk to me about the food at the wedding." No one was coming. "I forgot. Sorry, Juliet."

"I see the waiter now bringing the champagne."

"I'm sorry, really. I don't want them standing outside the door waiting. You two can share the extra glass." She stood up, took the coat off the back of her chair. "And thanks so much for the help with the dress."

She'd told James that her school had put on *The Merchant of Venice* when she was thirteen and she'd played Portia. She hadn't told him that she'd been given the lead role not because of her acting abilities, but because she was the only one in the class who could memorize all the lines. When it came time to perform it, she spoke in a monotone, the dullest Portia who had ever set foot on a stage. She was speaking in exactly the same way now; if she let any emotion whatsoever into her voice, she knew she'd break down entirely.

As quickly as possible, she walked out of the wine bar,

hailed a taxi, jumped in the back, and let the tears finally escape.

Chapter Twenty-Six

TREZ

Trez had arranged for James to come down for the day on his own. And she'd managed it so James was keeping the trip a secret from Nicola.

She'd told him that every woman wants surprises in her life and that she needed to instruct him on the best way to surprise Nic, to make the wedding as perfect as possible. "Tell her you're coming to see Hugo and it's about shooting next year. That it will bore her silly and you won't be long. A tiny lie like that won't hurt, not when it's for her benefit."

She hadn't told him Juliet would be there too.

Hugo had buggered off again, saying he had to visit his second cousin Myles in Windsor, which was strange because he didn't really like Myles, and did his best to keep a distance from him. "I know, I know, he's a royal pain in the ass, but I have to keep up family ties. Besides, I'm hardly the person to give romantic advice—to anyone."

Hugo had lost weight recently, and if she didn't know him better, she'd say he was moping. She'd find him sitting alone in the library, staring out the window, or sitting in the drawing room staring at the fire. Whenever she'd come upon him alone like that in a room, he'd sit up straight and say: "How is the baby?" and she'd say: "The baby is wonderful," and he'd say, "That's very good news."

It had turned into a little ritual, that conversation between them. The point was, he wasn't moping, he was thinking about the responsibility that came with fatherhood. He was being an adult.

Juliet arrived just before James. She was wearing jeans and a chunky white turtleneck jersey that Trez recognized. It made her face look like a heart.

"You had that jersey when we were in Cambridge. It was a present from James, wasn't it?"

Juliet glanced down at the jersey.

"Oh God, you're right. I forgot. It's so warm. That's why I've kept it. For days like this. You're looking cozy, sweetheart. All pink-cheeked and pregnant."

"Thanks. I get tired easily, but otherwise I'm in good shape. I hear a car—that must be James. I hope you have some helpful tips for him. I haven't been concentrating on it, I'm afraid."

"Don't worry, I have."

When James entered, he came straight over to her and

gave her a kiss on both cheeks, then said hello to Juliet, but stayed standing.

"Take a seat, Jimmy." Juliet motioned to the far end of the sofa she was on.

"This is a strange meeting." He sat down, raised his eyebrows. "Trez didn't tell me you were coming. She said she was going to give me some advice about the wedding, but honestly, I'm not entirely sure what I'm doing here."

"You're being instructed." Juliet pulled her legs up to her and hugged her knees. "First things first. Do you want some tea? Coffee? Whiskey? Mescaline?"

"I'm fine, thanks."

"All right, then, I'll start this off. Where are you taking Nic on her honeymoon?"

"I was planning a trip to Chile."

"Oh, Jesus, no."

"What?" James looked over at Trez, put his hands in the air, and Trez copied him.

"You want a beach. Total relaxation. The West Indies. Mauritius. Zanzibar. Somewhere like that."

"I thought Nic would enjoy Chile."

"Maybe. But I *know* she'd enjoy a beach holiday. Chile is worthy, I suppose, but not romantic."

"Okay, I guess I can have a think about that again. I haven't booked anywhere yet."

"Have you booked a hotel in Uzès for her family yet?"

"No. Not yet. It's just her parents. I assumed they'd stay in the house with us."

"With 'us'?"

"With me and Nic and my parents."

"You really are hopeless, Jimmy. You can't stay in the same house the night before your wedding. You have to be apart. And it's much better to have her and her parents staying in a hotel. No siblings? She's an only child, then?"

"Yes. She had a twin brother, but he died shortly after he was born."

"Oh no. Don't say that. That's so sad. Her poor parents. They must have been heartbroken." For the past week, Trez had felt as if her skin was porous, that she could feel people's pain in a way she'd never felt before. Even watching television, she'd find herself in tears when someone was hurt in any way, shape, or form. The idea of a baby dying was especially horrific.

She wished she hadn't made that announcement at Annabel's. It was too soon; she hadn't reached twelve weeks yet. Telling everyone was tempting fate. What if something went wrong? The thought terrified her.

"It was heartbreaking for Nic too. She talks to him sometimes. Has conversations with him."

"What?"

"Jules—don't look so surprised." Trez, for the first time she could remember, was stern with Juliet. "Of course she misses him. They were in the womb together for nine months. I think it's perfectly natural for her to talk to him. Did they name him?"

"Yes, Daniel."

"I'm glad they did. He deserves a name."

"She doesn't like to talk about having conversations with him. I don't know why, but I think she's embarrassed—she shouldn't be."

"No, no, she shouldn't." Trez hugged herself.

"On to more cheerful subjects: We've settled that you'll go to a decent honeymoon destination, Jimmy, and that you'll find hotel rooms for Nic and her parents in Uzès. Who is going to perform the ceremony?"

"I don't know." James crossed his legs, uncrossed them. "We're not getting married until May. We have time to work these details out."

"You may think so, but the sooner you sort things, the better. Nic has already chosen her wedding dress."

"She has?"

"Didn't she tell you? She found the perfect one when Bella and she and I went to Harrods. She was worried about not being able to afford it, but I've taken a sneaky photograph of it and I'm going to get a brilliant little seamstress in Hong Kong to whip up one just like it for her."

"You didn't tell me that about the dress, Jules. That's so nice of you." Trez felt like clapping. Who else could make such a lovely gesture in the same situation Juliet was in?

A line of an old pop song ran through her mind: *It should have been me.* Juliet had nominated one of the days the four of them had spent together in Saint-Maximin as "International Card Game Day." They'd made pitchers of sangria—and laughed about making a Spanish drink in

France as they were making them—and sat all day playing cards at the table outside by the pool. Old Maid,
Hearts, War, Snap. Every card game they could think of.
For hours. By the middle of the afternoon, they were all
cheating as much as they could, and yelling at one another,
and laughing—to the point where they were in uncontrol-
lable hysterics. Then they'd try to stop, but end up starting
again. That kind of laughter that makes life seem as if it
will always be bright and fun and funny and full of love.

She could envision the scene: James and Nicola saying
their vows—and when the time came to ask if anyone had
an objection, Juliet standing up and singing out, *It should
have been me.*

"It's easy peasy to get a dress made in Hong Kong," Juliet let go of her legs, reached her foot out, poked James's
thigh with it. "I suppose it's horrendously difficult to make
hotel reservations and book a honeymoon and do what
you're supposed to be doing. Come on, Jimmy. It's time for
you to get your act together."

"Okay, I take your point. Maybe I should start organizing things."

"Maybe?"

"Okay, Jules. Got it. I will."

*That's the first time I've heard him use "Jules" since she
came back*, Trez thought.

"Finally. Whew. So you'll sprinkle rose petals over her
hotel room and have a guitar player in the corner singing
'We've Only Just Begun,' too?"

"That's not funny," he said, but he and Trez both laughed.

"Say yes and then my work here is done. Rose petals, the Carpenters, Fiji for the honeymoon—Bob's your uncle."

"I'll take your invaluable advice on board," James said—half grudgingly, half gratefully.

"Excellent. Now it's time for lunch."

"I can't stay for lunch. I have to get back."

"Christ—you've been here for all of what? Ten minutes or so? It's a two-hour drive from London. Don't be silly, Jimmy. Stay for lunch. I'm sure Trez has something in the kitchen, don't you, Trez?"

"Yes, absolutely. We can make sandwiches."

Juliet, she could see, was studying James, narrowing her eyes as she zeroed in on his face.

"Are you frightened of me, Jimmy?"

"Jesus, Jules, why would I be frightened of you?"

"I don't know." She shrugged, pulled her legs back to her chest. "People say I can be scary."

"Seriously. You, scary? Tell me—what did they put in the water in Hong Kong?"

Raising her eyebrows, tilting her head, and giving a little nod, Juliet said: "Touché, Mr. Shuttleworth."

It should have been Jules. It really should have been.

Chapter Twenty-Seven

NICOLA

Nicola couldn't concentrate. She knew she should be doing something useful, but her thoughts kept leaping around: from James on his knee at the lighthouse, to James struggling to get on one knee in a punt. She had looked up the word "punt": a long, narrow flat-bottomed boat, square at both ends and propelled with a long pole, used on inland waters chiefly for recreation.

Or chiefly for hilarious proposals.

It sounded like a gondola to her. She pictured James, in a striped gondolier top, using the long pole to propel his way into Juliet's heart.

"You proposed to Juliet." She'd blurted it out as soon as he'd come back from work on the shopping-at-Harrods day.

"Hold on a second; let me take my coat off." When he

had hung it on the coatrack by the door, he came and sat beside her at the kitchen table. "You're right, Nic, I did. I was really young."

"And really in love."

"Isn't everyone really in love when they're really young?" Taking her hand in his, he rubbed it with his thumb. "Listen, I understand it's not easy for you having her around, and that I haven't been understanding enough about that. I'm sorry. Really sorry. And I'm old enough now to say that and mean it."

His words and the look in his eyes made her anxiety evaporate.

"I was proposed to before too."

"I'm sure you were. Who wouldn't propose to you?"

"We were standing by the jungle gym in the school playground. Roy Mabrey proposed to me when we were both five years old. It was really romantic."

"Jesus. You better tell him you've broken it off."

"I know. I'll have to track him down somehow."

"I assume he didn't pass out after proposing. Bloody hell. Don't track him down, Nic. He's too much of a threat."

He stood up then, pulled her up, and led her upstairs.

"I bet—no I *hope* you and Roy didn't do this by the jungle gym."

That's what he could do so easily: make her feel happy and loved and safe. The whole rest of the evening and far into the night, they stayed in bed, making love. Juliet receded from her thoughts, skating further and further away until she'd disappeared altogether.

At breakfast the next morning, back at the kitchen table, she'd taken his hand in hers and said: "Thank you for what you said yesterday. I have to admit that when Juliet told me you'd proposed to her, it did upset me. And having her around hasn't been exactly easy. It helps so much that you understand that."

"I do now. She told me when she came round to the office that I should realize it's difficult for you. I didn't really get it before—I didn't see any reason why it would be a problem because we were together so long ago—but I get it now."

"Oh."

I'm the fucking pheasant and I've been shot. Right in the heart.

"So it's all fine. Although I'm still worried about poor Roy Mabrey."

She managed to say, "I think he'll be okay," grabbed the breakfast plates, and went over to the little kitchen, turned on the tap, found a brush, and started to scrub them.

"Thanks for doing these." He was beside her. "I'll try to get back early tonight, and we can do something fun."

"Great."

He kissed her and left.

As soon as she heard the door close, she threw the brush in the sink and started to pace around the house, from room to room, upstairs and downstairs and back again.

Who the fuck is this woman who insinuates herself into

every single bit of my life?

Why are men so stupid? Why did he have to tell me that? I was fine before.

Should I find her, tell her to lay off James? Go back to Hugo, Jules—go kiss him again. Who knows—the way you play these games, you might just win and he'll leave his pregnant wife for you.

You're smart. And sly. I can't say: You bitch, why did you tell James I might be upset having you around? Oh, Nic, I was only trying to help. Like I am only trying to help finding the dress for you. Aren't you overreacting?

She had to get out, get some air, try to get her bearings.

It was another bleak wintry day; she was beginning to truly understand why the English talked about the weather so much. Hyde Park was desolate, full of barren trees. She headed for Kensington Gardens, trying to imagine how pretty it would all look in the spring. For a moment she stood beside a statue of a man on a horse, then she saw a pond in front of her and walked to it. It wasn't as windy as it had been that day in Maine, but it was strong nonetheless, and as she circled the pond, the wind lashed her face, bringing tears that were already lurking, to her eyes.

She had to dig herself out of this hole of self-pity and jealousy, she knew. Worrying about Juliet and James's past was never going to help her. If she forced herself to look forward, she'd be able to see her wedding, her honeymoon, her life here with James, which would include some form of work. She had put the idea of a career on hold again after the proposal because she had the wedding to organize. When they got back from the honeymoon, she'd get serious about finding a job. It would be a lot more fruitful if she started thinking about what kind of job now instead of obsessing about proposals and whether Juliet had turned Bella into her second best friend—Trez, obviously, being the first best.

"Hello."

The male voice came from right behind her. She jumped and felt a hand on her arm.

"Nicola, it's me." He gripped her arm tighter. "Stewart. Sorry, I didn't mean to frighten you."

"Stewart?" He'd come up from behind and was now facing her. "God. You scared me. What are you doing here?"

"I needed some air. This city stifles me. I was walking, and I recognized your coat. I'm pleased it wasn't someone else in your coat. Nice weather, isn't it?"

"Beautiful."

The English might care about irony, but sarcasm was clearly right up there with it.

"So shall we walk together?"

"We shall."

As they continued around the pond, she searched for a topic that might make him say more than two sentences.

"James is really looking forward to next weekend in Scotland. Do you prefer shooting grouse to pheasants?" When in her life had she ever thought she'd ask a question like that?

"Yes, they fly a lot faster, as I said when I arrived at your house a soaking mess."

"That's right. I remember now."

"I'm thinking of giving it up."

"Giving up your job?"

He was taking such long strides that she was struggling to keep pace with him.

"Yes, I think after this weekend in Scotland, I'll stop."

"Why?"

"The birds, the animals—they haven't done anything wrong."

"Can we sit down on the bench for a second? "

He went straight up to the bench a few feet away and sat, perfectly straight. She took a seat a little away from him.

"I don't understand. I mean, they *never* did anything wrong, did they?"

"No, you're right. I didn't used to think in those terms, though. I thought of it as sport."

"And now you think you're helping to kill innocent creatures?"

He nodded.

"James says that we eat them, that that's what makes it all right. Like eating a steak, except cows don't get any chance to live at all."

"There was a Russian man on one of the shoots early this year. He told me that in Russia they hunt bears. One very snowy day out bear hunting, he came upon a bear—it was only about fifteen feet away from him. He had a rifle, of course. He was about to shoot it—and he was a good shot. But the bear got up on his hind legs, looked straight at him, and put his paws up in the air." Stewart put his own hands up in a gesture of surrender. "And he couldn't do it. He couldn't shoot it. He left it in peace."

"God."

Nicola didn't know what to say. The story had nothing to do with eating the animals you killed, but that didn't matter. She was picturing the bear in the snow, rising up, lifting those huge paws.

Wordlessly pleading for its life.

"I think it might be a good idea to give it up, Stewart." She might be able to convince James—not now, but later on—to give it up too.

"Do you know what you might do instead?"

"Not a clue."

"Well, join the club. I have no idea what I'm going to do for work either."

"You won't have to work, will you? I heard about your engagement. Congratulations."

"Thanks. I *want* to work. I'd feel ridiculous not working."

"I thought that might be the case."

Yet again she wasn't sure what to say next. Something about his presence made small talk seem stupid. They sat in silence for a few minutes; they were both watching the swans floating gracefully on the water.

"They're beautiful, the swans," she said.

"Yes. You'd never think how vicious they can be."

"Swans? Vicious?"

"Yes. They turn vicious when they feel threatened. Like many people. Except swans are protecting their young, not just themselves. You should see them when they start hissing. That beauty vanishes. All you see is their ugly rage."

It felt as if this was a life lesson, a tale by Hans Christian Andersen. Instead of the ugly duckling, they had the vicious swan.

"I have to go." He stood up, put out his hand to shake hers. "It was very nice to see you again, Nicola. I hope we run into each other accidentally again soon."

"I hope so too." She shook his hand and then watched as he strode away, seemingly purposefully. But where was he going? What was he doing in London?

At least he'd taken her mind off Juliet.

She walked back to the statue of the man on the horse and read the plaque underneath. It was called *Physical Energy*. It wasn't only energy that it represented—she was taken aback by its strength and resolve. The man on the horse had his hand over his eyes and was looking to the horizon. To the future.

Another life lesson: Forget the past. The past trapped you.

All she needed was some of that resolve. Reaching out, she touched the cold stone, patted the horse's hind hoof, and vowed to herself if she ever felt as jealous again, she'd come here and reflect, gather her resolve and turn it into positive energy.

A half an hour later, when she was back in the house, finishing washing the dishes she'd left in the sink, the doorbell rang.

It was a delivery of flowers: a big bunch of tulips—her favorite.

The card read: *I'll let you off the hook, but I'll never forget you. Love, Roy Mabrey*

Chapter Twenty-Eight

TREZ

Stewart had found the perfect lodge in a village called Tomintoul, at the northern end of Aberdeen's Cairngorm mountains, close to the moors and near the River Spey, so there would be fishing as well as shooting to occupy the weekend.

Given that Juliet was coming too, there'd probably be after-dinner games on Friday and Saturday evenings; Trez, as she unpacked her bag, hoped they'd be less dramatic than Lava. Something simple like charades would be good.

After ages going through her address book, and Hugo's, she had come up with one potential man for Juliet. Luke Carr. He was thirty-four, an investment banker, an acquaintance of Hugo's. She remembered meeting him at a dinner party and thinking he was very good-looking and very funny. She made a few discreet calls and discovered he was still a bachelor and had no girlfriend. Doubting his single status would last much longer, she made the call and invited him for dinner the Saturday before Christmas.

She wouldn't tell Juliet she was setting it up, and she'd be careful not to seat them side by side at dinner. They'd find each other one way or another that evening. All they needed was to be in the same house at the same time.

So there were two big events to look forward to: Christmastime and James's wedding in the spring. He'd already asked Hugo to be best man. Nicola hadn't asked her to be matron of honor. That didn't surprise her—Nicola was probably flying in a friend from the States.

"You've landed on your feet," Trez recalled Hugo saying. It was a tactless, rude thing to say, but Hugo was right. Nicola had come out of nowhere and within two months had a ring on her finger. That really was fast work.

It wasn't like her to jump to bad conclusions about people. She couldn't work out why she had even had a whiff of a bad thought about Nicola. She'd been feeling edgy for the past couple of days, in a way that frightened her. The last time she'd felt her nerves jangling like this for no apparent reason, she'd heard the next day that an old school friend of hers had been killed in an avalanche on the ski slopes.

Nothing bad was going to happen this time. The moors and the river, the beauty of the Scottish Highlands, would put her soul at rest. Meanwhile, she had to concentrate on being positive. Nicola wasn't a gold-digger; she was a perfectly nice woman. And she made James happy. This weekend would be the perfect time to make an effort to get to really know her.

The real "event" to look forward to, though, was the arrival of the baby in the summer. She and Hugo hadn't discussed names yet. "Let's wait awhile," he'd said, when she'd asked him what he might like to call a boy or girl. "Okay. Let's do it on Christmas Day," she'd suggested, and he'd nodded. She'd never admit publicly that she wanted a boy, or that the only reason she hoped it would be a boy was because of Hugo. He did care about maintaining the family name, even if he didn't say so. If it was a girl, she knew she'd keep trying until she had a boy, but it would be a relief to have a boy first.

Juliet would be a godmother and James would be a godfather. Hopefully that wouldn't upset Nicola. They could always make her godmother to the second child.

"Trez? Can I come in?" She and Hugo had arrived after Badger; Hugo had then gone to find Stewart to discuss the next day's shooting, and she had just begun to unpack.

"Yes, Badger, come in. I'm fully dressed."

"Good. Good." He entered the room, sat down on the bed, began to snap the elastic band on his wrist.

"Are you all right? You seem nervous."

"I have a bad feeling. I don't know why. As if something unholy is going to happen."

"That's so strange. So do I. I wouldn't say 'unholy,' though. What an odd word to use."

He shrugged.

"But it's nothing a walk won't cure, I'm sure."

"I'm sure you're right. Did you know that we're in the heart of the whiskey distilling industry here? Near places like Glenlivet, Glenfiddich, Macallan—all those famous names. And we're approximately eighty miles east of Loch Ness. Maybe that's it. Maybe the Loch Ness Monster will rise from the loch and make its way here, trampling everything in its sight, and we'll have to defend ourselves from its mighty, monstrous powers."

"God, Badger, you definitely need some fresh air. Go downstairs, and I'll join you in a second." When he left, she finished unpacking.

"We're the first ones here, aren't we?" Badger asked as she joined him outside and they set out for their walk.

"Yes, Nicola and James are taking the train then renting a car, Nigel and Bella are flying then renting a car, and Juliet is with them. They should all be here in a couple of hours."

"I was surprised by the engagement, but I like Nicola. I hope they'll be very happy. I was worried Juliet might get back together with James."

"Why would that worry you?"

"I don't believe they're suited to each other."

"I see. Let's head to the river—Hugo showed me a map of the estate when we got here. If I remember correctly, we can get there if we walk down the path over there to the left. It's only a few minutes away." She was breathing deeply, savoring the air, starting to feel less anxious in the brisk sunshine.

"You may be right about Juliet and James not being suited, or you may not be, but it's not up for discussion anymore, is it? I've already started to find a man for her."

"For Juliet?"

"Of course for Juliet. Oh, look—the sheep!" Four sheep were on the path in front of them, unbothered by their presence, looking as if they owned the place. Badger and she walked around them; he kept twanging the elastic band.

"Badger, cheer up. I think those sheep are a sign of good luck, good things to come. They cancel out our nervous feelings."

"What do sheep have to do with luck? And I don't see why you're finding Juliet a new man. She doesn't need one."

"She needs a man to love her, Badger."

"She has one. She has me."

Trez stopped so quickly she almost lost her balance.

"Badger."

"Don't." He strode quickly ahead, like someone on a mission. His red hair was lit up further by the sun; his whole persona seemed on fire.

"Badger, hold up!"

He didn't look back or slow down.

They all knew he'd had a crush on Juliet in Cambridge, but she'd assumed he'd gotten over it by now. When she reached the river and saw him standing with his back against a tree, his arms crossed, she was swamped with a sense of regret. They'd taken him for granted, all of them.

Badger with his love of books and facts, Badger who never went on a date; the person you'd always call if you needed a spare man.

"Badger, I'm sorry." She went and stood by his side at the edge of the river. "I didn't know you had those types of feelings for Juliet."

"You don't think I'm good enough for her, do you?"

"No, no. I don't think—to use your words—that you're suited to each other, that's all."

"She came to me first when she got back. Not you or James. Or Nigel. To me."

"I know, but—"

"You have no idea what it felt like in the Cambridge days. To sit by and watch her and James. I have a heart, Trez. I'm not the buffoon you all think I am."

"No one thinks—"

"You do. I don't have a job. I sit and read. I know all these facts. That's all I'm good for. Knowing facts. I have a heart. No one seems to understand that. I've loved her all these years. And there you go setting her up with someone else. Not even giving me a chance. It might take a while. I know that. I don't have enough money to keep her happy, but I can get a job, Trez. I'm a Cambridge graduate. I can make money if I put my mind to it. I should have the chance, Trez. Give me a chance."

She'd never seen Badger cry. She'd never imagined Badger crying.

"You say we're not suited." He took a step away from

the tree, toward the river, wiped his eyes. "You don't know that for a fact."

"I do," she wanted to say. "I know that with one hundred percent certainty." Instead, she went up to him, put her hand on his arm.

"I won't set her up with anyone, Badger. You can have your chance. I won't interfere."

"Thank you."

They stood, staring at the river, which was running fast, racing toward the ocean. The water looked so clean, inviting. She imagined finding a boat, pushing off into it, and floating along at speed, watching the scenery whiz by.

Poor Badger. His heart was racing too. Toward an ocean of despair. He was doomed to be unhappy in this love. It wasn't fair.

"You won't say anything, will you? I will say something to her. This weekend. Let me say it—don't go running to her making a joke of it."

"Badger—God. I won't—it's not a joke, I understand. I'm so sorry that you think I don't know you have a heart. I've been your friend for years—if you don't think I know you have a heart, that's my fault."

"It's okay. It's not as if I advertise it." His smile was wry. "It's a well-kept secret."

"Maybe, when you talk to Juliet—"

"Time to get back," he cut her off. "You know, if you climb one of the Cairngorm mountains and look north, you can see across Morayshire to the Moray Firth—up to the Orkney Islands and the North Sea and then the North Pole. Perhaps we should take a long trek and go visit Santa Claus."

He'd reverted to the old Badger. But she'd seen his pain and how deep it ran, and it shamed her. They'd all tease him, the way they all teased one another, never considering that he might be wounded by it.

We're supposed to be great friends.

Yet how well do any of us really know one another?

Well enough to know that Badger will be crushed when he takes his chance.

Chapter Twenty-Nine

NICOLA

It was called Kilfiddich Lodge, but it looked nothing like a lodge, at least not any lodge Nicola had ever seen. Three stories of brown granite blocks were topped by steep angled gables and strangely incongruous round turret towers at each end. If it had been more colorful, it could have been a castle in Disneyland.

She should have been getting used to these mansions by now, but the sight of it still made her draw in her breath and think: *Oh my God, here I go again, another place that makes me feel out of my depth.* Inside, the living room was as big as the one at Langley House, with a fireplace so tall she could have walked into it without bending. The walls were covered with huge portraits of men in kilts, probably ancestors, and hunting and shooting scenes. And yet more dead animals.

And so much plaid—or, as James had informed her, tartan. The sofas were covered in tartan fabrics, the pillows on the sofas were tartan, even the rug was tartan.

Their bedroom was the same. Tartan curtains, a tartan bedspread over the dark wood four-poster bed, two chairs covered in tartan. It looked, frankly, ridiculous—the Disney World of tartan. She imagined a Disney character showing up, Mickey Mouse in a tartan outfit. Cinderella with tartan slippers.

The bedroom window looked out over the top of the pine forest behind the lodge to the river. The view was breathtakingly beautiful. She and James stood beside each other, staring at the river in silence until he put his arm around her, drew her to him, and said, "Not bad, right?"

"That's what my boss, what Tony Kellow, said to me the first time he met me. 'Not bad.'"

"I've been looking for hit men in Buffalo. I'll make another call on that, but let's unpack first."

When they'd finished unpacking, they went down to the living room. Hugo was piling logs onto the fire.

"Hugo, that's enough."

He didn't seem to have heard Trez, and threw another log on.

"Juliet and the others should be here soon, shouldn't they?" Badger asked.

She hadn't noticed Badger, who was sitting in a corner armchair, his foot tapping the floor.

"I'm sure they'll arrive soon, Badger," Trez replied.

There was something in the way she said it that made Nicola curious. A softness to her tone, almost a pitying tinge to it.

"It's gorgeous here. The forest and the river and the moors. I'm surprised they call it a lodge, though, it's so big."

"It really is glorious, isn't it, Nicola? Sit down. Tell me how your trip to America was."

"I have a new career goal." James sat on the sofa, patted the place beside him, and she joined him. "There should be a Dunkin' Donuts on every street corner in London. Glazed donuts, Trez. You wouldn't believe how delicious they are. And the coffee. Honestly, I'm a convert. I'd live in a Dunkin' Donuts shop if I could."

"Well, that sounds exciting. How were your parents, Nicola? Did they approve of James? I've forgotten—what does your father do for a living?"

"Absolutely—they approved of him, although my father said James didn't need to ask his permission. He and my mother both work, at a garden center. They run it together."

"That sounds lovely. We'll have to get some tips from them over the wedding to pass on to our gardener."

Maybe you should hire them to weed for you.

Stop it, Nic. She didn't mean to be patronizing.

"Nic's parents are great. They're funny and they're friendly and they forgave me for shooting birds."

"What's to forgive?" Hugo, who had been facing the

fire, turned around to face James.

"Having a son-in-law who shoots harmless birds."

"Did you tell him we eat them? Is he one of those idiotic vegetarians?"

"Hugo—calm down. And sit down, will you? We're supposed to be having a pleasant conversation," Trez said.

"He's not a vegetarian," Nicola suddenly felt fiercely protective of her parents. "Neither of them are. They don't like killing, that's all. They went on marches against the Vietnam War."

"Good for them." Hugo sat down, clearly irritated. "I assume they would not have demonstrated against World War Two, or are they pacifists? What are those people called? The ones who don't speak?"

"Quakers?"

"Yes."

"No, they're not Quakers. And for your information, Quakers do speak," James answered for her. "Hugo, you're being very silly and aggressive. What's gotten into you?"

"Nothing." He paused. "I apologize, Nicola. I didn't mean to be rude."

"It's not a problem."

It wasn't a problem—because she had figured out where his testy mood was coming from. Juliet was about to arrive.

Shit—he really was in love with her. Or desperately infatuated. Why didn't he convince her not to come on this weekend? There must have been some way for him to con-

tact her and tell her not to come.

Now he's sulking. But what will he do when she gets here?

"Maine is a stunning state," James went on, directing his words to Trez. "You'd love it. The coastline is a little like Cornwall."

"We should all go there," Trez stated, but she was looking quizzically at Hugo. And Badger was still sitting in his armchair, tapping his foot.

"Have you ever been to America, Badger?" she asked, trying to draw him in.

"No, but I'd like to go."

"Really?" It was Hugo again, sounding grumpy. "You wouldn't like it, Badger."

"How do you know what I would or wouldn't like?" Badger shot back.

"Boys." Trez held up her hands. "I don't know why you're squabbling. We'd all love to go to the States. We *will* all go sometime, I hope."

Just as Hugo started to say, *I don't want to,* the sound of a door opening stopped him, and within a few seconds Nigel and Bella and Juliet came in.

"God, I need a bath." Juliet went over to the fireplace, stood in front of it. "I loathe the smell of airplanes." She sniffed her black turtleneck sweater. "I'm revolting. Which rooms are we in, Trez, sweetheart?"

"I'll show you. And you and Bella too, Nigel. Follow me."

When they left, there was a difficult silence; Hugo was slumped in the high-backed armchair by the fire, Badger was slumped in his across the room, his arms crossed.

"Well, this is a barrel of laughs," James said. "You two are acting like teenagers. We're in Scotland, in a fabulous lodge, about to shoot grouse, for Christ's sake. Nic and I are engaged; Trez is pregnant. Cheer the fuck up."

"Do you want me to do a Scottish jig?"

"No, Hugo, I want you to play the bagpipes and recite a poem by Robbie Burns."

That got a smile from Hugo, and Nicola could see Badger's face relax slightly too.

Stewart appeared at the threshold. "Excuse me."

"Stewart, come in. Great find, by the way," Trez stated. "This lodge has everything we need."

"Thank you. The catering staff comes recommended. I'm slightly worried about the shooting because we're at the very end of the season, but there's nothing to be done about that."

"I expect you'll do some fishing, won't you?"

"I'd like to, yes."

Nicola half expected him to bow, or tug at his cap, and hoped what he'd said before was true, that he really was going to give it all up, and not only because he didn't want to kill animals anymore. Yes, he was an employee, but the subservience he had to show in this job had to rankle.

"Some of us might want to try our hands at fishing too."

"Well, there are plenty of fish in the river."

Stewart said it with a straight face.

"Ha. I get it. Plenty of fish in the sea." Hugo clapped his hands in a dismissive way. "We'll see you tomorrow morning, then."

Stewart turned and walked out: Nigel, Bella, and Trez walked in, closely followed by a youngish girl in a black-and-white maid's uniform bearing a tray of full champagne glasses.

The rich definitely were different. They were rich.

"Nic." Bella took two glasses of champagne from the tray and headed to her. "James, do you mind? I want to have a chat with Nic."

"Girl chat, I assume. I'll get out of your way." He rose, letting Bella take his seat.

"I wanted to say something before Juliet comes down." Bella took a quick look around the room. "The outsiders have a chance now, so I'm taking it."

Badger, Hugo, Nigel, James, and Trez were all standing by the fireplace, talking, champagne glasses in hand.

"Listen, I know I was all over Juliet that day at Harrods. She got to me, you know? With that way she has. It's like you feel honored if she likes you. Really fucking mad. I've never met a woman like that. Anyway, when we were coming up here today, she was doing her usual charming Juliet routine, telling me how great I am. Does anyone ever not like someone who compliments them? Seriously—it's a foolproof way to get fans. But then she slipped. She started asking me all these questions about you."

"What questions?"

"What your background is—as if I'd bloody know—had you had other boyfriends? All that kind of thing, and she was asking in a causal way, but I'm not stupid. And I'm telling you now I didn't say anything about that bloke with the divorcée, and I also kept my mouth shut about you seeing her and Hugo kiss. I admit, she got into my head for a while there, but after about her fifth compliment, I was thinking: *You're laying it on too thick, mate. And there's that little tiny hint of condescension in your voice.*

"The point is, I can tell when someone is playing me. Nigel always says I'd be a great poker player. He's right. I should quit my job and—oh, shit, here she is. Act like we're talking about some TV program. You like *Monty Python*, I get it, but have you ever seen *Yes Minister*, Nic?" She raised her voice as she asked the question. "It's about English politics but it's really funny. You should watch it."

"Sounds riveting, Bell." Juliet had approached them. "We didn't get that in Hong Kong. How are you, Nic? It's so good to see you—and speaking of Hong Kong, your dress is being made as we speak. Squish up so I can sit with you both."

"I'm fine, thanks." Bella and she were about to move to the side of the sofa, but Juliet pushed in so she was sitting between them. "And thanks again, thanks so much for doing that for me."

She couldn't pull the plug on that dress—not yet, not in front of everyone.

"My God, an extravaganza of tartan here." Juliet looked around the room. "Really. I bet you anything Arabs own this place and that's all they know about Scotland—tartan. Having said that, I've always wanted to do the Highland Fling. I have no clue how to do it, but I could learn. We all could. While we're here, I'll find a local to teach us. And then all we have to do is convince Trez to give a party with a Scottish theme. We can finally put that ballroom of hers to use. Wouldn't that be a good idea? At Christmas. I can see it now."

Not another party at Langley Hall. With Juliet swirling around the ballroom doing Scottish dances.

She'd been grilling Bella for information that she'd use somehow, but how? What was she planning?

"I'm going over right now, and I'll talk to Trez about it. She'll love the idea, I know. Brilliant—we three work terrifically together, don't we?"

Without waiting for an answer, she got up and walked over to the rest of the group, gave Hugo a quick kiss on each cheek, hugged Trez, then kissed Badger on both cheeks and added a third one.

"You get three because you're so lovely lending me your car so often," she said, loudly enough for everyone to hear. Badger blushed. And bowed.

"My pleasure," he said, running his hand over the top of his head in an effort to push his hair down. It sprang right back up.

"Wow—talk about having people in the palm of your

hand," Bella whispered. "Look at Badger's besotted face."

"I know."

"At least James isn't kneeling at her feet. You don't have to worry there."

Don't I?

Fuck this.

"Let's go over." She stood up. "Let's interrupt her."

They did, and Nicola's first question to the group at the fireplace was, "How many grouse do you think you can shoot tomorrow?" The conversation turned quickly to the number of grouse they might kill, a debate about whether grouse tasted better than pheasant, the best way to cook a grouse, all topics that didn't allow Juliet to dominate.

By the time it came to a natural end, the girl who had served them champagne came back in and announced that dinner was being served.

Nicola was getting used to people serving her, and to three-course meals and all that cutlery. What was unusual about this dinner was that nothing eventful happened. They talked about Scotland, segued from there into Wales and the unpronounceable words in the Welsh language, and then on to the monarchy.

Badger had regained his composure, and although Hugo was looking dour, he was participating too. Juliet didn't take over; if anything, she was being demure. It was actually a pleasant hour or so—until they'd finished dessert and Juliet announced: "Time for another game."

"Nothing strenuous, please, Jules." Trez sighed.

"No, no one has to move an inch. Well, one person does. One person has to go out of the room and the rest of us make up a story and the person comes back and asks yes-or-no questions and tries to discover what the story is."

"That sounds impossible, Jules." Nigel put his arm around Bella. "How could anyone possibly guess?"

"By asking yes-or-no questions, dummy."

"Still—"

"Come on, let's try it. You'll see. Nic . . ." Those Juliet eyes zeroed in on her with a challenging glint. "You should go out. We'll make up a story for you."

"I'm not sure—"

"Come on, be a sport. It will be fun."

They were all staring at her waiting. James gave her a little nudge with his elbow. "Go ahead, Nic. I bet you'll guess it quickly. We're not the best storytellers; none of us are exactly creative."

"Speak for yourself." Badger sat up straight. "I think it's a brilliant game. And I can be creative."

Was this how she could redeem herself from the Lava disaster? It didn't involve any leaping, simply asking questions. There was no way it could end in disaster. Even if Juliet had been the one to suggest it.

"Okay. I'll go."

"We'll call you back in when we're ready."

"Great."

She spent the next five minutes back in the living room, figuring out what kind of questions she could ask. Basic ones to begin with. Establish the sort of story it was, where it was set, what characters were in it. She probably wouldn't guess it, but she wouldn't embarrass herself.

When they called her back in, she saw that all of them were smiling.

"Should I stand or sit when I ask?"

"Stand, I think."

"Okay. First question. Does the story take place in Scotland?"

"Yes," they all replied.

"Nice one, Nic." James smiled an encouraging smile.

"Does it take place in this lodge?"

"Yes."

"Does it feature Badger?"

"No."

"Trez?"

"Definitely not." Nigel shook his head. They all smiled again.

"Hugo or James?"

"No."

"Are Bella or Nigel or Juliet in it?"

"No," Badger answered her.

"Okay, wait a second. It takes place here in this lodge, but it's not about any of you. Is it about me?"

"Yes." Trez nodded.

"Okay."

What story would they have made up about her?

"Is it a fairy-tale kind of story?"

They were all exchanging glances.

"Maybe." That was Bella, and she was nodding. "Maybe."

"A kind of fairy tale. Okay. And it's about me. Do I get to live happily ever after?"

"No." From all of them. Except James and Bella, who were silent.

She didn't get to live happily ever after. That didn't leave her much room to go forward.

"Does something horrible happen to me?"

"Yes." An emphatic "yes" from Hugo.

"Hugo—maybe we should—" Trez suddenly looked worried.

"No, let's keep playing." That was Hugo.

"Trez is right," Bella chimed in. "I think—"

"Yes, she's right. We should stop now," James cut in.

"Wait—I want to go on." She needed to know now just how terrible this story was. "Do I die? Do I die a terrible death?"

"Yes, you die a terrible death." Hugo again.

"Hugo!" James stood up. "Nic, it's—"

Juliet was sitting there grinning, a grin that made Nicola's psyche snap, like one of Badger's elastic bands.

"You've made up a story about me dying a terrible death. Jesus Christ. Do you all hate me that much?" Her eyes locked on to Juliet's.

"Yes," Juliet said and then burst out laughing.

She wanted to run away, but she couldn't move. Juliet

was still laughing. Badger was laughing. Hugo was laughing.

"Nic . . ." James came, enfolded her in a hug. "It's not a real story. We didn't make up any story. I'm so sorry. It wasn't supposed to be—"

"What do you mean?" she pulled away from him. "What do you mean it's not a real story?"

"It's a game. We didn't make up any story. We answered your yes-and-no questions alphabetically." He tried to draw her back into his arms, but she wouldn't let him.

"What?"

"You ask yes-or-no questions and we answer according to the last letter in the last word of your question. If it falls between 'a' and 'm,' we answer 'yes'; if it ends between 'n' and 'z,' we answer 'no'—unless it ends in a 'y,' then we say 'maybe.'"

"I don't understand."

"You make up your own story, Nic." Juliet leaned back in her chair, took a sip of wine. "That's the point of this game. When you asked: 'Is it about me?'—'me' ends in 'e,' so the answer is yes. If you'd asked, *Is it about the happy life I'm going to have?* That ends in 'e' too, so we would have said yes to that. If you'd asked, *Am I going to be eaten by a bear?* the answer would be no because 'bear' ends in an 'r.'"

She still wanted to run away. She still couldn't move.

"The last time I played it," Juliet continued, "the story ended up being about a flying squirrel who had hijacked a plane to Cuba. See—you make up your own story."

She hadn't made up her own fucking story. She'd asked questions and been told she was hated and was going to die a horrible death.

"Of course we don't hate you," Juliet added. "Nobody hates you, Nic. I don't know why you'd think that, why your mind would even go there."

"Because you said you hated me," she heard the quavering rage in her own voice. "That's why my mind went there."

"She didn't mean it, Nic." James put his arm around her. "Nobody meant anything. It's a stupid game that went wrong, that's all. Horribly wrong."

"Forget flying fucking squirrels. You know what my story would have been?" Bella stood up, came over to her. "I would have asked if it was about me. Yes. Then I would have asked: Is it about my sex life? Yes. Then I would have asked: Is it about how bad I am in bed? And when everyone said yes, I would have ransacked this bloody lodge, found a gun, and shot all you wankers. Come on—you're coming outside with me."

Taking her by the hand, Bella practically dragged her outside and led her about ten feet away from the front door.

"Juliet made up that game. She was the one who told me to go out of the room. I bet she was hoping something like that would happen. I hate *her*. I hope *she* dies a horrible death."

"Nic." James must have followed them. "Nic—she

didn't mean it. Don't—"

"Bugger off, James. I'm talking to her. You can talk to her later, but right now *I* am." Bella waved him back into the lodge.

When he'd gone, Bella fished a cigarette and lighter out of her pocket.

"Don't let Juliet get to you, Nic. Don't let her win. You have to play it cool, all right? She got lucky with that shitty game. Do you want a ciggie?"

"No thanks. But thanks so much for rescuing me. I was drowning in there. The way they were laughing at me. It was so mean. So nasty. And James didn't . . . I don't know. He should have—"

"Stopped it dead in its tracks. Stood up for you more. I know." She lit up, inhaled. "But you have to understand. He's English. They're not good at scenes. They're good at wars and shit, but they're like little boys some of the time. A lot of the time. Especially when they're in a group. James loves you, Nic. He might not be great in a situation like this, but that doesn't mean he's not great in other ways, you know? He should have stopped the game, but I should have too.

"And listen—I don't know exactly what Juliet's playing at but she isn't going to win—unless you let her. You need to walk back in and be cool, okay? Don't you dare cry." She took another deep puff of the cigarette, threw it down, and ground it out. "Jesus, I'm becoming like them, aren't I? Expecting some slave to come pick that up?" She bent over, retrieved the butt, put it in her pocket. "You know that book *Rebecca*? They made it into a film too. Alfred Hitchcock. With Laurence Olivier. Have you seen it?"

"Yes. Why?"

"It just hit me. Juliet is like Rebecca, except she isn't dead. She's haunting you, though, just like Rebecca. You can't let her get into your head too much, you know."

"I can't go back in there and face them all."

"Yes, you can. You have to. I bet they'll apologize and you'll want to smack them even more than you do now, but you should say something funny and that will be the end of it."

"Something funny? Like what?"

"Search me." Bella turned her around, made her face the door. "Here we go. Time for the outsiders to go inside."

Bella was right. As soon as they entered, apologies flew at her from all of them. Which was infuriating.

"Have you all been talking about me?"

"No, no," Trez sputtered.

"You're supposed to say yes." She forced herself to smile—and to pause for a few seconds. "The question ended with an 'e.'"

"Ha!" Hugo's voice boomed, followed by the group's nervous laughter.

"I don't think I should participate in any more after-dinner games." She walked over and sat down beside James. "Either I break the furniture or I break the party mood."

"You're a good sport, Nic."

And you're an evil bitch, Juliet.

* * *

THEY WERE LYING in bed, facing each other. James put his hand around the back of her neck, was pulling her toward him. She drew back.

"I need to say something." She had been gathering her courage from the moment they'd come upstairs after dinner. Now was the time to put it out there.

"You said you understood how difficult it was for me having Juliet around, and then we come on a weekend away, yet *another* weekend away, where Juliet is. I can't do this anymore."

"What do you mean exactly?"

"I can't keep going to places where she is. You keep taking her side. You think she can do no wrong. You—"

"I never said that, Nic. I said she didn't mean to hurt you with that game, that's all."

"And you said she couldn't possibly have kissed Hugo when I know she did."

"Not that again."

"See—you take her side." She sat up. So did he.

"It's not a war. How many times do I have to tell you there's nothing between us anymore?"

"Then why's she asking Bella all these questions about my past, my family, my ex-boyfriends?"

"I don't know. She's curious. She's always been curious about people."

"You're being naïve. She was out to get Hugo, then Trez got pregnant, so she's switched her attentions to you."

Getting out of bed, she started to pace around the room. This was it—their first fight. The thought of it terrified her, but she couldn't back down—she just couldn't.

"Let me get this straight. You think she was out to get Hugo—who has been a friend of hers for ages. Who is the husband of her *best* friend. Now you think she's out to—as you put it—'get' me. She has proved this by—"

"By—"

"Let me finish, please. She has proved this by coming to my office and telling me it must be hard for you having her around. Oh, and also by helping you get the wedding dress you want, sending off to Hong Kong for that help. Definitely, Nic. Those are sure signs of her being out to get me."

"She's smart, James. She knows how to manipulate things."

"Is her way of manipulating giving me tips on how to plan our honeymoon?"

"What?"

"She and Trez gave me tips on the wedding and the honeymoon—all to make you happier."

"When did this happen? What tips?"

"You know when I went on my own to Langley Hall that morning? I said I was going to see Hugo. Except I wasn't.

Trez asked me to come on my own because she wanted to give me advice about the wedding and honeymoon. And Juliet was there too. Wanting to help with advice."

"You're fucking kidding."

"Nic!"

She stopped pacing. "I can't fucking believe this."

"Calm down, will you? You're—"

"Overreacting? Because your ex-girlfriend, the woman you proposed to, is giving you tips on how to make me happy? I'm overreacting? Because you never told me she was there when you went to Langley Hall that day? I'm overreacting? Because she plays some game that makes me look like a paranoid nutcase? I'm overreacting?"

"Because you're not being rational." He said it quietly, in an even tone. He was still sitting on the bed, his arms crossed. "I didn't tell you she was there because I didn't see the point."

She walked over to the window, drew the curtain away from it, stared out.

Nicola knew she was seconds away from turning around, walking out of the room, going downstairs, and spending the night crying on the big tartan sofa.

This is exactly what she wanted. Don't fall into her trap.

But I can't pretend none of this is happening, Daniel.

Yes, you can. Because you're never going to win this argument, Nic.

She's been too clever for you. Give it up. Or this first argument could be your last.

"I will be rational." She drew the curtain back over the window, went over to the bed, and sat on it. "I just need to know you're on my team, that your loyalty is to me. I'm here on my own, James. These are your friends, not mine; your country, not mine. I don't mean to sound self-pitying, but I think you forget that sometimes."

"Come here." He held out his arms. She folded into them. "I'm sorry. You're right. I do forget. I know that game was awful, and I'm so sorry it worked out that way. Just to set the record straight, I didn't know Juliet was going to be at Trez's when I went. And it was all about doing nice things for you. I got it wrong, obviously. Nothing like that will ever happen again. But were they right? Would you prefer an exotic beach location to somewhere like Chile?"

"They were wrong."

They were right, but she wasn't about to say it.

"Have we stopped fighting now? Because . . ." He began to tickle her. "I can win any fight by making you laugh."

"Stop!"

He was tickling her mercilessly.

"James!"

"I'm going to tickle you to death."

An hour later, she lay awake, staring at the ceiling, her hands clenched by her side.

People always talked about how terrific make-up sex was. She preferred non-make-up sex, when you weren't thinking of the things you should have said or the things you shouldn't have said. When you weren't worried about what was going to happen the next day, what move Juliet would make next.

Is she going to shoot me? And blame it on Trez?

Closing her eyes, uncurling her hands, she turned on her side and faced her sleeping fiancé.

English men aren't good at scenes, Bella had said. They're like little boys.

James looked about ten years old, his face relaxed and peaceful.

I wish we were back on a plane, holding hands, counting to thirty-one.

I wish I felt safe again.

Chapter Thirty

TREZ

The journey up to the moor above the lodge was beautiful in itself. They traveled through the low pine woodland, then up and out into moorland, with its wide, ranging views of the surrounding countryside. Trez had always loved coming to this part of Scotland, how the heather with its purplish flowers stretched for miles over the hills. Langley Hall was stunning—she wouldn't trade it for anywhere else in the world, but she did get a thrill from being high up, looking down on the farming land of the valley, which sloped toward the dark, fast-running streams that fed the River Spey.

Today the sun broke through a smattering of clouds, giving a sharp clarity to the contrast between the treeless moors and the greener valleys below. As they got out of the Land Rovers Stewart had organized to drive them up to where they'd be shooting, she was thankful that she wouldn't be doing any shooting herself. She didn't think she could ever trust herself to pick up a gun again.

Stewart had driven her, Nicola, James, Bella, and Nigel and had taken it upon himself to tell Nicola some details of the shoot.

"We shoot from what are called 'butts,'" he'd said. "The butt is designed to hide the guns, and anyone in the butt with them, from the oncoming birds—so the birds don't shy away. They're dug into the peat ground a few feet, then a turf wall is constructed in the front so that the guns are hidden from sight. They're placed about forty to sixty yards apart from one another."

"Does that mean it's safer than pheasant shooting?" Bella asked.

"No, actually. It's more dangerous. Because the birds fly lower and faster, if you don't shoot them when they're out in front of you, you can make the mistake of shooting to the side—what we call 'swinging through the line,' which means you can potentially shoot the person in the next butt. The way we teach people when they're first shooting grouse is to tell them to always shoot in front—and then, if necessary, take the gun off their shoulder, swing around, and shoot them behind. The point is never to shoot across."

"Are there beaters on grouse shoots too?"

"Yes, grouse aren't like pheasants—they're wild birds, so they're not as closely confined. The beaters go out a long time before the guns and walk for half a mile or more to funnel the birds toward the guns."

"Don't worry about the beaters, Nicola, I'm not shooting today," Trez said, and saw Nicola and Stewart exchange a look in the rearview mirror. What was that about? She couldn't interpret it, but then she hadn't been able to work out what was going on when they'd all had breakfast either.

There was none of the usual joking or banter; everyone was preternaturally quiet and, seemingly, lost in their own worlds. That after-dinner story game had been a disaster, which might have accounted for Nicola's silence, but she didn't understand why the rest of them, including Juliet, were so subdued.

She couldn't work out either why Hugo had chosen to go in the Land Rover with Juliet and Badger, telling her she should go with the others. There should have been four in one car and five in the other, not six and three. Not that it made a huge difference. The moor was close to the lodge, so the drive was fairly short. She would have liked to ride with Hugo and Juliet, though.

After breakfast, Juliet had pulled her aside, taken her to the study in the back of the lodge, and said: "Jesus Christ. That was a fuckup with Nicola. How was I supposed to know how insecure she is? Because you do make up your own story, you know."

Trez agreed but wondered what story she would have made up. "Is this baby going to be a boy?" "Maybe." She might have asked if Hugo and she were going to live happily ever after too, however. In which case she would have been freaked out by the "no," just as Nicola had been.

"Jules, I should warn you now. Badger is desperately in love with you. I think he's going to tell you this weekend. Be kind to him, please. He'll be heartbroken when you turn him down. He told me he's loved you since Cambridge days."

"Oh, shit." She sighed. "That's all I fucking need."

"Be nice to him, Jules."

"Jesus." She ran her hand through her hair, looked up at the ceiling. "Badger. Now I won't be able to borrow his car if I need to."

"Jules!"

"Just kidding. I'll be nice, I promise. Of course I'll be nice."

Now they were up on the moor, and she was in the butt with Hugo, looking over at Juliet, who had put her hair in a ponytail again. Badger was in the butt on the other side of Juliet. Nicola was in the next one over with James, and Bella was with Nigel at the far end.

They were all standing quietly; it was always a long wait until they saw any birds on a grouse shoot. Not that long ago, she and Hugo would talk to each other as they stood in a butt together. They'd chat about silly, inconsequential things and laugh. His attitude the night before had surprised her. She knew he had his rude moments, but he'd never been nasty: making Nicola continue with the game, laughing when he'd said "yes" to her question about dying a horrible death—that wasn't like him at all.

"Hugo, last night you—"

"Shh."

Why "shh"? the birds wouldn't be coming for a half an hour. The "shh" was like a slap. He hadn't even turned around when he'd said it.

"Hugo, is something wrong?"

She could tell, even from the back, that he was taking a deep breath. After a second, he swiveled to face her.

"Nothing's wrong. I'm a little tired, that's all. I need to concentrate on the shooting."

The sun had decided to hide itself behind a cloud, and its disappearance made the moor look bleak and feel chilly. An image of a woman wearing a long black coat and carrying a baby, traipsing over the hills in the rain, came to her; it took her a moment to recognize that it came from the dream she'd had the night before.

"Oh God, I just remembered. I had this awful nightmare last night. This woman was carrying a baby and—"

"Trez, please. Can we talk about it later?"

He might as well have said, *Shut up.*

Tears started to form. She put her hand on her stomach and searched the skies for a sign of good luck.

Chapter Thirty-One

NICOLA

Grouse shooting was definitely less gruesome than pheasant shooting. Nicola didn't like it, but she wasn't as appalled as that day at Langley Hall. There weren't many birds, which helped, and the ones that came after long waits in the butts did fly at real speed, so most of them managed to escape. She couldn't deny the pull of the scenery either. The moorland was beautiful and wild; after each "drive," they'd walk on to the next strategically placed row of butts. Because the next butt destination was always at a distance, she had time to take in the countryside as they walked across the heather.

Stewart joined them each time they moved, and spent a lot of the time conversing with James about shooting in general. Which was a relief—she and James were back on even ground after their night of lovemaking, and she didn't want any tremors shifting it. She needed time to get a handle on her feelings. The only thing she knew for certain was that she loved James. She was ninety-nine percent certain that Juliet was trying to get him back, but she wasn't one hundred percent certain. She was one hundred percent certain that Juliet had been after Hugo, but there was no way she could prove it.

"I hate fighting," James had whispered at about one o'clock in the morning, a few minutes after they'd finished making love. "And I know you're not a jealous person, Nic. I need you to know there's no cause to be. You're the woman I love. You're the woman I believe in and trust. You're going to be my wife, Nicola Harris. Which reminds me—are you going to take my name? Will you be Nicola Shuttleworth?"

"That's a long name to take. And isn't there a game called 'shuttlecock'?"

"Please. Think about the jokes I've been on the end of on that one. Spare me and never mention it again."

"Right. God, there are some times I'm really glad I'm not a man."

"I'm really glad you're not a man—the whole time."

The day had gone smoothly, and they were walking to another butt for the last drive. Nicola was secretly pleased that Juliet hadn't managed to shoot any of the few grouse that had come their way. Maybe the Superwoman image would fade as time went on.

When she managed to find a job, she'd meet new people;

she and James would have new friends. It wouldn't always have to be the Club.

Stewart walked ahead with James and Bella, while Nigel lagged behind and joined her.

Badger was with Juliet at the front; he'd been walking with her each time they moved butts.

"Oh God." Nigel shook his head. "Look at Badger. Still with Juliet. I hope to God he isn't telling her how he feels. He was on at me early this morning, professing his undying love for her, saying no one believes he has a chance, but that he deserves one. I tried to reason with him, but failed. God—that woman. The damage she does."

Nicola's heart lifted.

"Damage?"

"Look, she broke the heart of one of my friends—sorry, Nic, but that's the way it was back then. She buggered off with no warning. James didn't have a clue she wanted to leave him and head to Hong Kong. Now she's about to break Badger's heart too. I'm tired of her. Also, I think there's something fishy going on. I heard from a friend of a friend in Hong Kong that she was more or less forced out. They wouldn't say why. But Bella told me about that bullshit *too many junks* comment—it's total crap."

"I think she's after James." There. She said it. And prepared herself for a *don't be ridiculous* rebuttal.

"It wouldn't surprise me. Nothing she does would surprise me."

"You said before everyone was in love with her back

then—were you?"

"I fancied her, yes. But was I in love? No. Juliet's a collector. What I mean is that she likes to capture people, make them think she's dazzling and wonderful, but deep down? I don't think she gives a shit about anyone."

"I don't—"

"Hey." James had turned around and was calling out to them. "Come join us. Stewart is telling us about red grouse."

Nigel made a move forward, but she put her hand on his arm, stopped him. "Thank you, Nigel."

"I don't know what you're thanking me for. But I'll take it. Keep your wits about you, Nic. If she is after James, you'll need them."

"Did you know these little things can fly at seventy miles an hour?" Bella asked when Nicola and Nigel reached them. "Christ, they're like the racing cars of the bird species. Tiny fucking Ferraris."

Nigel laughed, and Nicola was simultaneously pleased and envious. Bella didn't have to deal with Juliet. Not dealing with Juliet had to be the biggest bonus in the world right now. What new diabolical party game was she going to come up with that night? What perfect outfit would she wear?

At least she'd put a stop to Tony Kellow when she'd punched him. It would be so satisfying to slap Juliet's enchanting face, see the look of shock on it. That was hardly going to bring a halt to Juliet's influence, though. Avoiding her altogether might be the answer. After this weekend, she could make sure James and she didn't have any more meetups with the Club. If another weekend or a party was coming up, she could get sick. There had to be ways of steering clear of them. Having dinner with Nigel and Bella would be fun, if they kept it to just the four of them. Even Trez and Hugo on their own would be okay. Just no more group activities. No more humiliating games. After tonight, she'd make sure Juliet wasn't part of their lives.

After the last drive, they all walked back to the cars and drove back to the lodge. The air and the views up on the moor had been exhilarating; Stewart had said the season for shooting grouse started in August, and she could imagine being up there in the warm sunshine, but there was something special about the cold air, that sharp light and briskness, which didn't heat her body but revved her soul.

"Hey," Bella said as they exited the car at the lodge. "Come walk with me for a second, will you?"

"Sure."

"Right, you two. Are you being naughty again? Do you have a hip flask, Bella?"

"I wish, James."

"See you later, then." He gave Nicola a kiss on the cheek. The others had already headed into the lodge.

"Let's pretend we're Trez and Juliet. We'll walk arm in arm."

"What's up? Do you need a cigarette?"

"Of course, but that's not why I asked you. Nigel asked

me to come meet his parents. While we were standing in the last bloody butt. That has to be good news, doesn't it?"

"It's brilliant."

Was it? Or would they look down on her? Nicola felt like crossing her fingers and making a wish: *Please let them be decent. Please.*

"That's what I think. I think maybe it's sixty-forty that he won't ditch me now. Come here." She dragged her over to a tree, pulled a cigarette and lighter out of her pocket. "Thank God I've brought mints. And I might even be able to brush my teeth too before Nigel gets up close to me. If I'm lucky. Okay, now we have to discuss what I'm going to wear when I meet his parents while I smoke this. Maybe not the see-through blouse?"

"Maybe not."

Chapter Thirty-Two

TREZ

She sat down on her own in the living room, by the fire. Her feeling of impending doom wouldn't go away, even after a day outside on the moor. Why had she had that nightmare about the woman and the baby? The way the woman was dressed, all in black, and the way she was holding the baby as she tramped across the moor in the rain, as if it were dead—it was so mournful, so full of loss. She never remembered her dreams. Why now? Why that dream?

Closing her eyes and crossing her fingers, she wished: *Let me forget that dream. Let this baby be healthy and happy.* A thought sprang up, unbidden. *Let no one die a horrible death.*

That was it—the reason for her nightmare: that silly game. It had put terrible thoughts into her head.

Once, when she was eight years old, she'd decided to run away from home. Except she didn't want to go anywhere; what she wanted was not to run away but to hide. Then her brothers and her parents would miss her. And be so happy when they finally found her, hiding under the bed in the spare room.

She waited. She spent hours on that floor under the bed, waiting. No one had come to find her. No one had noticed that she was gone. Finally, she crawled out, went downstairs to the drawing room. Her parents were watching television. Her brothers had both gone off playing outside. Looking at the clock, she saw that she'd been hiding for five whole hours.

When she'd told Juliet that story one night, Juliet's response had been: "You can see that one or two ways, Trez. Either you can feel abandoned and miserable, or you can congratulate yourself on having so much fortitude and stamina. Five hours. That's bloody impressive, sweetheart."

Fortitude and stamina: that was what she needed to vanquish the increasingly uneasy feelings she was having.

But what if I went off and hid somewhere now? How long before Hugo, before anyone came to look for me?

She pounded her right fist into her thigh ten times. Then took a deep breath, stood up, and climbed the stairs to her room. Hugo was lying on the bed, fully clothed, his hands covering his face.

"Hugo? Are you all right?"

"Yes. Merely contemplating."

"What?" She sat down beside him, gently removed his hands from his face. "'Merely contemplating'? That's a funny thing to say."

"Never mind." Getting up, he stretched his arms. "I think I'll go for a walk. Get some air."

"Hugo. You've been out all day. You don't need any more air. Besides, I want to talk to you about Badger and Juliet. You went to sleep last night before I could tell you anything."

"Tell me what? What about Juliet and Badger?"

"He's in love with her. He admitted it to me yesterday. Absolutely besotted. And I think he's going to tell her at some point this weekend. Possibly tonight."

"That's ludicrous. Completely ludicrous. As if she'd have any interest in Badger. He's useless."

"You don't have to be so cruel. She likes Badger. Granted she's not in love with him, but he's a good man, Hugo—he's not useless. There's no need to demean him."

"There is when he acts like such a prat. She'll put him in his place, though. You can count on that."

"I told her to be nice to him; I warned her he might say something to her."

"Well, good—she'll be nice to him—that's that, then, isn't it?"

"Hugo? Why are you so angry? And why do you seem so angry with me? What have I done wrong? I didn't shoot anyone today. Is that why you're angry with me still? Because of Matthew?"

"I'm not angry. I'm tired."

"So am I."

"What?"

"So am I. I'm tired as well. If I hid right now, or if I ran away, would you come looking for me?"

"For God's sake. If you ran away? If you hid? You aren't going to do either. I'll tell you what you *should* do. Take a leaf out of Juliet's book. She's strong, she's confident. She's funny."

As soon as he saw her tears, he put his arm around her, whispered: "It's all right. It's all going to be all right. Don't cry, Trez."

"I don't want anyone to die a horrible death. I—" She was saying the words and sobbing into his shirt.

"What? What did you say?"

"I have a feeling something terrible is going to happen. And that dream, that nightmare—"

"Shh. Don't be silly. Nothing horrible is going to happen. We're all going to go on the way we were and live the lives we've been given and try to be grateful for them."

Chapter Thirty-Three

NICOLA

As soon as Bella finished the cigarette, they headed back to the lodge, and she bolted up the stairs to see James, to tell him Bella's news.

He was half lying on the bed, his upper body against the headrest.

Juliet was lying beside him.

"Nic, hi! I needed a little chat with Jimmy. I hope you don't mind."

Juliet didn't move from her position beside James. "Come sit down." She patted the bedcover. "Jimmy said you were chatting with Bell. Any good gossip?"

"What did you need to talk to James about?" She stayed standing.

"Badger." Juliet sighed. "I was telling Jimmy that up on the moor Badger declared himself to me and that I don't think I handled it very well. I wasn't as kind as I should have been."

"You didn't want to lead him on," James said. James was making excuses for Juliet.

"No, I didn't. But I worry that I was too blunt."

"He's one of your collection."

"What?"

"Everyone is in love with you, Juliet. You have a collection of ardent admirers."

"If only that were true." She swung her legs over, got off the bed.

"Are you angry with me, Nic?"

"Why would I be?" She was back playing Portia, back to that expressionless monotone voice.

"Exactly. I thought Jimmy could help me soften the blow a little, that's all. He's known Badger forever. He knows what might help."

"And did you help?" She turned her eyes to James.

"I hope so. I said it would be a good idea to take Badger aside and say she cares about him and wants to be his friend."

"You didn't say that to Badger before?" Her eyes swiveled back to Juliet.

"Not exactly, I'm afraid."

"It seems pretty obvious to me. I'm surprised you didn't say that to him already."

"You're so right, Nic. I should have. I'll do that now. Thanks, Jimmy. And thank you too, Nic. Other women

might not have been so understanding seeing an ex in bed
with their fiancé."

"I understand, Juliet. Don't worry, I get it."

As Juliet was walking out, she stopped, gave Nicola a
hug.

"You're a sweetheart, Nic."

"Thanks."

She knew she had a choice. She could try to control herself or she could let all that rage fly. But if she did the latter,
it would turn back on her like a boomerang and smash her
in the heart. Because she was keeping up with Juliet now:
this was another supposedly acceptable thing for her to
have done. Why not go to an old friend and talk about the
difficult situation with Badger?

How could she complain about that without sounding
shrewish and jealous?

*I'm wising up, Daniel. Bella was right—I can't let her
get to me. She thinks if she provokes me enough, I'll make
a scene and have a fight with James and our relationship
will take a hit.*

*She knew I'd come in and find her here like that. No
way will I give her the satisfaction. I couldn't act in Shakespeare, but I can act now.*

Nice one, Nic. I'm proud of you. You're kicking ass.

"Nic? Nic?"

"Sorry, I was lost in thought. Wondering what I'm going
to wear tonight."

"You're not really upset about Juliet coming in, are you?

It wasn't—"

"I'm not upset. I'm fine. I need to take a shower, though. It's been a long day."

Chapter Thirty-Four

TREZ

During drinks, Nicola was on one side of the room talking with Bella, in a huddle, as if they were sharing a secret. Badger stood at the far end of the room, staring out the window into the darkness. Hugo was in front of the fireplace, with Nigel, and Trez sat on the sofa beside Juliet.

Juliet had told her about Badger and his profession of love, how she'd tried to handle it the best possible way, but what could she say except that she didn't share his feelings? Trez was trying to concentrate, but her thoughts kept floating back to Hugo's statement: "We'll live the lives we've been given and try to be grateful for them."

Try? Why did he have to *try* to be grateful? Juliet had said before that she was disappointed by life; now Hugo sounded disappointed. Disappointed and resigned. It didn't make any sense. They were happily married, and they were going to have a child. Why did it require an effort to be grateful?

"Trez?"

"Sorry, Jules. Hugo's been strange lately. It's worrying me. He seems so distant and, I don't know . . . morose."

"Don't worry about Huge, sweetheart. He's probably anxious about becoming a father. It's very grown-up, you know. Being a parent."

"I suppose so."

Nigel broke away from talking to Hugo and walked over to Badger. James followed him. *The boys to the rescue*, she thought. *They'll tell him some jokes, distract him. Poor Badger.*

Trez knew that she shouldn't be so wrapped up in herself, she should think how upset Badger must be.

Juliet leaned closer to her.

"I think there may be trouble in paradise."

"What do you mean? What trouble, what paradise?"

"Jimmy and Nicola. I think they may not make it to the altar. Nic's so insecure. And jealous. That's not good for Jimmy."

If Juliet had said the same thing a week ago, Trez would have leapt at it, willing a breakup, willing a rekindled romance between James and Jules. Hearing it now scared and upset her. She didn't know why. She didn't know why she suddenly wanted to get up off the sofa and go to Badger and take him upstairs and cry with him.

Unrequited love. If James really was going to break up

with Nicola, that was unrequited love too. Poor Nicola.
Poor Badger. Glancing at Hugo, she saw a sad expression
in his eyes. Like a sick dog.

"We should have brought Buster here with us."

"What? Trez, are you all right?"

"Sorry. My hormones must be making me a little crazy."

"Did you hear what I said about Jimmy and Nic?"

"Yes."

"Trez?"

"I'm sorry. I need some air."

She couldn't get out of the room, the lodge, fast enough.
Outside, she leaned against the front door and took deep
breaths. The woman in her dream the night before had
been wearing black. She was wearing black—a black skirt
and a black jumper. If she set off to the moor now, she
might discover what that dream meant. The moon was giving enough light for her to make a start. If she took a long
enough walk she might be able to make sense of things.

Trez, pull yourself together. Go back inside.

But my name isn't Trez. It's Jane.

I abandoned my name.

*When I give this child a name, I'll want it to keep that
name.*

*Jane was my grandmother's name on my mother's side.
They named me Jane for a reason. She died before I was
born. She was strong and wise—my mother told me that.
"Your grandmother was a brave woman; she had a difficult life, but she never succumbed. She was indomitable."*

Why have I never asked about her difficult life, her bravery?

Why did I let Juliet rechristen me?

When I abandoned my name, I abandoned my grandmother.

I do what people tell me to do. I do what's expected of me. I'm not strong and independent and funny like Juliet.

I could be, though. If I keep walking, I could be someone else. I could be Jane.

Those sad eyes. Hugo has such sad eyes. As if he's seven years old and trapped back in boarding school.

Her foot hit a stone; she stumbled, fell, lay on the ground for a moment before turning over. The Scottish sky stared down at her.

You get so many bruises you should give a Black and Blue Ball.

"Trez." Nicola was standing over her. "God, are you okay?"

"Shit, that was a nasty fall." Bella was beside Nicola. She held out her hand and Trez took it, allowed herself to be pulled up.

"You found me."

"I heard the door open and close when you went out, and you'd been gone a while, and it's bloody freezing, so Nic and I came looking for you."

"Thank you so much." She brushed herself off. "I was taking a walk, and I tripped."

How far had she walked? She could see the lights of the

lodge about fifty yards away.

"You didn't fall on your stomach, did you?"

The baby. She'd forgotten the baby.

"No, no. My arm hurts. It must have taken the brunt of the fall. But it doesn't hurt badly. I'm fine."

"That's lucky." Nicola put her arm around her. "Come on, let's go back. We're about to eat. You need some food."

"I don't know what got into me." They started to walk back toward the lights. "I thought I needed fresh air. I was feeling faint inside. I thought a walk would do me good."

"Well, it probably did." Bella put her arm around her as well. "You know, I bet they'll serve something tartan for dinner. Some sort of layered dessert that looks like a kilt."

"Bella, you're wonderful. I don't know if Nigel deserves you. I think I know that James deserves you, Nicola, but right now I'm not sure of anything. All I want is for people to be happy, you know. I want everyone to be happy. I don't want anyone to have to try to be grateful. Gratitude should come naturally, shouldn't it?"

"I guess." Bella tightened her grip. "But nothing is ever easy. Is it, Nic?"

"No. It may seem easy at first, but I think things always get complicated."

"Listen to us, the philosophers. Jesus Christ. I know what they'll do. They'll make a cake in the shape of a man with a kilt on and a hole in the skirt where his little pink willy sticks out. That's what we'll have for dessert."

If Juliet had been with them, she and Juliet would have

exchanged glances. The proper word was "pudding," not "dessert."

For the first time in her life, she was glad Juliet wasn't there.

Chapter Thirty-Five

NICOLA

Juliet sat at the head of the dining room table in a dark blue high-necked silk dress she'd likely bought in Hong Kong. Her black hair was up, fastened with wooden sticks. Nicola was in a red dress Bella had helped her find at a charity shop in Fulham.

She wasn't going to compare herself to Juliet, except she couldn't not. She wouldn't have any idea how to fasten her hair up like that, not to mention that her hair was only shoulder-length, so it wouldn't have created that pile of beautiful black. For a second she smiled, thinking of bats nesting in it, laying their eggs. Then she focused again on what Nigel was saying to her, his story of playing cricket with James, how they managed to win some important match they'd been playing on a village green.

He was trying to explain what the term "leg before

wicket" meant, and she was trying to follow, but she stole a look at Trez too, to see how she was after that strange walk in the night, and her fall.

She seemed to have regained her composure, and though she wasn't saying much to James or to Badger, who were sitting beside her, she was smiling and clearly not in any pain so the baby couldn't have been hurt.

"What were you and Nic talking about on your walk, Bell?" Juliet's voice was loud enough to stop the rest of them talking.

"I was telling Nic I'd love to visit the States. I'd love to take that Route 66 road and drive across the country and chat with people in diners, people wearing cowboy boots."

Bella wasn't about to say she'd been discussing going to see Nigel's parents. She was dodging the question well; Bella was a better match for Juliet than she herself was.

"Jimmy, do you remember that nutty couple we met in Greece? How crazy they were? Really . . ." She was looking around the table at all of them, taking them all in one by one. "They wore matching clothes, if you can believe that. Every single day they'd come out of the hotel room in matching outfits."

"They were mad." James smiled. "Their names rhymed too. Kenny and Jenny, that was it."

"God, yes!" Juliet clapped. "I'd forgotten that bit. Kenny and Jenny. You should have seen some of those outfits. They were spectacularly awful."

"Excuse me." Stewart stood at the threshold of the dining room. "I'm sorry to interrupt. I wanted to say though that if anyone would like to go fishing early tomorrow morning, I've hung some waders up in the hallway off the kitchen, and there are rods all prepared there as well."

"Fishing. Yes! I'll go definitely, early tomorrow morning. That's a huge treat. I'll catch a fish for lunch."

"I can join you, Jules." Those were the first words Nicola had heard Badger speak at dinner.

"No, Badger. Thanks so much, but I actually want to go on my own. I want the solitude. I *need* the solitude. Not to be rude to anyone, but sometimes it's nice to be on one's own in the countryside."

Badger's body seemed to shrink as he sat back in his chair and his face sunk in on itself. Nicola wished she could magically transport him to a huge library, sit him down, and tell him there was life after Juliet.

"Good night, then."

"Good night, Stewart, and thank you for all your work."

"My pleasure." Was there a hint of sarcasm in his voice? She wasn't sure.

The waitresses moved round the table seamlessly. Did they go back in the kitchen and let rip with their own sarcastic remarks about all of the guests? She would have, for sure. These people in their thirties drowning themselves in champagne and wine, eating three-course meals, living the high life. There'd be a lot of fodder there for criticism. Jesus—they didn't even make their own beds.

"So—I always ask the crucial questions." Juliet leaned

forward. "Have you thought about names for the baby, Trez?"

"No, we're going to talk about it at Christmas."

"Really? I think we should all give our suggestions. You don't have to take any of them, but you never know, we might come up with something fabulous. We should go around the table. Girls' names first. I'll start it off."

"It might be bad luck." Trez looked frightened. "It's still early days."

"Come on, sweetheart. We're only a few weeks away from Christmas. You and your superstitions. I thought you would have dropped those by now."

The comment wounded Trez, Nicola could tell.

This wasn't the type of best friendship Trez needed. There was no equality: Juliet was top dog and always had been. Trez was her acolyte. A disposable acolyte obviously—if Juliet had succeeded with Hugo, Trez would have been left by the side of the road in a heap of misery.

Nigel was right, Juliet didn't care about anyone except herself. Most people like that didn't hide it as well as Juliet did, though.

"I choose Alexandra for a girl. What about you, Jimmy?"

"Esme. I've always loved that name."

"Excellent. Not as good as Alexandra, but excellent. Bella?"

"Sophia. But she'd be called Sophie."

"Another nice one. Badger?"

"Diana."

"Goddess of the moon. This is going very well."

"Trez—you're not playing, are you? Then Hugo shouldn't either. Nigel—it's your turn."

"Cleo. I'd choose Cleopatra, but that would be too much to live up to. So she'd only have to live up to about a half of it."

"Interesting. Nic?"

"Portia."

"Whoa. Portia as in *The Merchant of Venice* or Porsche as in the car?"

That got a laugh from the entire table, even Badger. She'd walked right into it, but she couldn't think of another name and hadn't worked out the similarity.

"Sorry, Nic, I couldn't resist. Portia is a lovely name. Now it's time for boys' names. Starting with Nic and going the other way round."

She chose George, Nigel chose Henry, Badger chose William, Bella chose Sam, James chose Benjamin.

"All good solid names." Juliet put her thumb up. "I think boys should have good, solid names. Now it's my choice. I choose Daniel. I love that Elton John song 'Daniel.'" She paused. "Wait a second. That's your brother's name isn't it, Nic? Your twin who died? I'm so sorry."

"How do you know?" Confusion coursed through her. "How did you know that's his name?"

"Jimmy told me. I think it's so wonderful that you talk to him as if he were alive. I'm sure I'd do the same if I lost someone that close to me, even if you never knew him. I mean, you were so close in the womb, weren't you?"

Greg announcing that he was going off with the divorcée was betrayal, a rocket aimed at her heart, but this was nuclear. Her biggest secret: one she had shared with James because of her love for him. She'd never even told Greg. No one. No one ever.

Juliet knew her secret. The whole table did.

Juliet had killed Daniel.

Chapter Thirty-Six

TREZ

"How could you?" Nicola aimed that at James. Trez was stunned by the tone of hurt mixed with fury.

"And you . . ." Nicola turned to Juliet. "You don't think I know exactly what you're doing? I fucking hate you." Tears burst from her eyes, and she fled the room.

"God, Jimmy, I'm sorry. I didn't know that was such a sore subject."

Before Juliet had finished the sentence, James got up and left too.

"Why are you looking at me like that, Nigel? What did I do wrong? I had no idea I was hitting a raw nerve."

"You know, you've never given me a nickname, Juliet." Nigel tipped back in his chair. "I think that's because I'm one of the only ones who sees through you."

"Fuck off, Nigel. Stop being the absolute prat you are."

Hugo's eyes weren't sad anymore; they were livid.

Nigel said something mean back and they were argu-ing and her mind floated away. To a walk she and Juliet had taken together in Cambridge. They were arm in arm, walking down a side street. She couldn't remember which one. What she did remember was that there was a dog on the side of the street and the dog was barking. It yapped and yapped as they approached it: a little mongrel dog. And Juliet was in the middle of a story—it must have been an important one—because she kept yelling at the dog to shut up, but the dog didn't, and when they walked past it, Juliet kicked it. Not hard, but she kicked it.

She remembered she drew her arm away and said, "Why did you do that to the poor dog?" and Juliet took her arm back and said, "I didn't mean to. Let's go get a sausage or something and give it to him to make up for it."

They'd done that. Walked to a shop, bought a sausage roll, gone back, and given it to the dog.

And that was the end of that.

Except she'd kicked a little defenseless dog.

Trez had thought about returning for it at some point, adopting it, but then she'd forgotten.

There were things to do—much more fun things to do.

"Trez?"

"Yes."

"*You* know I didn't mean to hurt Nic." Juliet was at her side. Everyone else must have decamped from the dining room to the living room while she was thinking about the dog.

"Yes, I know. But James told us she was embarrassed about talking to her brother. You do thoughtless things sometimes, that's all. You'll make it up to her somehow, won't you?"

"Absolutely. But really, I'd forgotten he'd said that about the embarrassment. And anyway, it's so silly to be embarrassed."

It had been one of those long, drunken nights they'd spent together. They hadn't gotten to the really drunk part of it yet when Badger had been talking about Anthony Trollope, some novel called *Phineas Finn*. "That's my favorite male name—Finn," Juliet had stated. "Finn. It's such a strong, perfect name for a boy."

"What happened to Finn?"

"Sorry? Finn who?"

"It used to be your favorite boys' name, remember?"

"Really? No, I don't remember. It's a good name, though. It must have been my favorite before that Elton John song came out."

"Right."

She was so tired.

How can you not mean to kick a dog? Either you kick it or you don't.

All she wanted to do was go to bed.

"Trez. What's going on in that head of yours? Nigel's been awful to me; now you're acting so distant. You're not cross with me too, are you?"

"No, Jules. I'm tired. I've had a funny feeling for ages now. As if . . . as if something is fundamentally wrong and it's going to get worse. Like the world is off-kilter."

"Sweetheart, you need some rest. But give me a hug before you go upstairs, please."

They hugged. Trez felt the silk of Juliet's dress against her skin.

"Would you like me to come up with you, chat awhile before bedtime?"

"No thanks. Good night, Jules."

"Sweet dreams, sweetheart."

She wanted to sleep a dreamless sleep, wake up refreshed and back to her old self. She wanted to spend a beautiful Sunday morning in Scotland with all her old friends and her happy husband.

"Jules?" She was on her way out of the room, but stopped and turned back. "Tell me it's all going to be fine. Tell me we'll go back to being the way we were."

"You definitely need cheering up. So think about this: The Beatles are all alive. The Fab Four can still stage a brilliant reunion."

On her way to her bedroom, she passed James and Nicola's room.

"I can't believe you can't see how manipulative she is." Nicola's voice was high-pitched, out of control.

Trez walked on quickly.

"You didn't give me a nickname because I'm one of the only people who sees through you."

It couldn't be. Juliet wasn't like that. Juliet was a wonderful force of nature, a brilliant, shining star. She wouldn't hurt anyone on purpose.

"Give Peace a Chance." "All You Need Is Love." She hummed a few bars of those songs as she got ready for bed.

But then other Beatles songs invaded her brain: "Help." "I'm a Loser."

"Baby's in Black."

No. No. Stop it. Baby's not in black. My baby isn't in the arms of a woman on the moor. What's wrong with me?

I'm pregnant. I'm a good wife. Juliet must have gone into whatever room the others were in. The living room. But why isn't Hugo up here with me now? He should be with me.

She undressed then went back downstairs in her dressing gown, covering her ears as she passed James and Nicola's room just in case. When she reached the ground floor, she headed to the living room, and could see, before she went in, that Nigel and Bella were there but the others weren't. Walking toward the dining room, she looked to the right and saw a light on in the study at the back. She went toward it and saw, when she was around ten feet away, Hugo bowed over the desk, writing.

It had to be something about Langley Hall. Some kind of business. She wasn't going to disturb him—for some unknown reason, seeing him like that, his head down, concentrating, comforted her. She'd seen him in the same pose at home when he was busy.

My Hugo. I adore him.

*It's going to be fine for you, my little one—whatever
we name you. You're going to have happy parents and a
happy life.*

*Nothing horrible is ever going to happen to you. I
promise.*

Chapter Thirty-Seven

NICOLA

I told you I'd never told anyone. You knew how important it was to me. How could you have, James? I trusted you. I don't understand how you could betray me like that."

"I didn't mean to. Trez asked me about your family, and I said you'd had a twin brother that died. Should I have lied? Really?"

He was pacing around the room. She was sitting on the end of the bed, still crying.

"You told them I talk to him. And his name. You told *Juliet*, your ex-girlfriend, your ex-fiancée, my secret. Did you not mean to do that?"

"They were both saying how sad it was, and I said you still talk to him. Because I think that's a good thing, Nic. Not something to be embarrassed about or ashamed of."

"No, talking to dead people is just great, isn't it? *Oh,*

here's my fiancée—my second fiancée—and she talks to dead people. You'll love her."

"Would you stop saying Juliet was my fiancée? She wasn't."

"Only because she didn't accept the proposal. But now she wants that proposal back and she wants to accept it and she wants to break us up and she's been working hard at it, setting me up, and she's smart about it—I have to hand it to her, she's fucking smart."

"Listen, I really am sorry I told them about Daniel, but you're being paranoid. She hasn't set you up for anything. She didn't bring that up on purpose tonight. We were talking about names and it came out, that's all."

"Why can't you see how manipulative she is?" Her voice was rising with each word she spoke. Her hands were shaking. "First she goes for Hugo—and don't you dare tell me again that that kiss wasn't a kiss. I saw it. Then Trez gets pregnant, so that didn't work, did it? Poor Juliet. Time to move targets. So she switched over to you. And she does that by making me react the way I'm reacting right now, and I know I shouldn't, I should keep quiet and play it cool, but this is too much. Talking about my dead brother in front of everyone was too much. I can't be cool. She's a snake, and she has slithered her way in between us. She's poisonous. Nigel can see it. Bella can see it. But you can't. Why can't you see it, James? Tell me—why can't you see how manipulative she is?"

"We're going around in circles, Nic. I understand it must

be hard to have my ex-girlfriend around so much, I really do. But she's not out to get me. She hasn't made one move in my direction. When she came to my office, she was being sympathetic to you. She was trying to help."

"There is not a bad bone in Bobby Tappan's body."

He won't see it. He refuses to think that way.

"And as for her being after Hugo—he's a great mate of mine and has been since we were children, but he's not the most attractive man on earth. Even if he weren't the husband of her best friend, Juliet wouldn't be attracted to him."

"She would be attracted to the title he's going to get—and the house, and the money."

"Wow." He stopped pacing. "You've really got it in for her, don't you? That's an unbecoming thing to say about someone you don't really know."

The disappointment in his face, the disappointment in his voice made her feel as if there were a rope tied around her heart and that rope was tightening, strangling it.

"I know, James. I know what it sounds like, but just please let me defend myself. Just listen, okay?"

He nodded.

"Okay. I'll skip the Hugo part of it because I know you'll never believe me. But I need you to hear the other parts, and I'll say it all rationally, okay? I won't raise my voice. First of all, she goes to your office—supposedly to be nice about me, to congratulate you on our engagement—all that—but then she comes to supposedly help me pick a dress and what does she do? She tells me about when you proposed to *her*—on the day I'm looking at wedding dresses. Then she arranges it so you go down to see Trez to get helpful hints or whatever and she just *happens* to be there? I don't believe that was a coincidence.

"She asked you questions about my family to get information on me. She asked Bella questions about my family too—Bella said she grilled her about me. Which is one of the reasons Bella doesn't trust her either. Then she sets up that guess-the-story game and who has to play it? *Me*. She makes me play because she knows it can go wrong—which it did. Dramatically. *Then* she oh-so-coincidentally starts talking about names and oh-so-coincidentally asks everyone to name those names and oh-*so*-coincidentally, her favorite name is my brother's name, and she then informs everyone that I talk to him. Oh, wait—I forgot—she just *happens* to be lying on this bed next to you when I come back from town this afternoon. To tell you how madly in love with her another man is. Don't you see? It's all part of a plan. It's not inadvertent."

He stood, his arms crossed, looking up at the ceiling. She waited.

"James?" She couldn't wait any longer. "Tell me—don't you see what she's doing?"

He blew his breath out, dragged his hands down his face, then looked straight at her.

"You're missing a fundamental point, Nic. Why would she make this elaborate scheme to get me back? Juliet doesn't love me. I doubt that she ever did, actually. What does she gain by all the supposed maneuvering she's doing?"

"She wants you now. She couldn't get Hugo, so she wants you."

"Why? If she loved me so much, why wouldn't she have told me as soon as she got back? And according to you, she wanted Hugo. Is your theory that she wanted Hugo for the title?"

"Yes, and the house. All of it."

"Then why me? I don't have a title or a big house."

"But you have money, James. You lead the same sort of lifestyle, the one she wants for herself."

Once again, he blew out his breath in a huff.

"Juliet's from a good family. I'm sure she has enough herself to lead that lifestyle."

"Are you? Are you so sure? Maybe they don't. Maybe—"

"Stop." He clenched his fists. "Just stop. You're saying so many awful things, I honestly can't stand to hear another. Juliet's a scheming shrew. She was going to steal her best friend's husband so she could have a title and a house. Now she's going to steal me from you—not because she loves me. Of course not. She probably has no feelings for me whatsoever. *But* I have enough money to keep her in the style she's accustomed to. That's a wonderful thing to hear my fiancée say. Isn't it? I'm at a total loss here, Nic. What the hell has happened to you?"

"I didn't mean she's not attracted to you. God, I'm sorry,

James. I didn't mean . . ."

"This is exhausting. I want to go to sleep. We can talk about it all when we get back to London. But if you care about me, if you love me at all, please, please, please don't bring this subject up again until we get back. I'm afraid of what might happen between us."

"Stewart thinks she was the one who shot the beater, not Trez."

"Nic—I asked you. Now I'm begging you."

"I'm sorry. I couldn't help it. I'll stop, I promise. I just wish she weren't in our lives. I wish someone would say 'presto' and she'd magically disappear. That's all. I'm not going to say another word. I promise."

It's what happened when you were so sure you were right in an argument: You couldn't let it go. You wanted to pound it in to the person until they saw the truth.

She'd hurt him. That comment about Juliet wanting his money had wounded him, and she hadn't even considered that it might. So angry at Juliet, so sure if she kept going on long enough he'd see, she'd forgotten James and his feelings.

He was sitting in the chair now, looking defeated.

"I'm sorry, James. I really am. Can you come to bed? Please?"

"In a few minutes."

They undressed at opposite ends of the room, went and brushed their teeth separately, and finished getting ready for bed, neither of them speaking. She didn't trust herself not to start up again, to try to justify what she'd said. When they finally both got under the covers, he didn't touch her. He slid to his side of the bed and said a feeble "Good night," before switching the bedside lamp off.

There was no way in hell she could sleep. She'd never had an argument like that before—aside from her losing control with Tony Kellow—but she hadn't tried to argue her case then, she'd punched him. She and Greg had had arguments, yes, but never as intense as this one, where everything felt at stake. When Greg told her he was leaving her, she'd been shocked and appalled, she'd questioned him mercilessly about his affair, but she hadn't been trying to make him believe her side of a story.

I want witnesses. Bella and Nigel are on my side. Stewart can tell him he thought Juliet was the one who shot the beater. He'll understand that Juliet taking the blame for it, then shifting it on to Trez, was another diabolical move, getting kudos from Hugo, making Trez feel shaky.

But what am I supposed to do? Line them up and have them testify for me tomorrow morning? I promised I wouldn't talk about it again until we get back to London. I can't stage a trial at breakfast.

She had no idea what time it was when she got out of bed and made her way downstairs. All she knew was that she needed to be on her own, not lying in a bed beside the man she loved when she might lose him forever.

Flopping down on the living room sofa, pulling one of those tartan rugs over her, she lay down and tried to imagine the future. The only future that could possibly work was if, when they got back to London, she took back everything she'd alleged. If she didn't, they'd have the same fight again, which would lead to nothing but disaster.

I didn't mean any of it, James. I don't know what I was thinking. Can you ever forgive me? I'm sure Juliet wasn't plotting against me. I was imagining she was conspiring against me when she wasn't at all. Mea culpa.

That might just work. Then I could return to the strategy of avoiding her. Otherwise I'll return to America. And Juliet will comfort him. Jesus. Juliet will be jumping with joy the moment I step foot on the plane.

"Oh, poor Jimmy, this is so awful. I hope I didn't play any part in it."

Fuck off, Juliet. Fuck off and die.

She must have fallen asleep for a while because when she woke up there was a shard of sun that had pierced the not-fully-closed curtains and hit her eyes. It was seven in the morning. However many hours of sleep she'd gotten hadn't managed to help. Going over to the curtains, she opened them up and saw Juliet gliding across the back lawn in long overalls with big pockets, carrying a fishing rod and a big straw basket. Juliet was going fishing—those overalls were waders. Her hair was in a ponytail again.

It was seeing that fucking ponytail again that did it. Nicola didn't hesitate. She didn't give a shit that she had on only a pair of wool pajamas; she didn't care that this was probably the worst thing she could do. She ran through the house and out the back door, not even bothering to grab a coat. Catching sight of Juliet's back disappearing, she followed her all the way to the river, and watched as Juliet put down the basket and waded into the river, up to her knees, rod in hand.

For one tiny moment, she stood still, taking in the sight of this woman, her nemesis, standing calmly, drawing her rod back, taking a cast.

"You think you can get away with it, don't you?" She was on the edge of the river now, a few feet away. Juliet turned quickly, almost losing her balance.

"Nic." She shielded her eyes from the sun. "Good morning. Oh, look. You're in your pj's. How fetching."

"You're not going to get away with it, you know. I know everything. I saw you kiss Hugo. I know you arranged that meeting with James on purpose. Everything you do is on purpose. To make people miserable. All that bullshit about not having designs on James was just that—total bullshit. You have designs on him because Trez got pregnant and you couldn't have Hugo. I know what you're doing, Juliet. And I'm not going to let you get away with it."

"Wow. You're really worked up, aren't you? Did you have a fight with Jimmy last night?"

"You're evil, you know that?"

"I have no clue what you're talking about. I think you have problems, Nic. You should see someone." Juliet turned, tossed another cast into the air.

"I'm seeing someone right now." She stepped forward,

into the water. "I'm seeing a narcissist who doesn't care about anyone but herself. Who ruins people's lives. Who is devious and manipulative. Turn around and face me, Juliet."

"I'm fishing."

"Turn around and fucking face me!" She was yelling. Her feet were freezing in the cold river, her whole body shaking.

"Nicola." Juliet turned. "I'm not hurting anyone. You're hurting yourself by being so insecure and jealous and defensive. You've—"

"I know you shot that beater. I know you blamed Trez when you were the one who shot him."

"As I was about to say, you've made up your own story, just as you did at dinner on Friday. You're showing your true colors. And they aren't attractive colors. Now leave me in peace. Unless you want me to tell Jimmy how hysterical you're being."

"As if you wouldn't anyway. And you're the one who hates the word 'hysterical.'"

"If the shoe fits, sweetheart."

"Fuck off. And stay away from us. Just stay the fuck away. Oh, okay. Go ahead. That's right, turn your back to me again. But I swear to God you won't win, Juliet. I won't let you get away with this shit anymore."

She turned then, retraced her steps. Her feet and wet legs were so cold they were numb, but her body was on fire, full of rage and frustration. She should never have gone to the river. She should never have confronted her. All reason, all logical, strategic thinking had vanished, replaced by heedless fury.

When she got back to the lodge, she went straight up to the room. James raised his head from the pillow, looked at her, and frowned.

"Your pajama bottoms are soaking. What's going on?"

"Nothing. It's early. Go back to sleep."

"Nic?" He sat up. "What time is it?"

"Time for me to get changed." She threw off her pj's, went into the bathroom, ran a bath. "I'm taking a bath now."

"You slept somewhere else, didn't you?"

"Yes, downstairs. I was tossing and turning and didn't want to wake you up."

"Why are your pj's wet?"

"I'll tell you later. Actually, I was hoping . . ." She came back to the threshold of the bedroom. "I was hoping we could go back after breakfast. I think we can work everything out back in London."

"You're right." He swung his legs over the side of the bed, yawned. "We need to get back. We need to sit down and thrash all this out in peace on our own."

"We will thrash things out." She smiled a real smile. "Thank you, James."

"You don't have to thank me. Listen, we'll have a good Scottish breakfast and then get out of here."

Seeing him again had calmed her down. If Juliet managed to get him aside before they left, then Nicola knew she'd just have to deal with it when they were back in London. The atmosphere would be different: they'd be by themselves and have time to talk quietly.

And yelling at Juliet might have been a mistake, but it had also been strangely therapeutic: at least she'd stood up to her; she hadn't taken her shit the way she had since the first moment Juliet had appeared.

She decided to wash her hair in the bath, clean herself totally and look as well as she could on so little sleep when they went down to breakfast.

* * *

WHEN THEY GOT to the dining room, she was pleased to see that Juliet wasn't there. Still fishing, no doubt. She would want to catch some amazing fish to bring back to show them all.

Nigel, Bella, and Badger were sitting discussing whether Scottish people did, in fact, hate English people or whether that notion was exaggerated.

"Believe me, they loathe us," Nigel was saying. "Hi, you two. Come sit down and join in the discussion. At least I think they do when I can understand what they're saying. Scottish accents are beyond me."

Trez walked in then, looking flushed. She sat down at the head of the table, dressed in blue-jean overalls with a frilly white shirt underneath.

"What do you think, Trez?" Nigel asked. "Do the Scottish really hate the English?"

"I have no clue," she stated, then looked around the table. "Where's Juliet?"

"She must still be fishing," Badger replied. "Remember she said she was going out this morning on her own?"

"Yes, of course." Trez nodded. "Well, no one has to wait for her. Or for Hugo. We should all have a good breakfast."

As she said it, Hugo strode in, took a chair beside Trez.

"Just what's needed. The perfect breakfast—eggs, bacon, toast, sausages, mushrooms, tomatoes, blood pudding. I can't wait." He rubbed his hands together. "Offal. I love offal."

"I'm not saying a word." Bella rolled her eyes.

"It's too easy a joke to make, isn't it? Even for me. Awful offal."

"It's too easy, but you made it anyway." Bella nudged Nigel in the ribs. "I hope to God you don't start spouting limericks too."

"There was a young man from Dundee, who—"

"Nigel! Stop!" Bella covered her ears. "Not in the morning. Please?"

"Okay."

"Where's Juliet?"

"She's fishing, Hugo." Nicola noticed how flat Trez's voice was.

Meanwhile, she was preparing herself for the inevitable:

Juliet waltzing in from her fishing with some huge catch, then telling the story of how Nicola had confronted her—Nicola in her pajamas.

She'll figure out a way to make it seem she's not pissed off at me. But she'll bring it up somehow. And I'll have to say I was just kidding. Or I was sleepwalking. Who the hell knows? But I might get away with it still—she might stay out fishing until we leave.

Sure. I'd never get that lucky.

It was easier to have normal conversations when Juliet wasn't around. They ate their breakfasts. Badger had recovered from Juliet's rejection enough to throw in a few random facts about Scotland; Nigel told a few more bad jokes; Hugo began to talk about how the run-up to Christmas was getting longer and longer and how much he hated certain Christmas carols.

"'Jingle Bells' drives me crazy. The repetition is mind-numbing."

"Children love it." Trez was sitting with her arms curled around her stomach. "Don't be a Scrooge, Hugo. Besides, I know you love 'Rudolph the Red-Nosed Reindeer.' So how can you really object to 'Jingle Bells'?"

"It's 'White Christmas' that gives me the hump. But only because how often do we get that white Christmas we're dreaming of in this country?"

"You should come to Buffalo, Bella. You'll get more snow than you've ever dreamed of there. And then it turns to sludge and icy mush, and it's a nightmare."

The sound of the telephone ringing stopped the conversation.

"Wrong number, I'm sure, but I'll get it." Hugo rose, headed out.

"Where's the phone in this lodge, anyway?" Nigel asked.

"On the desk in the study."

"Right—of course you know that, Badger."

The maid came in with a coffee pot in one hand and a teapot in the other.

"Would anyone like more?" she asked. The pretty young Scottish girl with that distinctive Scottish accent Nigel had been talking about.

"Yes, I'd love some coffee, please." Nicola wanted the breakfast to be over so they could go, but she also desperately needed another hit of caffeine. The girl poured the coffee and left the room.

"I don't . . ." Hugo was standing at the doorway. He looked as if he were about to keel over and reached out to the wall to steady himself.

"Hugo? What's wrong?" Trez rushed up to him.

"It's Juliet."

"What? We can't hear you, Hugo."

"It's Juliet. She's . . . I can't. I can't. She's dead." He sunk down onto his knees. "Oh my God, Juliet's dead."

"Don't be silly." Trez was yelling at him. "Of course she's not dead. What are you talking about? Get up, Hugo. Get off the floor. This is absurd. It's not funny." She tried to pull him up, but he shook her off, got up by himself, and staggered over to the table.

"That was Stewart on the phone." He sat down. "She drowned. In the river. She must have fallen in the river fishing. He was fishing down the river from her, and her body—I can't. I can't." Putting his head into his hands, he started to sob, his shoulders heaving.

"Juliet fell? Into the river? I don't believe it." Badger thumped the table with his fist. "Juliet wouldn't fall."

"Well, no one pushed her, Badger." Nigel said it quietly.

"Oh no, James. I'm so sorry." Nicola reached out, took his hand in hers. "This is terrible. I can't believe it."

They were all silent for what seemed like ages.

"Wait," Badger spoke up. "Wait one minute. What were you doing this morning, Nicola? I saw you. Why were you coming back from the direction of the river in your pajamas so early?"

"Nicola?" Trez had come back to the table and was staring at her. "You went out early this morning?"

"Yes, very early." Badger thumped the table again. "I saw you from my bedroom window. You looked like you were coming back from the river, Nicola."

"Is that why your pajamas were wet?" James turned to face her, took his hand away from her grip. "I don't understand. Did you go to the river?"

"Yes, I went to the river. I had an argument with Juliet. But that's all it was. An argument. She was fishing when I left."

"What kind of argument?" Hugo suddenly straightened, stared at her with his tear-filled eyes. "What kind of argument, Nicola?"

"I told her I wanted her to stay away from James and me. That's all. It really wasn't an argument. I said some things; she didn't pay any attention. Then she went back to fishing. That's all that happened."

"But you waded into the water—James just asked why your pajamas were wet. if your pajamas were wet, you must have gone into the river. Why?"

"I don't know, Hugo. I was angry, and she wasn't listening to me, and I took some steps closer to her to try to get her to talk to me."

"How close? How close did you get?" Badger asked.

He and Hugo were like two detectives, taking turns grilling her.

They thought she'd pushed Juliet. Badger and Hugo thought she'd pushed Juliet into the river.

"I didn't get close enough to touch her. Really. I swear. You can't think—"

"You must have been *really* angry to walk into the river barefoot in December."

"Badger, you can't think—I didn't . . . God . . . what's happening? This is . . ."

"So angry you pushed her."

"Hugo—stop it right now! Nic didn't do anything." It was Nigel. Nigel was coming to her rescue.

"Of course she didn't," Bella said. "This is ridiculous."

James didn't say anything. Not one word.

She replayed her time at the river, every second of it. She hadn't pushed her. She hadn't touched her. Juliet was standing with her back to her, casting, when Nicola had turned and walked back.

The fact that Juliet was dead hadn't really sunk in. It was horrendous and crazy, awful. And unreal. She half expected Juliet to walk in and say, "Fooled you!" to everyone.

But even if she did—even if she showed up now and everyone rushed over to her hug her, it didn't change the fact that Badger and Hugo were still staring at her as if she were a murderer and James was sitting there, silent.

"Look, let's be rational about this." Nigel took a deep breath. "Think about it. Juliet must have been wearing those waders, the ones that cover your whole body. She must have tripped or lost her footing and those waders fill up fast with water and then she started to sink, and Juliet was never a good swimmer. Even if she had been, the current in the Spey is really strong. It was an accident, a terrible accident. Blaming anyone—that's insane, frankly. We should be thinking about what we should do. What else did Stewart say, Hugo? Are we supposed to go to the police station or . . . I don't know, the hospital? What are we supposed to do now?"

"She can't be dead." Trez rose from her chair, sat back down. "Jules is *not* dead. It's impossible. Stop talking as if she were. All of you."

"You hate her so much" was what James said when he

finally spoke. "Why do you hate her so much, Nic? You told Bella you wanted her to die a horrible death. I heard you. And you made up all these crazy theories about her. I begged you to leave it alone until we got back. Why did you go to the river? Why?"

"I don't know." She hung her head.

Nothing could stop her tears. Nothing could help her now. James, the love of her life, the man she wanted to spend the rest of her life with, the man she trusted, the man who wasn't supposed to have a bad bone in his body, thought she had pushed Juliet into the river and watched her drown?

This wonderful, fun, funny man who did all the right things and made her so incredibly happy thought she was capable of doing that?

Raising her head and looking at him with all the love she had in her, she asked: "Do you think I pushed her? Do you?"

"I think you hated her, Nic. I think you imagined things. God, I don't know what I think. I *can't* think."

"I'm sorry to interrupt." All eyes swiveled to the new voice. It was Stewart, standing at the threshold, holding his cap in his hand. "I thought I should tell you what's going on. I've just come from the hospital."

"She's not dead."

"Mrs. Langley, I'm afraid she is. She drowned. It was a very sad accident."

"*If* it was an accident." Hugo snorted. "Nicola here had

a row with Juliet at the river this morning. The question is just how bad that row was."

"Excuse me?" Stewart looked confused.

"Nicola had a fight with Juliet this morning. At the river." Badger's voice was full of rage. "She waded into the river to fight with her. Even James thinks she pushed her."

"You don't believe . . . ?" Stewart took a step back, looked at Badger, then at Hugo, then at James. "You couldn't possibly think . . . ?" He switched his gaze and locked eyes with hers before turning back to Hugo. "I should tell you, then, Mr. Langley. I was at the river when Nicola was there. I was about thirty yards away, fishing myself. I was hidden around the bend, but I heard voices. I walked closer and saw Nicola there. I also saw her leave. When she left, Juliet continued fishing. I wasn't catching anything, so I packed up and went farther downstream—a long way farther. I suppose it must have been around a half hour later, I saw a body float by. I followed it and saw it get snagged in the weeds on the side. That's when I pulled her out. That's when I found her and called the ambulance and then called you. Nicola didn't go anywhere near her."

"Right. You better bloody apologize, Hugo—and Badger." Nigel stood up. "You better fucking bloody apologize to Nic, you assholes."

"I'm sorry." Badger said it first. "I don't know what got into me—I saw you coming back from . . . oh God, Nicola, I'm sorry."

"Hugo?" Nigel pressed.

"I'm sorry too, obviously. It's a very difficult time. I'm not thinking clearly. I apologize, Nicola."

"Thank you, Stewart." It was all she could say.

"Nic . . ." James reached out. She let him hold her limp, lifeless hand. "I'm so sorry. I should have . . . I must be in shock."

It was her turn to remain silent.

"What do we do now, Stewart?" Nigel was in control. Nigel was taking charge.

"I'm not sure what the protocol is when an accident like this happens. You'll have to inform her family—that's the first thing, obviously."

"Trez?" Bella sounded panicked. "She's fainting. Help her, Hugo. Jesus."

Trez had collapsed, slid off her chair, and fallen to the floor.

Hugo didn't move—it was Stewart who got to Trez, picked her up in his arms, and carried her out of the room, saying, "Someone get me water."

"I'll get it." Bella went to find water. The rest of them left the table and followed Stewart into the living room, where he had placed Trez on the sofa, sitting so that her head was down facing her knees.

"She's all right. Just give her some air—and thank you," he told Bella when she came in and handed him the water. "I'm sure this is a shock for all of you."

"I'm all right." Trez lifted her head. "I need to go up to bed, that's all. I need to lie down—by myself."

"Nic, come upstairs—we need to talk." James was at her side.

There was nothing to talk about.

She'd counted to thirty-one, but the plane had still crashed.

Chapter Thirty-Eight

TREZ

Juliet was dead. Juliet was actually dead. Trez, lying on her bed, closed her eyes and crossed her hands over her chest.

Juliet was dead.

I fainted.

Stewart picked me up when I fainted. Not Hugo.

Hugo.

Hugo. My husband. Who was lying beside me sleeping peacefully a few hours ago. A few hours that feel like a century. The world was a different world then. I was a different person.

She'd known, when she'd woken up that morning, those few hours ago, that she wouldn't be able to get back to sleep. She was feeling a lot better than she had in a long time, but she was still restless. Either she stayed in bed or got up; maybe she'd find a little snack in the kitchen. It would be quite nice to take a wander around the lodge on her own.

Managing not to wake Hugo up, she got dressed and headed down the stairs. The sun was just waking up too, she thought as she walked. We're waking up together. On the way to the kitchen, she looked down the corridor to the study, where Hugo had been sitting the night before. She smiled, thinking of him so studiously bent over the desk. That was the image that had comforted her, had brightened her mood.

Instead of going on to the kitchen, she turned and went into the study, switched on the lamp on the desk, sat herself down in the big leather armchair.

You should have run a company, Trez.

In another life. She could see herself sitting at a big desk like this, organizing things. Obviously, she had no idea what things she'd be organizing in what kind of company, but if she had gone to university or gone on working, even at temp-type jobs, typing, she might have risen through the ranks.

She opened the drawer to her right and found a ballpoint pen. Then she opened the drawer to her left and saw a piece of paper with Hugo's atrocious handwriting covering it. That must have been what he'd been working on last night. Usually he made more of an effort with penmanship when he was writing a business letter. She pulled out the paper and saw another page underneath, so pulled that out too, and started to read the first page.

You know that was the best time in my life. You know how I feel about you. I've never had that passion before. I've never made love like that before. I never thought I would make love like that. I never believed I could write a letter like this. I need to tell you. I can't express myself well, but I need to try. You've always been the most exciting person in the universe. You know that, Jules. You know everything.

She put the paper down. She picked it back up.

We can't go on. I understand. I have my duties now. I have a child on the way. But I can't bear it, really—I can't. I've loved you so passionately for so long and I never thought you'd feel that way about me. Never. We had those weeks, and it was bliss. Sheer bliss. Unforgettable. Magnificent.

I needed to say it to you. On paper. That makes it real. We'll go on as if it never happened. You're better at that than I am. You're better at everything.

Are you sure? Are you absolutely certain? People divorce all the time. It wouldn't be that much of a scandal, would it? I don't think you're right. We wouldn't be shunned. Couldn't it all be, in your funny way of saying things, tickety-boo?

What am I saying? It's over.

She put the first piece of paper down carefully. Picked up the second page.

But know this, Jules. You are the light of my life. Don't

go away again. Stay around so at least I'll be in your presence. I can smell your scent, hear your voice. Look at your amazing face. And remember.

I'll be good. I promise. You probably can't read this terrible handwriting anyway, but if you can, know this: you are my one true love.

She put the second piece down, as carefully as she had the first. And felt her whole world rise up in a tidal wave and wash over her. She put the papers back in the drawer.

Juliet.

Juliet and Hugo.

This wasn't a joke. This wasn't a game.

She opened the drawer again, took the pages out, reread them.

I have my duties now.

Sheer bliss. Unforgettable. Magnificent.

My one true love.

She sat.

Juliet and Hugo.

We had those weeks.

What weeks?

What weeks?

She sat and she put the pieces of the jigsaw together. One by one. Slowly. Very slowly, each piece slotted in: from the moment Juliet had come back to Langley Hall, to this, this—this heinous letter. Forming the picture of complete, utter betrayal.

She put the letter back in the drawer, shut it quietly.

Juliet and Hugo.

Hugo and Juliet.

Sheer bliss.

Light of my life.

Passionate, desperate Hugo.

In bed with Juliet. Making love as he never had before.

How was that, then? What did that mean? How different had he been with Juliet? What did that *mean*?

Had they had sex in Langley Hall?

What difference did that make? They'd had sex somewhere.

Juliet had slept with Hugo.

Hugo had slept with Juliet.

People divorce all the time.

Do they, Hugo? Do they divorce and marry their wife's best friend?

The friend that wife admired so much, was so entranced by? Told everything to?

Trusted?

It would have never even occurred to me. Not for one second.

Just how many lies has she told? Without a care in the world?

How stupid she must think I am. Dumb, dumb, dumb.

Bumbling little Trez, so easy to deceive.

Where are you, Jules?

You're fishing. That's right. You're fishing.

She walked out of the room, into the back hallway and

out the door. Then turned back. She was barefoot. She went back in, picked up a pair of green wellies from the pairs lined up on the floor, went out again.

It was a straight walk to the river. There were no sheep on the road. There was no Badger beside her, professing his undying love. For Juliet.

Juliet.

Who was standing in the river, cool as a cucumber, fishing. Just as Trez had known she would be.

"Did you want the title, is that it?"

"What?" Juliet turned around. "Trez, sweetheart. That's so nice you've come to see me. I'm getting lots of visitors."

"I said: Did you want the title? Or did you want to humiliate me? Or both?"

"Wait a second. I can't hear you properly." Juliet waded to the bank of the river, leaned over, and laid her rod on the grass. "Right, sorry. What did you say?"

"I didn't say. I asked if you wanted the title or if you wanted to humiliate me. Or both? Don't try to deny your affair with my husband. I just read a letter he wrote to you."

"Oh, shit. I didn't want you to find out." She took a step toward her.

"Keep away from me. Stay where you are."

"It didn't mean anything, Trez. Really."

"Oh, really? It didn't? Then why do it? Why?"

"I don't know. It happened, that's all. It was a silly fling. Hugo, well, Hugo was a little besotted in a schoolboy-crush kind of way. It was meaningless. We didn't mean for you to find out. I didn't mean to hurt you."

"Like you didn't mean to kick the dog."

"What? Trez—"

"I've worked it out. You think I'm stupid, but I'm not. I've worked it out. You thought I wouldn't be able to get pregnant. Because of what I said that first night. You thought you could entrance him and he'd leave me and you could get married and have the heir to the title. Were you going to kick me out of Langley Hall?"

"Don't be silly."

"Yes, you were, weren't you? You would have worked out a way to make it seem as if I were crazy or incapable in some way. Everyone would understand then why Hugo would have to get rid of me. You wouldn't have been . . . You wouldn't have been shunned. But a pregnant Trez? That was something altogether different, wasn't it? A lot harder to get rid of me comfortably then."

"You're bonkers right now."

"Drop it, Jules. I know. I *know*. You should read Hugo's letter. It's full of love and passion."

"How many times do I have to say this? It was a stupid fling."

"And then you switched your attentions to James. He was the next best for you. But that was such a quick turn-around, Jules. One second Hugo, the next second James. Why did you have to . . . oh . . . hang on . . ."

"Trez, just shut the fuck up, will you? You're not doing

yourself any favors."

"You had to be so quick because something happened in Hong Kong, didn't it? Something that people could gossip about and that gossip would get back here and then you'd be in trouble, wouldn't you? What happened in Hong Kong? You should answer me now, because I'll find out—you know that."

Juliet took a step toward her.

"You want to know what happened in Hong Kong? I wanted adventure. I got it. I had a boyfriend, someone who loved adventure too. He took me to visit an old Chinese man. The old Chinese man was an opium smoker. When in Rome, right?"

"You went to an opium den?"

"No. There weren't opium dens. We were in his flat. I tried it. I loved it. No, I adored it. I went back. On my own. A lot. I could tell you about triads, Trez, but I don't want to infect that innocent little mind of yours. Suffice it to say I was socializing with the wrong people. My boyfriend thought I'd gone too far. I think he must have said something to someone in his bank. In any case, someone got a whiff of it. And I had to leave. So you see, that story about too many junks was half-true. 'Junk' being the operative word."

"You were an opium addict?"

"No. I wasn't. But I might have become one. I was in trouble on a lot of fronts. I pissed some people off I shouldn't have. Simple as that." She reached back, took her hair out of the ponytail, shook it so it flew.

"Jesus. Opium? Triads? Jesus."

"Well, I was looking for adventure. I found it. It wasn't secretarial school, that's for sure. I came back with empty cargo, Trez. And I came back broke."

"Broke? Oh, Christ. Your parents lost all their money, didn't they? That's another lie you told me."

"Yes."

"So you needed a husband, a rich one. But why not someone else? Not Hugo, not James. You had Badger. But he isn't rich enough for you, is he? And you didn't have time to find someone else. Because you knew the gossip would spread. You knew you had to act quickly, get a ring on your finger before the truth came out."

"The truth? You want the real truth? You can have it."

Juliet looked ugly. How had she managed to hide such ugliness?

"I come back and I walk into Langley Hall and there you are, Queen Bee. About to be a countess. The little person who used to be my shadow. Who has no idea of how to be a countess, or anything except a vaguely proficient touch typist. And then I see Nicola, a common little American girl, and Bella, a common-as-muck English girl, and the three of you are sipping champagne and leading the life I should be leading. Fuck you all. Really. All of you. Huge and Jimmy, Nigel, Badger all went to Cambridge, to one of the best universities in the world, and honestly, they don't have a brain among the four of them. But they have the power, the money, the titles. And they'll all marry little drips—except Badger, who will never get married—and it's not *right*, sweetheart. Much as I love you, you really don't deserve a title and all that cash."

"And you do?"

"You bet I do. I'm more intelligent, more capable than all of you. I wasn't given a chance. But I have a chance now, and you're not going to ruin it, are you? Nicola's so jealous she can hardly speak. Jimmy can't stand that. Like I said, there's trouble in paradise. He'll come back to me— very soon. I'm not worried in the slightest about that. And you'll be fine, after all. You have the baby, the title. Huge. You can pretend none of this has happened, easily. You have to. If you confront Hugo about this, your life will change. If you don't, it will go on as is and all will be fine. Think of your baby, Trez. You want your baby to be happy, don't you?"

"So I say nothing to Hugo, I go on as if nothing has happened, I let you trick James into marrying you, and there will be world peace, and joy will abound?"

"That's about right. If you skip the world peace bit. We can still be friends. We're English, remember? We don't need to psychoanalyze everything and be up front and open and discuss all our feelings. We know that's bullshit."

"I see. You get involved in drugs and gangs in Hong Kong, and you come back here and try to ruin all our lives. What right do you have to be so bitter and cruel?"

"What right do I have? What right do *you* have? You

got lucky. You picked a bumbling oaf of a man to marry, and his uncle decides he's not even going to pretend he wants to get married and have a child. Now you're sashaying around a fucking mansion wearing ridiculous clothes and smugly patting your stomach."

Juliet was staring straight at her, delivering blow after blow—with relish.

"Oh my God, you're enjoying this. You hate me. You hate me with a passion. Because you always thought you'd do better than I did? You can't stand to see me happier than you? That's why you invited me to come to Sale e Pepe that night with Hugo. You wanted to sit there and gloat, didn't you?"

"Remember that bracelet I was wearing ? Hugo gave it to me."

The gold bracelet with the rubies. Hugo had never given her anything as beautiful as that bracelet, not even close.

She'd believed there had been a real mouse, she'd knocked over the glass of wine—had they laughed about that afterward? *Oh, Trez, she's so naïve and uncoordinated. How could you have ever married her, Hugo?*

"Sorry, Trez. I thought you should know. But it doesn't make any difference, don't you see? You go back to Hugo, I marry Jimmy, you have your sprogs, and one of them will be a boy, I'm sure. We'll all live happily ever after. No harm done, not really."

"No harm done? You've destroyed everything. No harm done?"

"Oh, for Christ's sake, don't stand there looking so wounded. Poor little Trez. My little treasure. I discovered you, remember. You looked so hopeless and helpless that first day. Now you're looking like a hopeless, helpless victim. That's another reason you shouldn't be a countess. You have no fucking backbone. Belt up, Trez. Belt the fuck up." Juliet picked up the rod, went right back to the spot she'd been fishing in, pulled her rod back to cast.

She went for her. She waded into the river and went up to that woman standing there with the haughty, cruel eyes, and she pushed her. Hard. She saw her fall, she saw the water splash, and she turned. Walked away. Heard her name being called out. "Trez!"

But it wasn't her name, not anymore. She wasn't Trez, and she wasn't going to answer to it. She was going to keep walking away. She was going to go back to the lodge and take off her boots and go into the kitchen and get a cup of coffee and get ready for breakfast.

She'd killed her. That one push had killed Juliet.

I didn't mean to. I pushed her, that's all. I didn't mean to kill her.

Yes, I did.

Juliet had cried out to her again. "Trez! Help!" She'd kept walking.

Because I wanted her dead.

I knew she wasn't the best of swimmers. Nigel was right: Juliet never suggested swimming in the old days—she'd go in the ocean or the pool, but she wasn't comfort-

able in either.

I heard her cry out for help, and I kept walking.

I wanted her dead.

But I didn't think she would die. Juliet? Juliet found a way around everything. Juliet could talk herself out of any problem—Christ, she'd figured out a way to graduate that secretarial school despite being god-awful at typing and shorthand. Juliet could fix anything, do anything.

Except rescue herself from a river.

I wanted to kill her.

And I'd do it again.

All that bullshit about not having been given a chance. Total, utter crap. She was supposed to go on to Hong Kong and have adventures and find some amazing career—all she'd done was what? Smoke opium. Then come back and seduce Hugo.

I'd do it again.

I didn't think she'd actually die, but I'm glad she did.

That cliché—the scales falling from your eyes—it's more as if I had been living my life with half a brain until I read that letter, and when I read it, the other half revealed itself. The other half that will never be taken for a fool again.

Everyone thinks it was an accident. No one is blaming Nicola anymore. She must have been down at the river awhile before I got there. That's why Juliet said she'd had visitors.

And Stewart? He'd seen Nicola, but not me. He'd gone by then, farther down the river.

I can be brave and indomitable. As long as I do what Juliet told me to do and keep my mouth shut.

Absolutely, Jules. I'll do that. Just like I used to do anything you said.

We will all mourn her. Hugo will be weeping buckets. Badger will convince himself she would have changed her mind and they could have had a future together.

The world will weep.

And then we'll get on with our lives.

We'll all live happily ever after.

No harm done, really.

"Trez! Help!" That second, final, call of hers had sounded so desperate.

But she wasn't Juliet's little treasure. Not anymore.

She was Jane.

Chapter Thirty-Nine

NICOLA

They'd all dispersed. Trez was up in her room, recuperating after her fainting fit. Badger had announced he was going to go to the hospital to find Juliet, to be with her. Hugo said he'd drive Badger there. Bella and Nigel had gone out for a walk together.

James and she were in their bedroom, sitting on the two chairs by the little round table. James had found some glasses and poured them both water.

"I don't know what to say, Nic. I didn't think you'd hurt Juliet, but I knew how much you disliked her, and I knew you thought she was trying to break us up, and you didn't say anything about seeing her when you came back in your pajamas—and they *were* wet. I know it's inexcusable that I didn't . . . It's all inexcusable."

She was twisting the engagement ring around her finger.

She was looking at his pleading eyes.

"Can you forgive me?"

"I think . . ." she started, then stopped, trying to keep her voice calm, trying to control her feelings. "I don't know what hurts the most—you basically accusing me of killing Juliet, or the fact that Nigel—Nigel, of all people—stood up for me and you didn't. I didn't think he even liked me much. You're supposed to love me, James. Remember? You're supposed to be my bulwark. Nigel and Bella supported me, and you sat there."

"I know. But I was in shock."

"So was I. But that shouldn't have . . . I don't see how you could have thought . . ."

"I wasn't thinking. I was remembering how upset you were with her and . . . There's no excuse. I know that."

He put his head in his hands.

"You still think I was imagining Juliet was trying to break us up, don't you?"

"I don't think . . ." He shook his head. "It's not relevant anymore, is it?"

"It is to me. You don't believe me. You don't trust me. You think I could drown someone, for Christ's sake." Her voice rose. "Remember how we joked about you murdering me? Not so funny anymore. Because you *have* killed me, James. You killed me down in that dining room. You killed us."

"It doesn't have to be that way." Raising his head, he looked at her with those pleading eyes. "We need to go back to London. We need to spend time together alone. I swear to God I'll find a way to make up for what I've done. I will."

They sat silently. Part of her wanted to reach out for him, but she couldn't bring herself to do it.

"Nic? Please?"

"We'll go back, but I'm going to ask Bella if I can stay at her place for a few days. I need to spend some time away from you, James. Right now I can't even begin to think straight."

"Okay. But please don't forget what we had, Nic. What we *have*, and what we can have in the future. We have so much going for us. I'll never do anything like that again. I'll never let you down. I promise. Don't abandon me—don't abandon *us*. Please?"

Don't abandon me.

Those three words that had meant so much in France.

James was crying. She was crying.

Is this a story about something horrible happening to me?

Yes, Nic. Yes, it is.

Chapter Forty

TREZ

"Mrs. Langley? I need to speak to you."

She was sitting in the library, in one of the comfy armchairs, glad to be back home in Langley Hall, pleased too to be alone. Avoiding Hugo was a priority at the moment: she couldn't stand to see his hounded eyes, his all-too-obvious misery. With time, he'd buck up and she'd be better at being in the same room with him. She'd never feel the same way about him, but she was now adept at pretending she didn't know anything, even more adept at hiding her feelings and continuing on with "normal" life. She had to—for the baby's sake.

Stewart breaching her privacy like this was a shock.

"Stewart, I'm sorry, but I'd prefer to be alone. Can you come back another—"

"Now's the best time."

He walked over to the armchair facing hers, sat down. Without asking.

"I'm sorry, Stewart. I haven't thanked you for helping me when I fainted that terrible day, have I?"

"No, you haven't."

"Well, thank you. Very much."

"You're welcome. Now you can do something for me."

"Of course. What can I help you with?"

"It's a simple request. I'll tell you what I want in a minute or two. You know, I saw you." He put his elbows on the table, rested his chin on top of his hands. "I saw you push her. I saw her get swept away. I tried to rescue her myself, but it was too late. The current was too strong. She was already gone."

"Wait—what are you saying?"

"I'm saying that I saw you push Juliet in the river and walk away."

Her eyes went immediately to the threshold—was anyone standing outside? Could anyone hear?

"Don't be concerned. We're alone here."

"I didn't mean to, Stewart—you have to believe me, I . . ."

"I'm sure you *did* mean to. But whether you did or didn't isn't really the point, is it? You pushed her. She fell. You left here there struggling. She drowned." He shrugged.

"But you didn't say anything before. You haven't told anyone this. Or have you?"

"I have not."

"Why not? I don't understand."

"I told you. I want you to do something for me."

"Do you want money—is that what it is?"

"Oh, please." He shook his head, looked up to the ceiling, sighed. "You're all the same. You're all so smug. And irritating."

"You seem to be blackmailing me in some way. I don't think you can take the moral high ground."

"You've grown up since killing your best friend, haven't you?" He looked straight at her. "I believe I can take the moral high ground. I haven't pushed someone into a fast-flowing river and not responded to her cries for help, have I?"

Her head dropped, she couldn't look at him.

"Before you think a little more clearly and tell me that if I say something now I won't be believed because I didn't say anything before, I think I should inform you that I didn't want to get my employer, the honorable Hugo Langley, and his very honorable wife in trouble. After all, think of all they have given me, me—the hired help—over these past three years, how generous and thoughtful they have been—but my conscience caught up with me. I couldn't live with the secret. That's an entirely believable explanation for not saying anything before."

"Jesus." She raised her head. "You loathe us, don't you? Why? I thought we'd treated you properly. We—"

"You know, your sort like to hunt stags. Back where we were, in Scotland, I've taken men stag hunting. All part of the job."

"Stewart—"

"It's not easy, stag hunting. It requires a lot more than grouse or pheasant or snipe shooting. You often have to crawl on your belly to approach a stag—and you have to crawl silently, sometimes for hours, in the rain, in the cold, in the mud. On your stomach. Slithering along like a giant snake. For hours. To get to the place where you see that stag standing. Where you stop crawling, get out your gun, take aim and shoot the stag. The poor stag, who is standing there, unaware. Minding his own business. Often you are looking them straight in the eyes when you shoot them. Other times, well—you crawl for hours and hours and no stag shows up. It takes skill to find a stag, yes, but it involves luck as well."

"I have no idea why you're telling me this."

"As I said, I have a simple request."

"Which is?"

He told her what he wanted, then added: "It's not much to ask given the circumstances, *Trez*."

"My name is Jane."

"Will you do it, Jane? Or will I have to clear my conscience?"

She sat back, unsure what to say—for approximately two seconds.

"I'll do it. But I want you to leave right now."

"Funny, I want to leave right now as well. We'll be in touch, obviously. You know . . ." He stood up, moved to the door, stopped just before opening it. "You may all be rich and entitled, but my God, you are such foolish, foolish people."

Chapter Forty-One

NICOLA

Nicola was sitting in Bella's apartment, watching TV. The program was called *Grange Hill* and took place in a school. She wished she could concentrate, lose herself in the characters and story line, stop thinking about her own life and the seemingly impossible situation she was in.

She'd been here two days now, and she still didn't know what she was going to do. Bella had been sweet and kind and had done her best to convince her to stay.

"James loves you, Nic. And look, Juliet was his first love, so her dying like that—well, it was bound to fuck him up, right? I understand how it's tough for you, but he's a good bloke, really. Look at all these bloody flowers he's sent."

The apartment was full of them. Bunches of tulips and a mixture of flowers she didn't even know the names of. Her parents would have. They might be delinquent at times, but they were good at their jobs.

He'd telephoned too—a lot. But she didn't want to talk to him—not yet. She had to get her head straight first.

Bella was right—Juliet had been James's first big love, Nicola understood that. Yet the fact was he'd chosen Juliet—every time it came to a crunch, he'd taken Juliet's side—or rather, he hadn't taken *her* side. He'd said she was imagining things, he'd said she was paranoid, and not only that, he hadn't said what he should have said. What Nigel had said.

"Of course Nicola didn't do anything."

If James had said that, then she'd be with him now.

Bella had commented about Juliet haunting her, being like Rebecca in that movie—except Juliet wasn't dead. Now she was dead. And Nicola felt she was haunting her from the grave and might just haunt her forever.

There would be her funeral, for starters. Then times at Langley Hall, times with Badger, hanging out with people who had accused her of murder, for Christ's sake. James couldn't ditch all his old friends for her, and if he did, well, he'd be miserable, wouldn't he? They were friends from childhood. Making him give them up wasn't good for a relationship.

The thought of seeing Badger and Hugo again was horrible. Trez—well, she was different. She'd been calling Bella daily, checking in.

"Trez is worried about you, Nic. She wants to make sure you're all right. She keeps asking me all these questions about how you are and what you're doing. She really cares."

"Trez is the salt of the earth," James had said on that first plane trip. It turned out he was right about her—Nicola hadn't expected that she'd be so concerned. She thought Trez would have been completely overwhelmed by Juliet's death.

But everything was tainted by Juliet; thinking about Trez only made her think again about Juliet. There was no getting away from Juliet. Omnipresent, omnipotent Juliet.

When the doorbell rang, she knew who it was before she heard his voice calling out her name. She knew too that she didn't have the energy—or the heart—to turn him away.

"Nic," he said when he came in. "Thank you. I wasn't sure you'd see me."

"I can't hide from you forever." She moved from the door, and he followed her into the tiny sitting room. Switching off the TV, she asked him if he wanted anything to drink.

"About five whiskeys, but no, no thanks."

"I don't know what to say, James."

"But I do." They were facing each other in the middle of the room, about three feet apart.

"I want to move to the States, Nic. With you. Start a new life there. A whole new life. We can do that, can't we? You wouldn't have to see anyone you didn't want to see. We'll make new friends, we'll have adventures, we'll get married there, not in France. We can do it—just say we can do it? Because I'm desperate here. Absolutely bloody desperate."

"You think that will fix things?"

"Juliet can fix anything." That was what Badger had said when the beater had been shot and the German was angry. "Juliet can fix anything."

Would there ever be a time when she wouldn't be thinking about her, remembering?

"Yes, yes, I do think it will fix things. We need to get away from here. I know how hard it's been for you, being in a different country with all these new people—and—and me being such a stupid fucking idiot. It will be different there—you'll see."

Could it be? Could it be different?

Maybe.

Just maybe.

"I don't know. I wish I did. I wish I could be certain."

"You've taken chances with me before, Nic."

"Yes. I have." She almost smiled. "I think the best thing would be for me to go back home, have some more time by myself in my world. But I'll think about it. I'll think about everything."

"And you'll call me when you've thought? I can fly over anytime. I *will* fly over anytime."

"Yes, I'll call you."

"Try to think positively, will you?"

"I will try. But you should go now. I'll let you know when I need to pick up the rest of my stuff from your house. On my own. I think it's better if I don't see you again. Until—I don't know. Until whenever."

"'Whenever' is a lot better than 'never.' You have to admit that." Now he smiled.

Shit. Those eyes. That face. The thought of not seeing him again was horrific.

Together in America? A brand-new start. He was the one who had offered to give up his friends, his life here. That had to mean something. Maybe? Just maybe . . .

"I'll call you when I have my ticket, and I'll come pick up my stuff and drop off my key. On my own. Really, I need to do it without you being there." *Or else I'll break down and throw myself into your arms. I can't do that. Yet.* "Does that sound okay?"

"If you call me as soon as you land in the States and tell me you want me to come over, then absolutely." He paused. "It would sound perfect."

He didn't try to kiss her. He must have known that was the right time to leave, the right line to make her want him back.

Fuck it, Daniel. This might work out. Am I being unbelievably stupid?

How would I know, Nic? I'm dead, remember. Juliet killed me.

* * *

TWA WAS DOING cheap flights, competing with the airline run by an Englishman, Freddie Laker. She had stood in line for a while outside the Kensington TWA building to buy one, but the wait was worth it. She bought the ticket on Wednesday, the day after James had come over, and she was flying on Friday.

"I'll pick up my things on Friday morning," she'd told James on the phone. "My flight's in the afternoon."

"I can come—"

"No, I want to go on my own."

"Okay, I'm not going to push you. Just do me a favor, will you?"

"What?"

"Don't run off with Roy Mabrey."

She laughed. She actually laughed.

Maybe there was life after Juliet.

On her last night, Nigel and Bella took her out to dinner at a fancy restaurant on Beauchamp Place in Knightsbridge. They were both incredibly kind, and Nigel did his best to entertain her—and to avoid mentioning Juliet's name.

"Trez keeps calling," Bella said, after they'd finished their main courses. "She wanted to know when you're going, Nic, what airline you're on—she said she could go to Heathrow with you to keep you company, but I told her you want to be alone."

"That's really kind of her, but I do want to go on my own."

"She asked if you were going to see James before you left. I told her you weren't, that you were dropping off his key and picking up the rest of your things from his place tomorrow morning. That's okay, isn't it?"

"Yes, of course. It's strange. I always thought Trez wanted James and Juliet to get back together, that she wasn't that keen on me. See? I can say Juliet's name. That's good, isn't it?"

"You and James will get back together. I know you will," Nigel stated. "I give him shit, but he's a really good man, Nicola. And he loves you. He made a mistake, that's all. Being around that woman—well, it made a lot of people make a lot of mistakes. Anyway, I think your wedding should be in New Orleans."

"Hold your horses, Nigel."

"Where are they? I'd hold them if I knew where they were."

Bella rolled her eyes. With affection.

Nigel wasn't going to ditch Bella. The outsider would become an insider—she could feel it.

It might work out for me and James.

I think I can, I think I can . . .

The next morning she made her way by bus to South Kensington. When she walked down the mews street, she felt loss: pure loss. The first time she'd come here with James, she'd been enchanted. And in that magical world of complete, uncomplicated, head-spinning love.

They'd been so happy. So amazingly, perfectly happy.

Opening the door, she stepped over the threshold. This house held all those memories too. She didn't have a long history in England, but she'd had two of the best weeks of her life here. Before she'd gone to Langley Hall. Before Juliet.

But Juliet didn't have to ruin everything. It could be salvaged. If James really was going to come to America. They could at least try . . .

Her thoughts braked, hard.

There was a bottle of whiskey on the coffee table in front of the sofa. It was almost empty. There was a glass standing beside it. There was an album beside the glass. A photograph album. One of the ones she'd looked at that afternoon on her own.

Nicola walked over to the sofa, sat down. The album was open.

To the page with the picture of Juliet, doing her cartwheel in the sun in front of those stone slabs.

He knew I was coming here today, and he didn't even bother to put it away. He got drunk last night and started looking at photographs of her. Juliet being Juliet. Juliet doing a cartwheel.

Her hair flying.

He didn't even bother to put it away.

Because he will never, ever forget her. He will obsess about her for the rest of his life.

She took off her engagement ring, placed it beside the album. And left.

PART THREE

They took what they wanted. They breezed through life, gathering all the goodies, not remotely concerned that they didn't deserve any of them.

Fancy prep schools. Eton or Harrow. Oxford or Cambridge. Banking. Insurance. Lunches in the city. Shooting weekends. Dinner parties.

Marriage. Babies.

And the cycle repeats.

She didn't belong with them. He knew that the first time he saw her.

"It was evidently a case of love at first sight, for she swam about the new-comer caressingly . . . with overtures of affection." Charles Darwin had written that—about a female mallard duck and a male pin-tail duck.

No one in that smug gang would think someone like him would have read Charles Darwin. But he had. And he remembered thinking: Can that be true? Can animals fall in love at first sight? Can people? I don't believe it.

Then she'd come down to breakfast and he'd seen

those green eyes, and he believed. All he wanted to do was walk up to her, take her hand, lead her away, and have her by his side for the rest of his life.

But she was taken. Spoken for. By one of them.

By James fucking Shuttleworth, who, back in those "glorious" Cambridge days, had actually been dumb enough to fall for Juliet. The scheming minx who claimed to have shot Matthew, then claimed her best friend had.

He'd seen through that little ruse from the start. Juliet was clever, he'd give her that, but she couldn't hide from him. The only thing he didn't know for certain was whether she'd shot Matthew on purpose or had just taken advantage of her mistake. It didn't much matter.

He could drop in early on a rainy day to have some time alone with Nicola, but he couldn't declare himself. He had to bide his time. Wait for the right opportunity. See how she was fitting in with them—or not.

Watching them carefully over the next months, he knew exactly what was going on. He'd seen Hugo Langley looking at Juliet with a mixture of lust and desperation. And all those trips to London? If Hugo Langley had shooting business there, he would have told his gamekeeper. Stewart, we need to talk about dates for the new shoots I've signed up. But not one word.

Men are supposed to get suspicious of their wives

if they start buying new, sexy underwear. Well, Hugo Langley was dressing better. And losing some of that appalling paunch of his. Solid, dependable Hugo Langley. I'll cheat on my wife—just please give me the chance Hugo Langley. I'm going to be an earl, so I can do whatever I want Hugo Langley. In thrall to a vixen.

And then the tide had turned. Mrs. Langley— Trez (please, Trez and all these stupid nicknames— does it get any more childish?)—fell pregnant, and Juliet switched courses and set her cap at James. If he hadn't loathed the woman so much, he could have kissed her. It was easy to make friends with the maids in Scotland and hear all about the dinner-party shenanigans—that silly yes-or-no game, then that "favorite names" game Juliet had engineered. She was playing right into his hands without knowing it. Juliet would break them up, and Nicola would be free.

Except then he saw Nicola at the river. He heard her challenge Juliet, say, "Stay the fuck away from us." He was proud of her for standing up for herself, but that anger—it had to mean she loved the idiot. She hadn't realized what a useless excuse for a human being he was. By the time she did, she would most probably be his wife.

Nicola walked off. Juliet tried to cast. As if she actually thought she was a skillful fisherwoman. He had a mind to reveal himself, go up to her and tell her she couldn't catch a fish in a bathtub. Luckily for him, though, he kept away. Luckily because, ten or so minutes later, out came Mrs. Langley. To have a cozy chat with her best friend.

Although not so cozy a chat as it turned out. Now it was Mrs. Langley's turn to go for Juliet. Aha. A wonderful fight ensued. He could hear most of it. He would have paid to hear it, actually. These two well-brought-up society women tearing each other to shreds. To the point of physical violence.

That push. Juliet landing on her ass in the river. Mrs. Langley striding away, not looking back. Not answering those calls of Juliet's. Those pathetic "Trez-es!" and "Helps!" as she struggled in the water, as her waders filled up, as the current began to get its grip on her, dragging it into its hold, carrying her downstream. Toward him. Right toward him.

Her head disappeared underneath the water, then popped up again.

She saw him.

"Help!" she cried out, her hands came up in the air. Like that bear in the snow. "Help, Stewart!"

It was interesting. If he'd saved her, she would have gone on with her plan and probably succeeded, captured the idiot Shuttleworth and left Nicola alone. Which would have suited him perfectly. But he couldn't do it. He saw that entitled face of hers.

Even when death was approaching, that face looked so fucking arrogant. He looked at her, and he just couldn't do it.

He couldn't have guessed—no one could have—just how stupid they were. They thought Nicola had pushed Juliet in the river. James Shuttleworth actually thought Nicola had done it.

He'd almost laughed when he walked into that dining room in the lodge and learned how James Shuttleworth had finally given himself away. That ridiculous Badger and Hugo Langley as well.

Not one of them would have suspected anyone in their circle. But an American girl? Absolutely.

He'd never forget the look on her face when he told them she'd had nothing to do with it. That "Thank you, Stewart."

On one of the shoots, a friend of Mr. Langley's, a man who was, he'd been instructed, supposed to be addressed as "Sir Malcolm" because he was a knight of the realm—that man had wanted to show off. He'd shot a gray dove. It was a drive in the woods, and the dove had landed neatly, not far from his peg. "Sir Malcolm" had walked up to it, grabbed it, taken a knife out of his belt, dug into the dove's chest, and ripped out its heart. Then eaten it.

"I was told a freshly killed dove's heart is delicious," he'd said. "It's true."

James Shuttleworth had ripped out Nicola's heart

and eaten it.

He'd wanted to kill Sir Malcolm. He'd wanted to kill James Shuttleworth.

But he didn't need to.

All he needed to do was keep watch and be clever. Cleverer than Juliet, cleverer than them all.

Nicola would get her heart back. And it would be a damn sight healthier than it would have been with that asshole.

Chapter Forty-Two

NICOLA

It was over, and now she knew: it was *not* better to have loved and lost than never to have loved at all. You didn't think about the "loved" part, you thought only about the "lost." If the timing had been different, if Juliet hadn't come back from Hong Kong—if Juliet hadn't died . . . they could have made it work. But the disaster had happened—so many disasters had happened.

When Juliet had talked about "The Road Not Taken," she couldn't have known that Nicola's favorite poem when she was a teenager was also by Robert Frost. "The Death of the Hired Man." "Poor Silas, so concerned with other folk/And nothing to look backward to with pride/And nothing to look forward to with hope/So now and never any different."

Nothing to look forward to with hope. That about

summed it up.

She'd go hide out in her parents' house for a while. Shit, maybe she'd even start smoking dope with them.

She wouldn't be laughing with James, making love with James, seeing that little bald spot on the back of his head and smiling.

She'd always wonder whether Trez and Hugo had a boy or a girl, whether Bella and Nigel got married, whether Badger found something to do in life other than read and drink.

The Club. Whose life would go on without her.

How long before Trez, despite how solicitous she'd been lately, was setting James up with another woman?

It hurt too much. It was too fucking painful. She had to stop crying.

* * *

HE'D BEEN CLEVER. *He'd found the way to gather the information he'd needed, he'd kept watch. Waited for the right time. Waited until the idiot left for work.*

All that education and they put the spare key under the mat in front of the house. Not so bright.

Then he'd slipped in and cased the joint, as they said in American crime novels—quickly, because he knew she was due to come in in the morning after all—found the album, found the inevitable photo he'd needed. The whiskey bottle. The glass. Set it up.

Then waited at a safe distance outside until he'd seen her rush off and away from the twee little mews house, which probably cost more than all the houses in his parents' village put together. Let himself back in again, tidied up.

Seen that engagement ring lying on the coffee table.

He hadn't had to be that patient, hadn't had to crawl through the mud. It had all taken only a few hours.

The stag was right in his sights.

* * *

SHE WAS STANDING in line at the check-in desk at Heathrow, wiping tears from her cheeks, nudging her suitcase forward, when she saw him. Or at least it looked like him from the back, but it couldn't be him. He was ahead of her, she didn't want to jump the line, but when he turned slightly, she saw his profile.

She picked up her bag, went up to him, grabbed his arm. "Stewart! God! What are you doing here?"

Acknowledgments

Huge thanks to Lucia Macro for being such a brilliant editor. Working with you is a true pleasure.

Thanks to my terrific agent, Charlie Viney, and to Asanté Simons and Emily Fisher for all their work.

As ever, I am massively grateful to Keith Barnes and the Colegrave, the Feige, and the Blake families for their support.

And a special mention to Handan, Erdo and Ece Aydin, and Osman Ince for creating such a special environment and so many wonderful memories.